GHOST
AN EVIL DEAD MC STORY

NICOLE JAMES

GHOST
AN EVIL DEAD MC STORY

NICOLE JAMES

Published by Nicole James
Copyright 2015 Nicole James
All Rights Reserved
Cover Art by Viola Estrella
ISBN# 978-1532849169

Author's Note ~

For those of you that have read the previous Evil Dead MC Stories, there are events that occur in the beginning of GHOST that overlap with events that occurred toward the end of WOLF. (But told from these new character's perspectives.)

This book picks up in Sturgis, SD where chapters of the Evil Dead MC from all across the country attend for the club's national meet.

For those of you that have not read any of the others in the series, this is a stand-alone story. It is not necessary to have read the other stories to enjoy this one, although it may make it a richer experience to know some of the other characters' backstory.

PROLOGUE

Two Months Ago…
  Evil Dead Clubhouse
  Birmingham, AL
  June 3rd
  Just after midnight

Ghost's phone went off just as he and the brothers were heading out of the clubhouse. He pulled it out of the hip pocket of his faded jeans and glanced down at the screen, frowning.

It wasn't a number he recognized.

"You need to take that?" Shades asked, looking back at him as they walked out the door.

Ghost's eyes connected with his VP. "Yeah, give me a minute."

"Make it fast," Shades replied as he and the rest of the boys headed to their bikes.

Ghost frowned as he hit the button and put the phone to his ear, wondering who the hell this could be. He wouldn't even bother taking an unknown call except for the fact that this wasn't the first time he'd gotten a call from this particular number. He'd had one yesterday, but hadn't picked it up, and whoever it had been hadn't left a message.

"Yeah?" he growled into the phone, a little pissed off that someone he might not know had his number.

"Billy?" a soft female voice asked. There was only one person that called him by his given name. *Holy shit.*

"Jessie?" he replied back in a stunned whisper. He heard her soft laugh through the phone. Only it kind of sounded sad, like she was overcome with emotion or choked up.

"Surprised to hear from me?"

"Hell yeah. But a good surprise." Ghost eyed his VP who sat on his bike not twenty feet away, watching him and trying not to look impatient. They had business to take care of tonight—the kind conducted in the dark of night, and Ghost was keeping the whole club waiting, their bikes idling behind the big clapboard house that was their Birmingham Clubhouse. "Honey, why you callin' me so late?"

"Is it late there? I'm sorry." Ghost frowned at her response. *Where the hell was she?*

"It's after midnight."

"Oh, I didn't realize. Its just past ten here." Her voice sounded kind of shaky. Or was that just his imagination?

"Ten? What time zone are you in?"

"Pacific."

"Pacific?" Ghost was thrown for a loop with that one.

"Ghost!" Shades snapped, motioning with a circular motion of his finger to wrap it up.

Ghost gave him a chin lift. "Babe, I really can't talk right now."

"Oh. Okay." That time he was sure he heard a sniffle through the phone.

"Honey, why you cryin'? Is everything okay?"

He heard her swallow, and then she put on a fake, bright voice.

"Yeah. It's fine. I just...wanted to hear your voice I guess."

"It's really good to hear yours, too. It's funny that you're callin' me tonight. I was thinking about you the other day."

"You were?" He could hear the smile in her voice as she perked up.

"Yeah. Drove by that snow-cone place you used to love."

She huffed out a soft laugh. "Chilly Willy the Penguin?"

"That's the place. What was your favorite flavor again?"

"Maui Mango."

"Right. Maui Mango," he repeated softly. She was quiet for a few moments. Ghost wasn't sure how much more small talk he could make. He knew there had to be a point to this call, so he decided to cut to the chase, his voice dropping low. "You still with him?"

It took her a moment before she whispered back, "Yes."

"Does he know you're talkin' to me? This gonna start a fight?"

As if on cue, Ghost heard a male voice growl in the

background, "Who the fuck are you talking to?"

A moment later, he heard a clattering sound, and the line went dead.

Cursing, he immediately tried calling back, but the phone went straight to automated voicemail.

"Let's go," Shades hollered.

Ghost jammed the phone in his pocket, promising himself he'd try her back later.

CHAPTER ONE

Yesterday
Wyoming/South Dakota State line
Interstate 90

The trucker looked over at the girl he'd picked up at a truck stop on I-90 just outside of Seattle. She'd said she needed a ride to Sturgis. Against his better judgment *and* his trucking company rules, he'd grudgingly agreed to take her. Maybe it was the air of desperation about her. Or maybe it was the long legs revealed by the black leather shorts she wore. His eyes skated down the length of them now, stopping at the funky, high-heeled ankle boots before glancing back at her face. She sure was a looker. Pretty face, long dark hair hanging in tangled curls to the middle of her back, luminous, pearly skin, and big brown eyes that were only partially ruined by the heavy liner and mascara she wore. Maybe the excessive makeup was the style, but he couldn't help but think it looked trashy. She was too skinny for his taste, too.

She glanced over at him, catching him studying her, and he jerked his eyes back to the road.

He needed to focus on his driving, damn it.

A road sign appeared on the right, drawing his attention with its artistic rendering of the faces on Mount Rushmore. The sign read, *SOUTH DAKOTA, GREAT FACES, GREAT PLACES.* It marked the state line as they rolled across from Wyoming.

He looked over at his passenger again as they passed another sign that proclaimed the mileage to the next three towns.

Spearfish 10

Sturgis 30

Rapid City 59

He cleared his throat. "Hey, look. I'm sorry I can't take you all the way to Sturgis, but I gotta take the turnoff in Spearfish heading north to Belle Fourche. Sturgis is another twenty miles out of my way, and I'm behind schedule as it is."

"I understand," she replied quietly, turning those big brown eyes on him.

"You gonna be able to find another ride in Spearfish?"

She forced a smile. "I'll be fine, Joe. Thanks for taking me this far."

Before he could respond, his attention was drawn by a roaring sound, and he glanced at his large side-view mirror.

Shit.

It was a large group of motorcycles coming up fast,

easing into the left lane to pass him. *Pass him* being an understatement. They blew by in an angry horde, barely giving him time enough to count how many there were, but if he had to guess, he'd put the number somewhere between fifteen and twenty. He did manage to catch the three-piece patches on their backs. The top rocker that indicated the name of the motorcycle club they all belonged to read *Death Heads*. The bottom rockers all read *Montana*. It was August, so he knew they had to be headed to Sturgis for the annual rally.

He glanced at his passenger again. If she was headed to Sturgis, she was most likely headed to the rally as well. His eyes skated down her again. Maybe the outfit and makeup made sense after all.

He noticed her eyes follow the bikers as they sped off ahead of them. She actually perked in her seat for a moment before slumping back.

A mile later, they passed a sign indicating a rest area, and she glanced over at him to ask, "You mind stopping for a minute, Joe? I need to use the restroom."

He grinned. "Sure."

He took the exit, his eyes sweeping over the area with its main information building. An unusual concrete statue made to look like some abstract teepee was set back a dozen yards. He was sure it was meant to be artistic, but to him it just came off looking like some weird monument to the KOA logo.

Pulling his eyes from it, he was halfway down the exit ramp before he noticed the line of bikes parked in front of the information building that contained the restrooms. Even from a distance he could see the black leather vests. *Shit.* It was the bunch that had passed them a couple miles back.

Taking the left split, he parked behind a tractor-trailer hauling logs. It was the only other rig in the lot. Bringing his own to a stop, he looked over at the girl.

"Maybe this isn't such a good idea. We could probably find another exit farther down. Find you a gas station or something."

He glanced around, taking in the landscape which consisted of flat grasslands, rolling hills, and a steep flat-topped butte of red rock in the distance. They were in the middle of nowhere. He knew there might not be another exit until they neared Spearfish. He watched her take in the men standing next to their bikes, then she turned back to look at him.

"This is fine."

"You sure?" He frowned, his eyes moving past her to the men.

She smiled. "Who knows, Joe? Maybe I'll find a ride into Sturgis right here." Then before he could protest, she grabbed up her purse and yanked open the door, jumping to the ground.

"Hey!" he called out as he leaned across the seat to look down at her. "I'll wait around, just to be sure."

She grinned and nodded. "If I don't come back, thanks for the ride, Joe."

He watched her walk away. No, not walk, *strut.* It didn't take more than a second before the eyes of every one of those bikers were turned in her direction.

As his truck idled, he watched her breeze right past them with her chin held high and head inside. A few minutes later, she reemerged from the building. With her hips swaying, she bee-lined straight for the curb where the bikes were lined up. Even from a distance, Joe could see her smiling up at one of the men, flirting with him. Damn, that girl had moxie.

A couple of minutes later, the bikers were all climbing on their Harleys. As they fired them up, Joe could hear the engines roaring to life.

He watched as the girl climbed on the back of one of the bikes, and then she raised her arm, waving to him as they rode off. He noticed every one of the bikers eyeing him as they all pulled out in a line.

As he put his truck in gear, Joe worried that maybe he should have driven the extra twenty miles out of his way to take her all the way to Sturgis himself. But it was too late. All he could do now was hope the little gal knew what she was doing throwing in with that bunch.

CHAPTER TWO

Present Day
  Sturgis, South Dakota
  August

Five bikes slowed on the rain soaked pavement, and then backed into spots in front of the tattoo shop, their back tires to the curb.

Three bottom rockers read Alabama. Two read California.

Ghost dropped his kickstand and threw his leg over the bike, turning to look up at the place. He pulled his daylight KDs off and wiped the water from his face.

Brothers Ink

Word was it was the best place in town. Just a temporary store, like so many others that popped up in Sturgis seemingly overnight this time every August.

This one was different. Four brothers owned it, and one

of them, a man named Jameson O'Rourke was gaining recognition in the tattoo world. He'd been on the cover of *Inked Up Magazine*, and rumor had it they were in talks about a TV show.

The MC came through the door, ignoring the clearly posted sign that read, *NO MC COLORS*, their broad, leather-covered shoulders filling the small shop. They were dripping wet, rivulets of water running off them to puddle on the floor.

Ghost saw his two California Chapter brothers, Crash and Wolf smile at a girl standing by the window.

Wolf even winked at her.

"Got a customer for you, Superstar," Shades announced, pushing JJ forward. They were here to get JJ his club tattoo. Club bylaws stated you had to be a member for two years and be accompanied by two patched members who already had their ink.

Jameson looked from Shades to the girl who obviously worked for him. It was almost as if he was questioning whether she wanted him to get rid of these men. Not that it would be an easy task, but apparently the man thought he was up for it. Ghost huffed out a breath. If Jameson was going to take on five members of the Evil Dead MC, he was either fucking stupid or he had balls the size of the Hulk.

Shades narrowed his eyes at the man, not liking his hesitation one bit.

"There a problem?" he asked with a growl.

The girl cut in, breaking the tension. "Not at all. I'll get the paperwork." She moved toward the counter. "Please gentlemen, this way."

Shades eyed Jameson, and then turned toward the counter, shoving the younger member ahead of him.

As the girl shuffled through the papers at her station, searching for a consent form, it was apparent that their VP was making her nervous as hell. That is until Crash leaned his elbows on the counter and grinned down at her.

"How's it going, Crystal?"

Shades looked over at him. "You know her?"

"Crystal used to run the bar at our clubhouse."

"That so?"

"Crystal, this is Shades, VP of the Birmingham Chapter." Then he indicated the others. "This is JJ and Ghost."

Shades and Ghost both smiled.

"Ma'am. Pleased to meet you." Ghost tried to put her at ease.

"You, too," she replied, giving them a nervous smile.

"Think you can relax now, darlin'?" Shades asked as he turned up the charm.

"Of course." She handed the paperwork to JJ. "Sign here and here, please."

Ten minutes later, Jameson was at work on a full back tattoo, working from the design on the club's cut. The man was a fast worker, Ghost had to admit, but even so, it would take several hours to complete a tattoo of this size.

They had a couple more customers that the other owners took care of, but in comparison to a normal day, they were pretty dead. The rain was keeping most people away. It varied off and on from a downpour to a drizzle and back again. *Classic Sturgis*, Ghost mused.

As the afternoon wore on, Jameson was getting close to finishing JJ's club tattoo. Ghost had to admit the man had talent. His lining was flawless, and his shading was phenomenal. Ghost rose and moved toward the front door, deciding to wait outside. He stepped out onto the boardwalk with its overhanging roof and slid his daylight KDs on with their yellow lenses, his eyes on the distant mountains visible at the end of the street. A group of brave riders rode past, a fine mist of rain spraying up from the tires of their big bikes.

Ghost glanced over to the end of the porch where Wolf, one of his brothers from the Cali Chapter, was talking to that chick, Crystal. Seemed they had some history. Ghost smiled. He'd heard stories about Wolf. The man had a line of women a mile long. But something about this one told him she meant something to the man.

The wooden boardwalk shook as three more pairs of booted feet stomped out the door. JJ's tattoo was finished, and they were ready to roll. Ghost saw Wolf twist to look behind him as they all glanced in his direction.

"You comin'?" Crash asked.

Wolf lifted his chin. "You go on. I'll be a while."

Crash nodded, and then they all headed toward their bikes.

The rain had slacked off to a light drizzle as Ghost and his brothers mounted up. A moment later, four Harleys roared to life and pulled out, heading back to the Evil Dead's Sturgis campground.

The Evil Dead MC was in Sturgis for Bike Week. It was

their club's national meet. Mandatory. Members from every chapter across the country were required to attend.

Ghost eyed the sky as his fellow Birmingham Chapter brothers rode ahead of him, and he suddenly felt a shimmying vibration in his bike and knew right away that he was getting a flat.

Motherfucker.

He eased up on the throttle and pulled to the gravel shoulder.

JJ glanced back over his shoulder, immediately noticing when the rumbling sound of Ghost's pipes were no longer at his side. He then gunned his engine to pull alongside Shades and Crash passing the word.

As Ghost climbed off his bike, he noticed all three of his brothers slow into a U-turn. He squatted down next to his rear tire to examine it. It was losing air fast. Dipping his head and following the hissing noise, it only took him a moment to locate the nail he'd picked up.

At least he had a repair kit with him, and as bike problems went, this was an easy fix.

He stood as the three bikes rolled back up to him. "Picked up a nail."

"You got a kit?" Shades asked.

"Yeah. I got this. You boys don't need to hang here with me."

"You sure?"

"Yeah. I'll meet you back at the campsite," Ghost assured him as he pulled the repair kit out of the leather bag strapped to his swing arm. The Evil Dead MC owned forty-four acres of land halfway between Sturgis and Deadwood. They'd bought the property back in the eighties and used it for a campground for their national meet during Sturgis Bike Week.

"All right then. See ya back there." Shades lifted his chin to him, and the rest of his brothers pulled out.

As the sound of their engines faded over the rise, Ghost bent down and got to work plugging his tire.

***

It took Ghost about fifteen minutes to repair his tire. Then he mounted up and pulled back onto the blacktop. A few miles down the road, he turned off into the gravel parking lot of a remote roadhouse, the neon beer signs in the windows calling his name. The lot was crowded with bikes, but not nearly as many as it soon would be. The rain earlier in the day had slacked off and riders were starting to get back out.

Ghost rolled slowly across the lot, gravel crunching under his tires. He found a spot and parked. Dismounting, he headed toward the front door, stretching his neck from side to side to crack his spine.

As he came through the door, he looked around. The place was medium size, rough-hewn wood floors and rustic décor, with tables on the right and a bar on the left.

He made his way through the crowd and found a place at the far end of the bar where it curved around to form a short L-shaped corner. Beyond the end of the bar was a doorway leading to a short hall that contained the bathrooms and a back door. From his spot at the corner end of the bar, Ghost could see both the front and back door, and that wasn't by accident. Sturgis, Deadwood, and the surrounding towns were crowded with many one-percenter clubs, many of which didn't get along, to put it mildly. Not a problem for a member if you were traveling in a pack, not so if you were the sole patch from your club in the place when another club walked in. Some bars were claimed by certain clubs as their territory while they were in town; other small places—like this one—were not.

Ghost ordered a beer and surveyed the typical biker crowd, riders decked out in leather against the chilly, rainy day. Although the Sturgis Rally was held in August, the South Dakota weather was always unpredictable and changeable. Temperatures could vary anywhere from the low fifties to the upper eighties. Today had started out wet and windy. It was temporarily clearing, but the horizon looked dark and the wind had picked up again.

A couple of women with bandanas around their braided hair, laughed at the jokes the men at their table in the corner were telling. A jukebox up front blasted out some music. He'd picked out only one other patch when he came in, but it was just that of a member of a military veterans club, nobody that would give him any trouble.

Ghost quietly sipped his beer, keeping to himself. It had been an honor taking JJ to get his club tattoo today. He'd glanced over at Shades while JJ sat under the needle, and he knew they'd both been remembering when they'd gotten their ink. It had been years now, but every now and then, like today, it seemed like just yesterday.

Ghost signaled the bartender for another beer and leaned on his elbows, his arms folded. Movement through the doorway behind him caught his eye, and he twisted his head, peering over his shoulder to see the back door open and a young woman dash in. His eyes swept down over her, taking in everything at once from the low cut, bright pink t-shirt that proclaimed in big block letters, *Punk Rock Rules* to the pair of black leather hot pants with the fishnet stocking under them, and cute little high heeled ankle boots. She may be wearing black leather, but she looked more like something off a London runway than blending in with any of this crowd. His eyes returned to her face. She had long dark hair and the heavily lined and shadowed eyes that also could be found straight out of some fashion magazine. But there was something else… Something about her rang familiar to Ghost. He just couldn't quite place it.

That feeling was quickly pushed aside by the expression on her face. She looked frantic, terrified, and maybe even desperate. Ghost frowned.

What the fuck?

She jerked to a stop when her eyes hit him, sliding down and taking in his cut and the patch on his back.

Ghost had seen that reaction in women before—the ones who saw the cut and backed away. But this was different. This was downright terror.

She stood beyond the doorway, still in the back hall, just out of sight from the crowd in the bar.

Ghost's frown deepened, and he straightened from the bar, but before he could react, his attention was drawn to a commotion at the front door. The crowd had suddenly gone quiet, and he saw the reason. Four members of the Death Heads MC had just come through the door. They stood there, just inside the entrance, their eyes sweeping slowly and painstakingly over every person at every table.

They were searching for someone, Ghost realized.

Then the terror he'd seen on the girl clicked, and his head jerked around to look. She had her back to him now as she stood at an old pay phone, her shaking hand punching at the buttons, oblivious to the danger that had just come through the front door.

Ghost glanced back to the Death Heads moving through the bar. If he was going to get involved, he had only seconds to do it. If he had any sense, he'd stay the fuck out of this shit. But something about the terrified look on that girl's face wouldn't let him leave it alone.

"Fuck," he cursed as he pushed off the bar.

***

Jessie held the receiver tightly to her ear, relief flooding through her when she heard the dial tone. Thanking God the old pay phone was still functional, she punched in *911* with trembling fingers hoping the call would go through even though she had no coins to feed into the slot.

Suddenly, she felt a presence at her back and the smell of leather enveloped her. She sucked in a breath as a muscular arm reached over her shoulder, two fingers pressing down on the cradle, disconnecting the call. The other hand yanked the phone out of her trembling palm and hung it up. Before she could react or spin around, the man grabbed her by the upper arms and was herding her into the women's restroom. The flimsy door banged against the wall as he shouldered his way through, pushing her ahead of him.

It was a small room with only two stalls, a low counter with double sinks, and a cracked mirror on the wall above.

She whirled as the man turned and locked the door before facing her. Her mouth fell open when she realized she was staring into the face of the man she'd come to Sturgis to find. Her shoulders slumped in relief. *Thank God.*

She watched his shocked expression as he got a good look at *her* face. It had been years, but something in her looks must have registered. She'd been seventeen the last time he'd seen her, and she could tell his mind was struggling to place her.

"Hey, Billy," she whispered. Her eyes moved over him. In the seven years since she'd last seen him, he'd matured. His brown hair was longer now, brushing his *much broader* shoulders, with the top half pulled back in a band. He had a close cut beard, and there were a few more lines radiating out from the outer corners of his golden brown eyes.

He frowned as if suddenly putting the pieces together, or maybe it was the sound of her voice that had triggered his memory.

"Jessie?" he asked in a stunned whisper as if he couldn't believe his eyes. They searched her face.

She was sure she looked different, the dark eyeliner and heavy shadow giving her the signature smoky eyes she'd adopted years ago.

She nodded.

"What the hell are you doing here?" he snapped.

Her eyes darted past him to the closed door, and then she watched him stiffen.

"Christ. The four Death Heads that just came through the front door? It's *you* they're lookin' for?"

She nodded and watched him run a hand over his mouth in shock.

"Holy fuck."

"I'm in trouble, Billy. If they find me…" she whispered, her voice breaking.

And suddenly he was all action. She watched as he pulled his cut off and tossed it on the counter, then he tore off the flannel shirt he wore, stripping down to a black t-shirt. He slipped the cut back on and put the flannel over it. Then it dawned on her what he was doing—he was covering his cut. It didn't take her long to figure out why he didn't want the Death Heads to see it, to connect his club with whatever shit was about to go down.

His eyes swept over her body, and all of a sudden she was self-conscious, sure she looked nothing like the girl he remembered. But she'd done the best she could with what she had. Besides, if someone didn't like her style they could go to hell.

"Take off your shirt," he ordered with a lift of his chin.

She frowned, confused, and then her eyes dropped to his hands that were already working his belt buckle. "W-what?"

"They see that hot pink, they're gonna know it's you."

When she didn't comply, he paused in what he was doing and reached for it, yanking it over her head and shoving it in the trashcan, the metal lid swinging back and forth with a squeaking sound. Turning back, his eyes took in her black lace bra that covered her small breasts. She'd always had a model-thin figure, all legs and arms, and she was never more aware of that than now.

"Ghost," she tried to protest, but he was already spinning her around and bending her face-down over the counter, and then his hands reached around, undoing her shorts like a pro and jerking them over her hips along with her fishnets and panties. "What the hell are you doing?"

"They're gonna boot that door any second. That flimsy lock isn't gonna stop 'em. We gotta make this look good. Time to show me your acting skills, darlin'. And whatever the fuck you do, keep your head down."

He put a hand to the back of her neck, shoving her down. Her long dark hair fell over her face, effectively obscuring her identity from anyone's view. She could feel him working his pants open, his movements just behind her ass. Then he was pressing his hips against her and bucking, although the two of them would be the only ones that would know he wasn't penetrating—that this was all for show.

The doorknob rattled, and two seconds later they booted it in, just like he'd predicted. It banged against the wall.

"What the fuck, man? Can't a guy get a piece of ass in private anymore?" Ghost snapped as Jessie heard them enter. He kept his hand at the back of her neck, pinning her as he continued thrusting, giving her the pounding of her life. She could feel the front of her hips slamming into the counter with every thrust. Hell, she'd be bruised tomorrow for sure, if she lived that long. Thoughts of what the Death Heads MC would do if they found her flashed through her mind.

With her head still bent, she could see their boots. She heard one of them move to the stalls, pushing the doors open to bang against each wall as they searched.

Ghost kept thrusting.

Jessie heard the other man mutter, "Nice ass."

She yelped as she felt Ghost smack her right ass cheek, agreeing with a growl, "Damn right."

"Let's go," the second man growled as he moved from the stalls to the door.

A moment later they both stomped out. Jessie lifted her head in time to see Ghost stretch his arm out to slam the door shut again. The moment it was closed, he backed off, buckling his pants.

Twisting to face him, she didn't miss when his eyes traveled over her naked ass just before she yanked her clothes back up, her face flaming red.

"What the fuck are you doing here?" he hissed.

"I really don't think we've got time for that now," she bit out sarcastically.

"Maybe not, but as soon as I get you the hell out of here, you're gonna tell me what the fuck the Death Heads want with you, babe."

She nodded. What else could she do? She crossed her arms over her chest, trying to cover herself. "My shirt."

"Leave it," he ordered. "They spot that bright fucking pink, you're done for."

"But I can't go out there like this."

"Why not? It matches the rest of the look you've got goin' on," he smirked.

"Don't be an ass." She glared at him.

The corner of his mouth lifted as if he was enjoying her discomfort, but a moment later he yanked his flannel shirt off and tossed it to her. "Here, put this on."

She slid into it quickly, knotting the tails across her stomach as the scent of him enveloped her, immediately calming her as she took a deep steadying breath.

She watched as Ghost opened the door a crack and peeked out. It must have been all clear, because a moment later he had her by the hand and dragged her out into the hall. He silently opened the back door and peered outside. She could hear the patter of rain. He hesitated only a moment before dragging her outside and off to the side of the building to what she presumed was his bike. He threw his leg over, quickly firing it up, and she wasted no time scrambling on behind him.

He turned his head, saying over his shoulder, "Wrap your arms around me and stay pressed tight to my back. I don't want them to get a look at my patch. And hold the fuck on."

She nodded, and he gunned the throttle. They tore across the gravel lot toward the highway. As they hit the blacktop, she saw the Death Heads running for their bikes, one of them pointing frantically toward them. Apparently, they'd fooled no one.

She tucked in behind Ghost, pressing her face against his leather and hanging on for dear life as the bike surged forward, and she knew he was gunning it for all it had, winding out every gear for all it was worth. They raced on into the open country between Sturgis and Deadwood. The rain picked up and stung her face whenever she dared to peek over Ghost's shoulder. Her arms and legs got so cold and wet that she soon couldn't feel the sting anymore, and she knew Ghost was taking the brunt of it.

She was afraid to look back, knowing the Death Heads wouldn't be too far behind. They flew over a rise, and it almost felt like the bike went airborne for a split second. They raced on, Ghost flying around curves, weaving in and out of traffic. Bikes, oncoming tractor-trailers, it didn't seem to matter, nor did the treacherous wet pavement. Fortunately, weaving in and out kept the bikes chasing them from catching up. On the other hand, they were still in sight.

As they went around a bend, Ghost slowed to take a turn onto a dirt side road. Jessie couldn't help but wonder what his strategy was, but she trusted him. Perhaps he knew they couldn't outrun them for long and it was best to hide while they were out of sight around the bend. She hung on as they tore up the road, disappearing into the foliage of bushes and trees along the way. Her hopes that perhaps they'd slipped away were soon dashed as she heard in the distance behind her the roar of several bikes.

Ghost made another turn, going off-road across the wet grass and into the trees. She couldn't imagine what he was doing as they bumped across the ground, knowing his bike wasn't made for this terrain. Then she saw where he was heading. There was a shed, barely visible in the bushes. It was falling apart, leaning to one side and she couldn't even imagine how old the thing was or how it stayed standing. Perhaps the overgrown vines that wrapped around it were holding it in place.

They slammed into a hidden ditch, and Jessie felt the left side of the bike jar against something hard. Ghost cut the engine, and they coasted to a stop. She scrambled into the grass that came to her knees as Ghost jumped off, pushing the bike with his hands on the grips. The 600 lb. bike wasn't easy to move in the foot-high overgrowth, but he was able to get it to the shed.

Jessie dashed ahead to get the door open, yanking and tugging until she got it far enough for the bike to fit through. Ghost hurriedly pushed the bike inside. She closed the door, leaving an inch gap to peer through as they heard the distant rumble of a pack of Harleys.

She heard Ghost drop the kickstand on his bike, and then she felt his heat at her back as he, too, peered through the crack.

"Do you think they'll find us?" she whispered nervously.

"I don't know, babe."

At his honest answer, she turned her head looking over her shoulder and up at his face. His golden eyes remained focused like a hawk on the distance. Her gaze slid down his neck to his shoulder and down his arm. It was then she noticed the gun he now held in his hand. She didn't know where it had come from. It didn't matter. She was just glad he had it. It may be all that stood between her and them. *He* was all that stood between her and them.

They waited, the sound of the rain pattering on the roof and the howling wind drowning out anything else.

"Maybe they didn't follow us?" Jessie asked hopefully, beginning to wonder if the bikes she'd thought she'd heard following them down the dirt road were really just the sound of bikes out on the highway.

"Maybe," Ghost muttered, then his hand closed over her upper arm, and he pulled her from the door, stepping in front of her. "Stay away from the door until we're sure."

***

A bolt of lightning flashed across the sky, and almost immediately the thunder cracked over their heads. They both flinched at the deafening sound. A moment later, the skies opened up, and the rain became a torrential downpour. Ghost eyed the sky and kept his vigil by the door, but his thoughts were half on the girl behind him.

Jessie, his bratty little stepsister. At least that's how he'd always thought of her years ago. He still couldn't believe she'd turned up here, out of the blue, in Sturgis of all places. She was so out-of-place it wasn't even funny.

His mind went back to the last time he'd seen her…

Rosewood Cemetery
  Seven years ago—

Ghost approached the gravesite. His stepbrother, Tommy, younger by only a year, had been dead two months, but this was the first time Ghost had visited the grave to pay his respects. He'd missed the funeral, unable to attend courtesy of the Jefferson County Correctional Facility. He'd been awaiting trial for some bogus assault charges at the time, unable to post bail.

Tommy had chosen the military. Ghost had chosen the MC. Their lives had taken very different paths.

The girl stood forlornly, staring down at the headstone. His stepsister, Tommy's younger sister.

His eyes swept over her. She was seventeen, way too young to have lost the big brother she'd adored. No, not adored. *Worshipped.*

When Ghost had been thirteen, his widowed father had remarried. Collette had been the woman's name. And as if having a new stepmother wasn't bad enough, she'd brought two children with her: a son named Tommy, who was twelve, and a daughter named Jessie.

He and Tommy took to each other like two peas in a pod. They were close in age and just fell into an easy friendship, bonding almost immediately.

Jessie was a different story. He supposed it was because she was only eight. Which made her the perfect age to be nothing more than a tagalong pest to the two boys. Still, Ghost had looked out for her, taking her under his wing just the same. Even though she could be a little brat, pestering the fuck out of both Tommy and himself, she'd grown on him over time.

His eyes moved past her to land on the boy waiting by the car, leaning against it in a bored manner. He was some punk kid that Ghost could tell in one glance wasn't anyone she should be hanging around with. He had "bad influence" written all over him. Tommy would have run his ass off within five minutes, but Tommy wasn't here to do that anymore, was he?

His eyes swept over Jessie. She looked different. He wouldn't exactly call her new look Goth, but it certainly had a dark, wild, and reckless edge to it, so totally opposite of her. He knew right away that her brother's death had hit her hard and left lasting scars. *Collateral damage.* That's what she was. That fucking IED had taken out more than the four men in the Humvee. It had taken out their loved ones as well. Destroying lives and causing pain that was long lasting and far-reaching.

"Hey, Jessie."

She turned at his soft-spoken greeting. She'd always been a brat, always a pain in the ass, always getting in their hair, always smarting off with more backbone than anyone he'd ever known. Now she just looked sad. No, not sad. *Devastated.*

"You okay?" *What a stupid question,* he realized, the moment the words left his mouth. How could she possibly be okay?

"I'm fine," she whispered, turning back to the headstone, and then she let a bit of that backbone shine through, along with that snarky attitude he always remembered. "Just peachy."

In reality he hadn't seen much of her the last year and a half since he and Tommy had gone their separate ways. In fact, he couldn't remember seeing her a single time since he'd joined the MC. She'd just turned sixteen the last time he'd seen her.

"Jess—" he broke off. What the hell did he say to her? His eyes moved to the headstone and the small bunch of wildflowers that she must have just laid on the grave. "He loved you."

"Right. That's why he left."

There was anger in her tone, and that confused him. "You're pissed at him."

She looked at him then. "Yes. I'm *pissed* at him."

He frowned. "Why?"

"I'm pissed he left. Pissed he ever joined up. Pissed he had to go and fight *and die.*"

"Sweetheart—"

"Don't call me that. I'm not your sweetheart. Thank fucking God."

"Christ, babe," Ghost said in a stunned whisper.

She'd stalked off then, almost as if she was embarrassed by her childish outburst. Even in her grief, she knew she was out of line, knew he hadn't deserved that.

***

Ghost shook the memory free, keeping up his vigil, watching the horizon.

He'd lost track of her over the years. There'd been a few phone calls here and there, but for the most part, they'd lost touch. Until that one phone call months ago. He'd tried to call her back, but the number had gone straight to a generic voicemail. He'd left messages, but she'd never called back. He'd even called his father trying to get her mother's number, thinking maybe he could track her down that way.

But his father didn't keep in touch with any of his ex-wives.

Now the fucking Death Heads were after her. How in the hell was that possible?

After about twenty minutes of standing guard, the muscles in his shoulders relaxed, and he turned from the door, satisfied that they were out of danger. His eyes met hers, drilling into them as he tucked the gun into the waistband of his jeans at the small of his back.

"Time for that talk."

She looked at him with wide, deer-in-the-headlights eyes.

"Why are they after you, Jessie?" He watched her swallow. Not a good sign, at least not if he expected to hear the truth come out of her mouth.

"I heard some things I wasn't supposed to hear."

His chin lifted. "What things? Why the hell are you in *Sturgis* of all places?"

"It's a long story."

Ghost looked at the ceiling as another boom of thunder shook the building. "Yeah, well it seems we're gonna be here awhile, so we've got time."

"I don't even know where to start."

"How about you start at the last time I saw you."

"You mean at the cemetery? At Tommy's grave?"

Ghost nodded, studying the woman before him now. She was no longer a girl. No longer a bratty little child getting into trouble, no longer even the teenage girl she'd been the last time he'd laid eyes on her. Now she was a grown woman, and the trouble she was in now was so much bigger.

"Tell me, Jessie."

"I'm in a bit of trouble, Ghost."

"No shit. Explain it to me."

She swallowed, dropping her eyes. "I've been in Seattle."

His brows shot up. "Seattle? Doing what?"

"I followed Kyle out there."

Kyle, the asshole. That's how Ghost thought of him anyway. He was the punk who'd been at the cemetery that day, the son-of-a-bitch who talked her into dropping out of school. He was also the jerk who, Ghost knew, did not give one fuck about Jessie.

"You remember Kyle?" she whispered.

"Yeah. I remember Kyle," he bit out. "What the fuck's in Seattle?"

"He's a musician, Ghost. I told you that."

Yeah, she'd told him that. She'd called him a couple of times over the years. He always tried to talk her into dumping the asshole and coming home. But she never had, at least not until now. "So he's a musician. What of it?"

"He said Seattle was the place to be. They have an amazing music scene there."

"Right. So you dropped out of school and followed him all over the fucking country?" Ghost couldn't help but think Kyle was a bum who wanted to play music while he dragged Jessie along to support them both. "Let me guess. You worked and he played."

She looked at him with wide, guilty eyes.

"Right. Don't bother denying it. You finally wake up

and figure out he was using you?"

She rolled her eyes and grudgingly admitted, "Sort of."

"And you thought you'd try *Sturgis*?" He let out a huff that was half disbelief, half sarcasm.

"Not exactly."

"Then what, *exactly*?"

"I knew you'd be here."

That threw him. Ghost frowned. "Say what?"

"I knew you were still with that club you'd joined." She lifted a hand toward him, her eyes dropping to his cut. "Knew you were still in Birmingham."

"And?"

"That's a long way, and I was broke. Kyle had the only car. I wanted to get home, but then I remembered Sturgis was coming up, and I knew you'd be here. I thought if I could just get as far as Sturgis and find you—"

"You are shitting me, right? You really thought you'd come to Sturgis and be able to find me in half a million bikers?"

"I suppose I didn't really think it through."

"Ya *think*?"

"All right, it was a stupid plan," she snapped at him. "You don't have to rub it in and be a dick about it. And I *did* find you, didn't I?"

He shook his head. "Unbelievable. How the hell did you get here if you had no car?"

"I hitchhiked."

"You *what*?" The words almost exploded from him. "Don't you know how dangerous that is?"

"A long haul trucker brought me most of the way. It wasn't so bad, Ghost."

He took a step towards her. "You're lucky you weren't raped or murdered. That was incredibly stupid, Jess."

"Maybe," she conceded. "But I'm okay."

"When, in this stupid plan of yours, did you end up crossing paths with the Death Heads? Why are they looking for you?"

"I overheard something I wasn't supposed to."

"And what was that?"

"It's complicated."

He folded his arms and stared at her. "*Un*-complicate it."

"They were talking about a man they had planted in some other gang."

"You mean another MC?"

She shrugged. "I guess so, if that's what you call it."

Ghost studied her. She may be clueless about the MC world, but she was far from stupid. "You catch the name of that other club by chance?"

"Devil something, I think. But then they used an acronym."

"The Devil Kings? The DKs?"

"Yes. That was it."

"What about them?"

"This guy they planted, they were talking about how they were going to use him to get all the information they needed to take that club out of Georgia. They want the state. Not just that state. If this works, they plan to do the same thing in Alabama and Louisiana."

His arms came unfolded at this news. "Those are Evil Dead states."

She nodded, shrugging. "I guess so. I don't really know about all that. I just know what I heard. They want the entire Gulf Coast under their control. I heard them say that the only thing standing in their way were the DKs in Georgia and the Evil Dead in Alabama and Louisiana."

"You overheard all that?"

She nodded.

"Jessie, nobody just 'overhears' MC business."

"*I* did."

"How? Where?"

"I...I was just in the wrong place at the wrong time, okay?"

"Jessie." He glared at her. "Tell me."

She blew out a breath. "I just happened to wander into the back of this bar in Sturgis. I was looking for the restroom, and I overheard a few of them talking."

Ghost knew there were holes in this story. MCs were not known for discussing business just anywhere, unless perhaps they thought of the bar as their territory. Clubs were known to stake claim to bars while they were in town. If that were the case, it was possible they would feel comfortable talking in a backroom. But hell, there'd be guards. Someone making sure no civilians got close. No. Something was off about this story. "You just happened upon a meeting and got close enough to hear every word?"

"Well..."

"Jess."

"I was hiding, actually."

"From who?"

"Um, well, this guy was hitting on me, wouldn't leave me alone. I dashed in the back, but instead of going in the restroom, I went down a hall and hid when he followed. I was going to come out when suddenly all these Death Heads trooped down the hall and I was trapped. I was in a tiny broom closet, but it shared a wall with some office behind it. I could hear everything."

"They found you?"

She nodded. "I got away. But they've been hunting me ever since."

"Jesus Christ." His eyes slid over her, taking in her words. "They're not gonna just give up and go away, Jess." He turned then, moving to the door, his arm on the frame and his eyes scanning the horizon as the ramifications of it all rolled through him. "Holy fuck."

"Ghost." He heard her soft voice whisper behind him. She had no clue. No fucking clue just how deep this shit was. It wasn't just that they were after her. It was what she knew. That was some damning information. They'd stop at nothing to silence her.

He turned, his hand dropping from the doorframe as he shook his head. "Jessie, I don't think you realize—"

"How much trouble I'm in?" she cut in. "I know, Ghost. I know those are dangerous men."

"They'll kill you." He couldn't be any more blunt than that.

She swallowed and nodded. "I'm sorry I dragged you

into this. I understand if you don't want any part of it, if you don't want to get involved."

"Christ, babe, you really think I'd walk away from this? From you?" he asked, stunned. "You really think that low of me? That I'd just throw you to the wolves and not look back?" He watched her eyes fill.

"No," she whispered. "But I'd understand if you did."

He clenched his jaw, looking away and shaking his head. "I need to know something, Jess." His eyes hit hers, boring into them. "This story. Are you telling me the truth?"

She nodded, but there was a hesitation that had him doubting her. He turned in frustration and moved back to the door. Leaning his shoulder against the frame, he stared out at the rain wondering how his life could turn on a dime like this. One minute everything was copasetic, the next, it was totally fucked.

Fucking hell.

***

Jessie watched the firm set of his shoulders. She knew he wanted details—details she wasn't prepared to tell him. There were things she couldn't yet trust him with. She could tell that he didn't buy her story, at least not all of it. Ghost was a smart man, very little got past him. He'd always been quick to pick up on the little things, and now he picked up on the telltale signs she inadvertently gave off, and he knew she wasn't being completely honest with him. But he didn't push her on it. For that she was grateful. Maybe he believed in her enough to trust in most of what she'd said or maybe he knew he'd get the truth out of her eventually.

She hoped she'd never have to tell him all of it. He'd never look at her the same, if he knew. She blew out a breath and closed her eyes a moment, letting the sound of the rain on the roof calm her for a moment. Then she opened them and took in her surroundings.

The shed wasn't very big, maybe eight-by-ten. There were no windows, but there were a couple pieces of boards missing on one side that let the fading daylight in. The roof was about eight feet high and rain leaked through in a couple of places, but at least it had a wooden floor, so they wouldn't have to sit in the dirt.

She leaned against one wall and slid down to sit with her back against it. Her eyes moved to Ghost.

Ghost. His club name. Not the one she knew him by. He would always be Billy to her. He came into her life when she was eight, and her mother married his father, the man who was her second stepfather.

Her father died when she was six. She barely remembered the man. After Daddy, there was her first stepfather; he'd been her father's business partner. That only lasted long enough for him to weasel her dad's half of the business away.

That's when Billy came into her life. They'd moved in with him and his dad. She was eight and Tommy was twelve. Billy was thirteen, a year older than Tommy and so instantly became Tommy's idol. Hers, too.

He was older, cooler, and worldlier. Just everything about him drew them into his aura. And what an aura it was.

She instantly fell in love with him. Well, perhaps love

was a strong word for an eight-year-old girl. But she'd crushed, *hard*. And that never changed.

Billy's was the hand that was reaching for theirs even before they had to ask. He always made them feel safer, feel braver. He was always there when they needed him most. There was a multitude of times he came to her aid without her even having to ask.

Tommy and she both knew, as did most kids on the block, if they were with Billy, they were gonna be okay. He watched over all of them.

And he always carried their secrets. They could unburden themselves to Billy knowing he was never going to break their trust.

He was the most fiercely loyal and protective person she'd ever known, and he'd come into her life at a time when she'd needed him most.

CHAPTER THREE

"Do you have a phone?"

Ghost turned to look back at Jessie to answer her question. "Yeah, but my battery died about an hour ago."

"Mine, too."

She was shivering with cold, running her hands up and down her arms. The sleeves of the flannel shirt he'd given her were soaking wet from their ride. The skin of her legs were also wet, her fishnets, soaking.

Ghost watched her, his eyes sliding over her legs, noticing her shiver. "You should get out of that shirt."

She wiped the droplets on her face with the sleeve. "Well, my shirt's in the trashcan, so this is all I've got."

"You've got a bra on. And I've already seen it, remember?"

She rolled her eyes.

"At least take those soaked fishnets off."

She glanced down at her legs, seeming to consider his

words, and then pushed to her feet. She glared at him. "Turn around."

"Already seen that, too."

"Turn around!" she practically growled, her hands landing on her hips.

Ghost grinned, thinking she was fucking cute when she was pissed off, but he did as she asked.

A few moments later, something wet slapped against him. He glanced down, pulling her stockings from his shoulder. The little brat had flung them at him. He turned back to her, raising a brow.

"There. Happy?" she snapped.

"Gee, a memento of our lovely day together," he bit out sarcastically with a grin, already shoving them in his pocket.

Her eyes got big. "You're not keeping those, are you? I was only being…"

"A brat?"

That shut her up, a feeling he had to admit he enjoyed the hell out of. He moved to his bike and bent down to dig through his saddlebag. A moment later he pulled out a pair of chaps and tossed them at her. "Here, put these on. At least they'll keep your legs warm."

She caught them. "Thanks."

Holding them out, she looked at the strange looking garment, and he could tell she had no clue how to put them on. He blew out a breath. "Come here."

She did, and he squatted down in front of her. He wrapped the belt around her hips and buckled it across her pelvis. Then he wrapped each leg in leather and zipped the sides up from ankle to thigh. They were too long for her, but at least they'd keep her warm.

They framed her crotch, drawing his attention to it, and thoughts of how her pretty naked ass had looked swam before his eyes. He glanced up and found her staring at him, wide-eyed, and he knew she'd caught him looking, knew exactly where his eyes had been aimed, maybe even knew exactly what he'd been thinking. *Shit*, he shouldn't have thoughts like that about her. She thought of him as a big brother, and he couldn't destroy her trust like that.

He looked away uncomfortably and mumbled, "Better?"

"Peachy."

He rose to his feet and made a move to step toward the door, but the touch of her hand on his arm stopped him. He looked back to see her looking up with big eyes, looking at him like she used to when she was a child. Like he was her knight in shining armor. Like he could do no wrong. Like he could fix anything.

He remembered that look on her face when she was nine and he was fourteen. She'd been walking home from school, and some bullies were teasing her. They'd cornered her by ol' Man Walker's picket fence. They'd knocked her book bag to the ground, and its contents had scattered all over the sidewalk. He'd come up and bloodied the biggest bully's nose, threatening him with worse if he ever dared bother her again or if he ever told who'd hit him.

The boys had run off, scared shitless.

He'd bent down, wiping the tears from her face with the sleeve of his flannel shirt. She'd looked up at him with those same big eyes, thinking he was her hero.

Up until that point, she'd always been Tommy's bratty little sister, the one who pestered them to no end, the one who was always tagging along, always being a nuisance.

But after that day, things changed, he was more tolerant with her, more patient. He'd begun to look out for her, to care for her like a real big brother would. It was a responsibility he took seriously.

He'd known she'd idolized him back then. Maybe even had a crush on him. But she was always just a little kid.

That is, until she grew up, and he began to take notice.

"Are we going to be okay?" she asked softly, shaking him from his memories.

He had no clue what the hell was going to happen with the Death Heads, but he'd die before he'd let them get their hands on her. He lifted his hand and cupped her face, his thumb brushing over her cheek. "I'm not gonna let anything happen to you, brat. Understand?"

She just stared up at him.

"You trust me?" he asked when she didn't reply.

She nodded, but that wasn't good enough for him.

"Say it."

"I trust you, Billy."

"Ghost," he corrected. "I go by Ghost now."

"Ghost."

He studied her a long moment, and then nodded. Dropping his hand, he lifted his chin toward the wall she'd been sitting against earlier. "Get some rest."

She sat as he moved toward the half opened door and

dropped down on the floor next to it. He leaned back against the wall to keep watch.

"When it stops raining will we be able to leave?" she asked.

He kept his eyes on the landscape. "Not until I fix my bike."

"Fix your bike?"

He turned back in time to see her frown.

"What's wrong with your bike?"

"Did you feel when we jarred against something right before I shut it off?"

She nodded.

"We hit something. Broke the shifter."

"The shifter?"

He nodded, pointing toward a metal piece that was flopping down on the bottom left of the bike. "The shift linkage. Can't ride if I can't shift gears. Hopefully, I can fix it when we've got daylight tomorrow. I can get a better look at it then."

"So we're stuck here tonight?"

"Looks that way."

As hours passed, the rain slacked off. Eventually Jessie put her head back against the wall and drifted off. Ghost kept his vigil by the door, determined to stay awake and make sure the Death Heads didn't return searching for them.

As night fell, the temperature dropped, and Ghost cursed the fact that he'd left his leather jacket back at camp. Not for him, but for Jessie. He knew she was cold.

As if his thoughts communicated to her, she came

awake, shivering. She wrapped her arms around herself, trying to keep warm. Her eyes moved to him. He could see them in the dim moonlight that shone through a hole in the ceiling.

"Why don't you sit over here? Isn't it cold over by the door?" she asked.

"I'm fine."

"Maybe our body heat would help keep each other warm," she suggested.

"Then come over here."

"Ghost."

He knew she thought he was being difficult. That wasn't it at all. He might as well admit it. "I have a problem with small spaces."

He watched her frown.

"You do? I didn't know that."

"Yeah, well, I do."

He felt her studying him, like she was trying to figure him out. And then she tilted her head to the side as if something had just dawned on her.

"Is *that* why you always took the stairs instead of the elevator?"

He grinned, wondering how she'd never put it together before now. But then he had to remind himself she'd just been a child. "Yeah, brat. That's why."

His use of the nickname he'd had for her back then made her smile and roll her eyes. Then he watched her stand up. His eyes followed her in the dim light as she moved toward him and sat down. He wrapped his arm around her, pulling her against his body. "Might also explain why I prefer riding a bike to being closed up in a car."

She laughed. "Probably."

They were quiet for a few minutes.

"Do you remember the year we came to live with you and your dad?" she asked.

"Of course. I was thirteen. Tommy was twelve. And you were, what? Eight?"

"Um hmm. I remember when we walked inside for the first time. You were sitting on the couch, all sullen and pissed off, looking like it was the last place you wanted to be."

"I tried to take off, sneak out the back. Dad caught me. Threatened to ground me if I didn't stay and meet you."

"No wonder you seemed so angry when you looked at us."

"Sorry, brat. I was an adolescent boy who had lost his mother and didn't want a new one."

"I know. I didn't want a new father, either. *Or* a new brother. Until I met you, that is."

He gave her a squeeze.

"Do you remember what you used to call me?" she asked.

"Brat?"

"No, before that."

"What did I call you?" he asked with a frown, struggling to recall.

"When we met I had on a polka dot dress, and all that summer you called me Polka Dot."

He grinned. "I did, didn't I? Hell, I'd forgotten that."

"I hated that dress."

"You hated all dresses back then. You were a little Tomboy, always wanting to tagalong with us. Remember when you wanted to enroll in Little League with us?"

"Yeah, Mom made me take ballet class instead."

"You hated it."

"Want to know a secret?"

"Sure."

"I really didn't hate it. I liked it. A lot. I just hated that I couldn't play baseball, too."

"*Really?*" He dragged the word out. "Interesting."

"I used to love when you'd let me play ball with you in the neighborhood."

"Well, you were the best third baseman we had," he admitted in a teasing voice.

She grinned, lifting her chin proudly. "I was, wasn't I?"

"Yup."

"We had some fun times, didn't we?"

"Sure did." He pushed her head down on his shoulder. "Get some sleep, brat."

***

Jessie eventually drifted off. Ghost could tell when her breathing changed, deepened, and her weight settled heavily against his side. He pressed a kiss to her forehead and continued to stroke her hair, his fingers sifting through the silkiness.

The curves of her warm body, soft against his side, reminded him that she was no longer a child. She was a grown woman now, and his body reacted to hers accordingly. He tried to tamp those feelings down, knowing the last thing he should be feeling toward her was desire. Somehow it felt wrong. He'd always been a big brother to her, and he was sure that wasn't the type of relationship she'd sought him out for. She needed protection, someone to look out for her, someone to fill the role of the brother she'd lost. He was fine with filling that role; he'd be whatever she needed. It was the least he could do, the least he could do in Tommy's memory.

His mind drifted to the trouble Jessie was now in, going over everything she'd told him about the Death Heads and the plans she'd overheard. If it were true, it was damned valuable information. Information his club could use. Information the DKs would also find valuable. And there was the rub of it—his club would use her and that information to make a deal with the DKs.

Question was, would he be comfortable with that? Using her for that purpose didn't sit well with him. It put her smack in the middle of an escalating biker war. Could he live with that?

CHAPTER FOUR

Jessie stretched, coming awake. It was daylight now, and Ghost had propped the door wide open, letting in the bright sunlight. He was squatted down next to his bike, fiddling with it. When he heard her movement, he twisted, looking over his shoulder.

"Mornin'," he said.

"Good morning," she replied, stiffly getting to her feet. She moved next to him and nodded toward the bike. "Did you figure out what happened?"

He looked up at her. "The bolt connecting the shift linkage snapped."

"Can you fix it?"

He stood, wiping his hands on a bandana, and answered sarcastically, "Yeah, you got a couple of five-sixteenth bolts on ya?"

Her mouth pulled up in a half smile. "Right. See your point." She eyed the door. "So what do we do? Walk?"

He huffed out a breath. "I'm not leaving my bike here."

"Then what?"

"I'll fix it. I just have to figure out some way to jury-rig it."

"Jury-what?"

"Jury-rig. A makeshift fix."

When she frowned, still not understanding, he expanded. "Improvise, Cobble something together, *half-ass it*."

"Gotcha."

He glanced around the shed. "Check the floor. Maybe we'll find something I can use."

The shed was cluttered with some garbage in the corner. They both scoured the place top to bottom.

***

Jessie dumped her meager pile of "found" items next to the bike. Ghost squatted down, looking them over, moving them around with his finger. A couple of nails, a paperclip, and a fat rubber band.

She looked at him hopefully, like she'd found the jackpot. His brows rose as he looked up at her indicating he had his doubts about what he could do with these items. Did she think he was goddamned *MacGyver?* He huffed out a breath. Maybe it was the hopeful look in her eyes. Maybe it was the memory of how she used to always look up to him as a child, believing he was capable of anything. Whatever it was, he found himself looking back at the bike and grinning.

"I'll try, baby doll."

She grinned back.

***

Hours passed as Jessie watched as Ghost tried one fix after another. He tried the rubber band, but the first time he climbed on and hit the shifter with his foot, it snapped off. Then he tried to fashion a fix with the jumbo paperclip, twisting it through where the bolt would connect. It popped off with the first tap of his foot. He studied the nails, and she knew he was trying to figure out a way to bend them to hold the connection, but that fix didn't pan out either.

Through every attempt, she expected him to get more frustrated and angry, but he never did. He remained totally calm, which in turn, kept her calm. She needed his unruffled, coolheadedness right now to allay her fears and make her believe everything was going to be okay. If he had been agitated, she would have gone over the edge. But his relaxed confidence reassured her.

Her stomach growled loudly.

He looked over his shoulder, trying to suppress a grin. His chin lifted toward his saddlebag. "I think there may be an energy bar buried at the bottom."

She quickly moved to the bike and dug through the bag like a starving animal. He grinned, shook his head, and continued to fiddle with the bike. A moment later, she came up with a bottle of water and a granola bar, holding them high in the air like she'd just found diamonds.

"Yes!"

She tore the wrapper off and took a bite. Then she looked down at him guiltily, and her chewing slowed. She swallowed and broke off half the bar, offering it to him.

He shook his head. "You eat it, brat. I'm fine."

"Are you sure?"

"Yeah. But I'll take some of that water."

She twisted the cap off and held it out to him. He guzzled down half, and then handed it back to her. She continued eating the bar and watching him. Her eyes fell to his wrist, and she paused.

"You still have the bracelet I made you," she murmured in a stunned voice.

His eyes moved to his wrist, and then he looked up at her. "Of course."

He said it so matter-of-fact, like it was the most normal thing in the world to keep a handmade gift from a nine-year-old.

She frowned. "All these years you've worn it?"

He nodded. "I have."

"Why?" she asked. It was his turn to frown at her.

"Why wouldn't I?"

She shrugged. "It was just a stupid childish gift. I never thought you'd keep it."

"Of course I kept it. You made it for me."

Her eyes again fell on the bracelet. It was a brown leather cord with knots tied in it. And between each knot was a silver nut she'd pilfered from the parts on the garage floor that summer when Ghost and her brother had put together their first dirt bikes. Ghost had always looked the other way when he saw her sneaking the little nuts and washers, but there had always been a sly grin pulling at the corner of his mouth, like he was on to her.

Her brother, on the other hand, would pitch a fit every

time parts went missing. She could still see him now in her mind's eye, scrambling around on the floor, cursing up a blue streak, insisting the damn nuts had been right there. But not Ghost. Ghost would just calmly walk over to the workbench to dig up some replacements.

She remembered when she'd given the bracelet to him. She'd purposely waited until her brother had left the garage to go get them a couple of sodas from the kitchen, knowing he'd tease her mercilessly if he ever found out.

Ghost had made her feel like it was the coolest thing in the world when she'd given it to him. He'd actually put it on, and for the years that followed before he'd moved out, he'd always had it wrapped around his wrist.

"I can't believe... all this time you've kept it?" she murmured again.

"It's on my wrist, isn't it?"

She blinked. It *was* on his wrist. What did that mean? Her hand strayed to her throat, her fingers touching the necklace she herself wore. She'd made it at the same time, out of the same dark brown leather cording. But for hers, she'd attached a large flat silver washer as the pendent. She rubbed her thumb over it now, stroking it like it was some kind of talisman. Perhaps it was. The washer had come off of Ghost's bike. He didn't know that, of course. But whenever she thought of him, whenever she missed him, she rubbed it.

He had no clue about the necklace *or* about her feelings for him, and those feelings had nothing to do with brotherly love—far from it.

"I wear it to remind me of the little girl who made it for

me," he said quietly from where he was squatted down, his attention on his motorcycle.

"That little girl is gone," she whispered. That brought his head around, his eyes to hers.

"Is she?"

She nodded.

"I don't think so."

She was uncomfortable with his scrutiny, and maybe with his words. The observation hit too close to home. So she changed the subject.

"You and Tommy were always fixing that first dirt bike you had."

He grinned. "Yeah, because your brother wrecked it so many times. I tried hard to teach him to ride, but he was such an uncoordinated guy. He laid that bike down more often than not. He just couldn't get the hang of working controls with both his feet and hands—clutch, shifter, brakes, balancing the bike, steering... it was too much for him to keep up with. But he could shoot. Damn, that boy could shoot. Every time we went hunting, he amazed me. I knew he'd do well in the military."

At the mention of the military, she cleared her throat, not wanting to think about how that ended.

"How old were you?"

He shrugged. "I don't know. Fourteen. Fifteen, maybe."

"I remember being terrified you'd laugh at me when I gave that to you."

"Never."

Her brows rose. "You teased me all the time. Worse than

Tommy ever did."

He had the decency to look contrite. "I guess I did. But I wouldn't have teased you about this. It was a gift. You'd made it for me. How could I make you feel bad about that?"

She rolled her eyes. "It was stupid, wasn't it?"

He shook his head. "Not to me."

She smiled, surprised that all these years later, his words about a long ago gift still touched something in her.

"I'd always wondered why you were constantly stealing these." He fingered one of the silver nuts.

"You never said anything to Tommy. Never once ratted me out."

"Of course not."

"Why?"

He shrugged. "I'm not a rat."

"I was a pest. Always getting in your hair. You used to hate when I'd get in the way."

"Maybe a little."

"A little?" Her hands landed on her hips.

He grinned. "I used to love watching you get all riled up. Kinda like now."

"You used to torment me. Constantly."

"You used to pester the fuck out of us. You were an annoying little brat half the time."

"I was not!"

"Oh hell yeah, you were. And you did it on purpose."

"I most certainly did not."

"Yeah, you did, Jess. And I know why, too."

Her brows arched. "Oh, you know why, do you? Do

tell."

"You were trying to get attention. Mine, specifically."

"I was trying to get attention? From *you*? That's a laugh."

He rose and took a step toward her. "Is it now?"

She backed off, but then her chin came up. "I eventually got your attention, though, didn't I?"

At the reminder, Ghost's head came back, and he sucked in a deep breath before taking a step away. His eyes skated down her, and he ground out, "That was a mistake. It should never have happened. I told you that."

"A mistake? Is that how you remembered it? Is that all it was to you?"

***

Ghost studied her, recalling the day that was etched in his memory like glass.

She'd just turned sixteen, had raced home from getting her driver's license, ecstatic to have passed the driving test on her first try. She'd dashed into the garage to brag to Tommy, who'd had to take his test three times. She'd skidded to a halt. The only one there was himself. He was squatted down next to his new motorcycle, the one he'd just bought the previous week. He'd been about to turn twenty-one that year. It was just before he'd moved out of his dad's house...

Ten years ago...

Ghost looked up from the carburetor he was adjusting.

Jessie skidded to a stop, the smile on her face bright. *Blindingly* bright. His eyes slid down her, taking in the whole package. She was not a little girl anymore, and she had the curves to prove it. Her low-cut jeans hugged her hips, a two-inch gap above the waistband giving him a peek at her bellybutton. Her short pink tank was scooped just enough to give a hint of cleavage swelling above her bra, the baby-blue straps of which showed a bit.

"I got it! In one try! I got my license, Billy." She was practically jumping with excitement. There wasn't anything he could do but rise to his feet and sweep her up when she practically threw herself in his arms.

"That's great, brat. Really great."

He lifted her off her feet and swung her around. When he set her down, he insisted in a teasing voice, "Let me see your mug-shot."

She proudly held out the paper copy of her license.

He took it, studying it. There was that bright smile again. Hands down, best DMV photo he'd ever laid eyes on. "Not bad, shorty."

She snatched it out of his hand. "Not bad?" She pointed to her head. "I did my hair and makeup and everything."

He grinned, his eyes skating over her face. She was beautiful. "Real pretty, hon."

Her hand went to her hip. "Well, Billy Taylor, I do believe that's the first compliment you've ever paid me."

His eyes narrowed. "Is it?"

"Um hmm."

"Well, that's because you'll always be a brat in my

eyes." He grinned down at her.

She smiled back, then bit her lip before saying, "Is that so? Well, then maybe you should look again."

Uh, oh.

He couldn't help but drop his eyes to her mouth. Why the fuck did he just do that? She must have taken that as a sign, because she took a step closer, and her palm settled on his chest.

Oh, fuck.

"Maybe you'd like what you see," she whispered.

When the hell did she acquire that sexy seductive voice? Did girls practice that shit? Or did it just come natural?

His eyes dropped to where her hand touched him, her warm palm burning a hole through his shirt. He blinked once, and then lifted his eyes to her. He shook his head an almost imperceptible inch. "That's a game you don't want to play, little girl. Not with me."

"Maybe it's not a game."

"Isn't it?"

"And I'm not a little girl, Billy."

No shit.

"Yeah. I noticed."

Her head tilted to the side, and the smile was back. "Did you? I was beginning to wonder."

His hand closed around her wrist, intending to pull it away, but when he touched her warm skin and felt her pulse under his thumb, he hesitated, holding her hand against him.

"I can feel your heartbeat," she murmured, her eyes gazing up into his.

Was it beating as fast as her pulse thrumming under his thumb?

"Jessie—"

"You've never thought about it?"

"About what?" *Fucking her? Hell yes, he had.*

"Kissing me."

Oh, that. Yeah, he'd thought about that, too.

The next thing he knew, his hand had released her wrist only to slide to her throat, his thumb and fingers cupping to gently tilt her jaw up as he walked her backward into the tool bench. When her ass hit it, he closed in, his mouth coming down on hers. Softly at first, lips just barely brushing, but after a few soft kisses, he pulled back a fraction of an inch to growl, "Open for me, Jess."

When he came back a second time, her soft lips parted. He didn't hesitate, his tongue delving inside. She surprised him. Her eagerness, her hunger, it seemed her need for his kiss was just as strong as his was for hers. Before he knew it, his hands were closing around her ass and lifting to set her on the waist-high tool bench. She gasped, but he didn't waste a moment wedging his hips between her knees and bringing his mouth back down on hers.

If he was going to hell for this, he might as well make it count.

He felt her hands clutch at his waist before they slid up his back to pull him closer. She wanted him, wanted this as much as he did in that moment. And he wanted it pretty badly. His hand slid up under the hem of her tank to close over her lace-covered breast. He wasted no time in pushing the bra down out of his way, that soft skin of hers filling his hand. He growled into her throat, breaking the kiss to trail his mouth down her neck with only one goal in mind: closing over her nipple.

He heard her breathing escalate as his mouth tracked across her collarbone, down her cleavage, to latch onto the prize.

Her back arched, her body offering itself up for him, and her fingers threaded into his hair to pull him closer.

Heaven.

Nothing better. Well, he could think of maybe one thing—sinking deep inside her.

Fuck. He was hard as a rock, and for some sick reason he wanted her to feel that, to know the effect she was having on him, so his fist clamped around her wrist and planted her hand against the erection that bulged behind his fly.

She gasped, and he released her nipple with a pop, his head lifting, his eyes connecting with hers. But still he held her wrist in a tight grip.

"Touch me," he growled. Her hand closed around him. "Feel that?"

She nodded.

"You want that? Cause this ain't a game."

"Billy—"

Was she even a virgin? He thought she was, but hell, it wasn't like he kept tabs on her sex life. She was in high school. There had to be boys. And maybe she was smart enough not to bring them around the house, because if she did, they'd sure as hell be run off. If not by Tommy, then sure as fuck by him.

His jaw clenched.

"Asked you a question."

"You're scaring me."

He backed off. "Thought so. Don't play this game again, Jess. You hear me?"

She'd nodded once, her eyes big.

"This was a mistake. Best we forget it."

She stared up at him, but he couldn't quite read her expression. Was she scared? Stunned? Disappointed? But he couldn't worry about that now. He needed to get her gone.

"Go, Jess. Get in the house."

She'd jumped down and fled. Embarrassed? Ashamed? He didn't know. Running a frustrated hand through his hair, he made a decision in that moment. It was becoming way too dangerous to be living in this house with her. Not with the way he was starting to feel.

He moved out the very next day.

***

Ghost shook the memory free and stared at the woman before him now.

"I crossed a line I never should have crossed. Thought we both agreed to forget that day ever happened."

"You mean forget that *kiss* ever happened?"

"Yeah. That's what I mean."

"We're not blood-related, Ghost. It's not like you're really my brother. My mom just married your dad. He wasn't the first stepdad I ever had, nor the last."

He squatted back down and began working on his bike

again. "What's she on now?"

"Husband number five."

He shook his head.

"How about your father?"

His brow furrowed. "Mmm, number six, I think."

She huffed out a breath. "Doesn't bode well for either of us, does it?"

Ghost chuckled. "I guess relationship longevity doesn't run on either side of this fucked up family."

She smiled, sobering. "I guess not."

Ghost continued working on his bike. He was glad to occupy his mind with something and that they were both able to drop the subject of the one and only time they'd kissed. He hadn't been lying. It had been a mistake.

Jessie sat back against the wall and eventually dozed off. After a while, Ghost took a break and wandered outside. He found a small bluff and was able to climb up and see the road. He spotted several small groups of Death Heads riding the highway.

He thought about leaving his bike and heading out on foot, but he didn't know how far they'd get, especially with Jessie in those damned high-heeled boots. There was no way she'd be able to hike through the vegetation, and if they kept to the roads, they'd be sitting ducks. He didn't want to think about what would happen if the Death Heads came upon them.

He looked to the west and saw another line of storm clouds approaching. *Goddamn it.* They just couldn't catch a break. He returned to the shed to find Jessie nervously pacing. When she looked up and saw him, she came to a dead stop.

"You came back."

He frowned. "I was just checking out the road."

"I thought you left me."

"Babe, I was twenty yards away."

She began twirling a piece of her hair nervously. "I just thought..."

He remembered that quirk of hers. Whenever she got nervous or anxious she'd twirl a piece of her hair, round and round. He wasn't even sure she was conscious of doing it. But for him it was like a tell in poker—a dead giveaway to how upset she was. Not that she'd ever been hard to read, for him anyway. At least, that had been the case when she was younger. Now, maybe not so much. "Jess, you really think I'd leave you here?"

"Well, I didn't think you'd leave your bike, but when I woke up you were gone..."

"Oh, so I'd leave you, but not my bike, is that it?"

"I'm sorry. Of course you wouldn't leave me. I guess I just... got scared."

Where the hell did this insecurity come from? It was so unlike the girl he'd known. She was ballsy and brave. Perhaps her brother's death had done more damage than he'd realized. That or the years since he'd seen her last had scarred her in some way. She'd obviously left Seattle with not much more than the clothes on her back. At some point he was going to have to draw that out of her, but now was not the time. Now she just needed to feel safe, and that was something he'd always been good at.

"Come here."

She hesitated only a moment before she walked to him. He pulled her roughly into his arms, holding her close. He dipped his head to her ear.

"Not goin' anywhere without you, brat. Okay?"

"Okay."

Lightning flashed and a crack of thunder boomed. He felt her shiver and pulled her closer, remembering how she'd always hated storms as a child. He remembered one storm in particular when she was just a kid, and he'd come home from school that afternoon before either of their parents were home and found her hiding in her closet, shaking with fear. He'd pulled her out and sat on the couch, holding her close, murmuring to her that he was with her and it would be okay. When that hadn't worked, he'd distracted her with stupid knock-knock jokes until he'd had her giggling, completely forgetting the storm raging outside. He saw a glimmer of that scared little girl in her eyes now.

"It's just a storm, sweetheart. We're safe here. Safe and dry." His hands rubbed up and down her back.

He pulled her down, leaning back against the wall near the door. He kept it cracked open a couple inches so he could breathe easier through his claustrophobia.

He held her close against his side. Her arm naturally lay across his stomach, holding him tight. With one hand he stroked her head, and soon his fingers began to play with her hair.

"Ghost?" she whispered.

"Hmm."

"Can I ask you something?"

"Anything, brat."

"When you moved out of your dad's house… Was it because of me?"

He was quiet for a moment, not sure just how much to admit. Finally, he blew out a breath. "Partly."

"Because of the kiss."

The kiss. Their one and only. He'd kissed hundreds of women since then, but still that one kiss he'd shared with her stuck in his memory like no other. "Yes and no."

Her head lifted from his shoulder, and she met his eyes with a frown. "What do you mean?"

"Because of the kiss, but mostly because you were growing up and…"

"And what?"

"I was starting to think about you in a way I shouldn't."

She grinned. "You wanted to fuck me, didn't you?" Blunt and to the point—that was Jess.

"Watch your mouth, brat."

"But it's true, right?"

"Yeah, I wanted to fuck you. That what you wanted to hear?"

"Yep."

"Wasn't gonna happen. No way in hell. So I did what I had to do. I left."

"And now?"

They looked into each other's eyes a long moment. He supposed they both were thinking about the "what ifs".

Which was a total waste of time. It was in the past. Done deal. Best she realized that. He pressed her head back to his chest. "Get some sleep, Jess. Tomorrow I'll get us out of here."

***

The next morning she awoke to find him going over his bike, studying every part.

"What are you doing?" she asked sleepily.

"Trying to rob Peter to pay Paul."

She frowned. "Huh?"

"Trying to find a place on the bike I can steal a bolt to use on the shifter."

"Oh. Any luck?"

"Nope."

"I've got to pee." She stood up and moved toward the door. He barely spared her a glance.

"Don't go far."

She slipped out and glanced around. The sun was up, burning off the chill of the night before and drying out the ground. She moved to some bushes a short distance away. When she returned, her eyes to the ground, she saw something in the dirt near the entrance to the shed. Squatting down, she realized it was two black cable ties half covered in mud. She dug them out and looked at them. Then she bit her lip, stood and moved into the shed.

"Ghost?"

"Yeah, babe?" he asked, still tinkering with his bike.

"Think these will work?" She held up the two black pieces of plastic.

He looked up, his eyes zeroing in on them and narrowing.

"Zip Ties? Let me see." He motioned her over.

She handed them off and watched as he looked from them to the shifter.

"Goddamn, girl. I think they may just do the trick." He quickly threaded them both through the hole where the bolt would go, connecting the two parts together. Then he looped the ties through and pulled them tight.

She watched as he yanked the shifter up and down.

"Fuck yeah." He grinned back at her. "I think we're out of here."

She grinned back.

"Let's go before your friends roll out of bed and come lookin' for you again."

With that her smile faded, and she nodded.

CHAPTER FIVE

Ghost roared back into the Evil Dead's Sturgis campsite with Jessie on the back of his bike, her arms wrapped tight around him. They used it during the Sturgis annual rally for their national meet. It was mandatory, and chapters from all across the country made the trip so the place was crowded with bikes and brothers.

It was now Monday, and Ghost knew the club should have pulled out by now. Hell, he hoped they weren't all still there just because of him.

Fuck.

He brought the bike to a stop and dismounted, eyeing his chapter President, VP, and some of his brothers standing in a group. He looked back at Jessie, ordering, "Stay there."

She gave an almost imperceptible nod. He caught her eyes moving uneasily around the campsite before he turned and strode toward his brothers, satisfied she'd stay put.

"Well, goddamn. It's about fucking time!" Butcher

muttered as he looked over Shades shoulder. Shades, Griz, Boot, and Hammer all twisted around.

"Where the fuck have you been?" Shades growled to Ghost once he'd stalked toward them. "You've been MIA for two goddamn days. I've got half the club out lookin' for you!"

"It's a long story," Ghost bit out.

"We got time," Griz replied with a glare.

"And who the fuck is that?" Shades asked, lifting his chin toward the girl they were all eyeing.

Ghost looked over his shoulder to where he'd left Jessie standing by his bike and muttered, "You ain't gonna believe it."

Shades studied him, his eyes narrowing. "Try me."

Ghost grabbed the beer out of Griz's hand and chugged it down, then wiped his mouth with the back of his hand, drawing the moment out. But in the end, knowing he couldn't avoid dropping this bomb, he just spit it out. "My stepsister."

There was dead silence for a split second, and then Griz let out a bellow of laughter that continued on and on, grinding on Ghost's last nerve. He could see even his VP was trying to hold back a grin.

With his brows raised, Shades asked, "Your *stepsister*?"

"Yeah," Ghost gritted out, then turned to Griz. "And shut the fuck up."

That only made Griz laugh harder. Hammer choked on his beer, spewing it on the ground, unable to hold his own laughter in.

Ghost ground his teeth together, already anticipating the

ribbing he was going to take from his entire chapter over this turn of events. Even now he could see them eyeing her up and down. *Fuck*. He was going to have to lay down the law and make it clear she was off limits to all of them.

"And she's here *why?*" Shades asked, not holding his grin back any longer.

Griz began making thrusting motions with his hips as if in answer to Shades' question, even grunting along for added effect.

Ghost slugged him in the shoulder. "It's not like that, asshole."

Griz stopped the thrusting, but he was still grinning. "Not yet, maybe. But I'll bet you've thought about it. Fuckin' *look* at her. A hot stepsister, isn't that every teenage boy's dream?"

"Grow up, dickhead."

"I'll ask again. Why the fuck is she here?" Shades asked in all seriousness.

"She's in some trouble."

"Yeah? So? Since when did you grow a heart?" Hammer asked.

"Fuck off, Hammer," Ghost growled, but Hammer just grinned back.

"And?" Shades snapped, drawing Ghost's attention back to him.

"She's got some information you're gonna wanna hear."

Shades cocked an eyebrow as if he truly doubted that were possible. "Right."

"I'm not lyin', bro. This could be big for the club."

Shades eyed her. "Get her settled, and we'll fucking talk. And you better have a damn good explanation for being AWOL the last three days."

***

Jessie stood nervously by Ghost's bike, watching him talk with his other club members, then chug down a beer like she wasn't left standing here waiting. *What the hell?*

Had he forgotten about her that quickly?

Then she noticed them all turn and look back at her, and a couple of them burst out laughing.

Oh my God, they were laughing at her.

Well, fuck that. She moved around the bike stalking straight for Ghost. He had another thing coming if he thought she'd stand there and be the butt of some joke.

His head swiveled, and when he saw her moving toward him, and probably more likely the furious look on her face, he moved quickly to intercept her.

He grabbed her by the arm and tugged her in the direction of a huge metal shed.

"Whoa, whoa, whoa. Come on, brat."

She had no choice but to stumble along in his wake, her arm firmly locked in his grip.

"What the hell? Let me go."

"No way, José. I know what you were about to do. I could read it all over your face, Jess."

"They were laughing at me."

"They weren't laughing at you."

She snorted a disbelieving breath.

"And you were about to let loose on them with that

mouth of yours, weren't you?"

"Maybe," she grudgingly admitted.

He huffed out a laugh. "No maybe about it, sugar-pie. You're in a mood."

"I am not. And don't call me that."

He looked back at her with lifted brows.

"Oh, all right, maybe I am, but I can't help it. I'm tired and dirty and *hungry*," she whined.

"Well, if you'd have given me half a second, I was about to fix that."

He continued pulling her along, moving around the corner toward a big grill fashioned out of a cut old oil drum turned on its side. An old grizzled biker stood over the hot coals, turning burgers and brats with a silver tongs. He had two long, graying braids and a headband tied around his head. The bottom rocker on the back of his cut read, Louisiana.

"Skeeter," Ghost greeted.

The old man looked over his shoulder. "Well, look what the cat dragged in. Where ya been, boy?"

"Had a bit of trouble."

It was then the old man's eyes slid beyond Ghost to land on her. "Trouble, huh?"

"Haven't eaten in the last two days, Skeet. You gonna feed us?"

He nodded. "I'll feed ya, Son. Grab a plate."

They soon had plates piled high and were sitting at a picnic table away from the others. Jessie didn't think that was by accident. Ghost seemed determined to keep her away from his club, which was going to be impossible since they were everywhere. She wasn't sure if that was for her benefit or his. At the moment, she didn't care. She was too hungry. She dug into her food like a starving person.

Nothing had ever tasted so good; she practically moaned with pleasure, her eyes sliding closed. When she opened them, Ghost was grinning. Then he winked.

"This is *sooo* good," she said around a mouthful of food. "Willie Nelson over there sure can cook."

He chuckled. "I'll tell him you said so. And do me a favor, don't call him that to his face."

She grinned, still chewing. "If the shoe fits."

"Just don't start shit, Jess, okay? Not everybody appreciates your mouth like I do."

She stopped chewing.

He paused. "That came out wrong."

She grinned. "If you say so, Tonto."

He rolled his eyes.

After they finished eating, he tossed their paper plates in the bonfire and led her into the cavernous, empty shed.

"The club built this place," Ghost told her as they walked. "It wasn't much more than a shelter from the rain when it was first built. There've been a few upgrades over the years. Now we've got a bunch of bunks. They're not much, just a place to unroll a sleeping bag when the weather gets wet."

She noticed there were about ten bunk beds made out of cheap lumber lining each wall on either side of them.

"Not nearly enough for everyone, but most of the guys

sleep out under the stars anyway, so it's all good. Another major improvement and favorite among the guys has been the recent addition of a shower room installed at the far end of the building." He pointed toward where they were headed. "It's got four stalls and, best of all, *hot water.*" He waggled his brows.

She followed him through a doorway. There were indeed four stalls on the right. On the left was a long counter with several sinks. She watched as Ghost leaned against the counter and folded his arms, and then nodded toward the stalls.

"Take a shower. I'll make sure nobody comes in."

She blinked. *Was he joking?*

"Now?"

"You want a hot shower, don't you?"

Her eyes slid to the right. A hot shower *would* be heavenly. But these stalls didn't even have curtains. She supposed bikers weren't shy. At least it wasn't one big communal shower, *but still.*

"Ghost, you want me to take a shower? Now? With you just standing here?"

He grinned and nodded toward the shower at the end. "Take the last one. I won't watch."

"But...you're just going to stand here?"

"You *do* want me makin' sure my brothers don't come in, right?"

Uh, yeah.

"Jess. Take a fucking shower."

Oh, man. That sounded like a challenge. Something

she'd never responded well to. She pursed her lips and flung her cross-bag on the counter with a bang. His eyes followed it and then returned to her, his brows lifting, but he didn't say a word.

Her hands moved to the buckle of the chaps that fastened low on her hips. His eyes dropped to watch. She pulled them off and then tossed them on the Formica counter as well.

His eyes bore into hers, waiting.

She lifted her hand and made a twirling sign with her index finger.

He grinned and grudgingly turned his back to her, grunting out a sigh.

She wriggled out of her leather shorts and tossed them up on the counter. When she did, she saw his head turn a fraction of an inch and his eyes fall on the discarded clothing as she continued to toss piece by piece onto the growing pile.

She unknotted his flannel shirt, pulled it off, and flung it up there.

Next her bra.

And lastly, her panties, like a cherry on top. She saw the muscle in his jaw clench when she got to those, and she couldn't help but smirk. At least she was having *some* effect on him. Maybe she could torture him just a bit in retaliation.

She wasted no time moving into the far stall. Turning on the knobs, she soon had hot water shooting out the showerhead to cascade down her body. It felt wonderful. She grinned and moaned with delight, loud enough for Ghost to hear, knowing the sound would get to him.

"Hmm, this is *heavenly*. The warm water running over

my body feels *so good.*" God, she should get an Academy
Award.

She heard Ghost clear his throat.

"That good, huh?"

"*Um hmm.* I may never come out," she purred, really
rubbing it in.

"I'm not standing here all night, babe, so move it along."

She grinned, knowing by the snap in his voice that she
was really getting under his skin.

She bent down and uncapped the body wash someone
had left, bringing it to her nose. It had a manly scent that she
actually liked. She poured some into her palm and began
washing. Then she shampooed her hair. As she was rinsing
the lather out, she heard Ghost growl, "Get the fuck out,
bro."

"What the hell, man?" a deep voice complained.

"Move."

"*Fuck.*"

Jessie panicked, crossing her arms over her chest and
huddling against the divider, wondering what was happening.
She heard a bang like a fist had hit the wooden wall, then
some stomping.

"Ghost?" she called hesitantly.

"He's gone. Hurry it up, brat."

For once, she did as she was told, dropping the seduction
scene and quickly rinsing off.

A few minutes later she turned off the water and peeked
out around the divider. "I, um, need a towel."

She watched as Ghost yanked his cut off to fling it on

the counter with her clothes, then ripped his tee over his head. Her eyes slid over his exposed chest. *Good God*, he was beautiful. That was definitely not the body of a boy anymore. He was all thickly muscled *man*. Before she could regain her tongue to ask what he was doing, he tossed his t-shirt to her.

"Here, use that," he growled.

She grabbed it up, looking at it with wary eyes. "Are you serious?"

"Hey, this ain't the *Hilton*. There's no towel service out here. It's that or nothing."

She rolled her eyes and retreated back around the divider to dry off as best she could. When she was done, she peeked back out, holding his damp shirt in front of her.

"I need my clothes."

Ghost was leaning against the counter, his booted ankles crossed and arms folded. He lifted his gaze to her, and then the corner of his mouth pulled up as he challenged, "Then come get 'em."

"Ghost!"

"Yeah?"

"Can you *hand* them to me?"

His brows went up. "That how you ask?"

She rolled her eyes and gritted out, "Please."

He grinned, his arms coming unfolded as he straightened. "Yes, ma'am."

He scooped up her clothes—minus the chaps—and strolled over to her. But instead of handing them over when she reached for them, he held them just out of her grasp.

She glared at him as she tried to grab them.

"Uh, uh, uh. Say thank you."

She huffed out a breath. "Fine. Thank you."

"*Nicely.*"

She rolled her eyes, and then batted her lashes up at him with a sugary sweet smile, turning on the southern charm. "Why thank you, sugar. Aren't you just sweet as pie."

He smirked down at her. "Darlin', sweet is the last thing I am. And don't try that game you were just playin' with me again, understand?"

"What game?" she played dumb, frowning.

He lifted his chin toward the stall.

"You know exactly what I'm talkin' about, *sugar.*" Then he gave her a cocky grin, kissed her on the nose, and handed over her clothes. "And you're welcome, you little smartass."

***

After getting Jess set up with a bunk and sleeping bag, Ghost headed out to talk to his brothers.

As he approached, Shades held out a beer toward him. "You get her fed, bathed, and all tucked in?"

Ghost glared at his VP's smiling face. He knew the man was teasing him, so he let it slide.

"Were those your chores when she was a little squirt?" Hammer added.

Now Hammer, on the other hand, got a punch in the arm, which probably hurt Ghost more than it did Hammer since the man was built like a brick house with tattoo-covered biceps as thick as a Christmas ham. That wasn't how he got his name though. No, he got the name Hammer because he nailed everything in sight. "Everything" meaning any woman with great tits and ass.

"Ow. What, too close to home?" Hammer grinned.

"Can we quit the juvenile fucking jokes now?" Ghost asked with a scowl.

"Probably not," Griz added with a grin. The man was six four, forty-eight years old and with his wavy blond hair and beard, he looked like the lead character in the seventies TV show, *Grizzly Adams*. Which was how *he* got his nickname.

"Okay, boys, cut the shit," Shades admonished, taking a hit off his beer. Then his eyes swung to Ghost. "You want to fill us in on what information *little sister* could possibly have that's of use to us?"

Ghost nodded across the fire to where his chapter President, Butcher, stood in what looked like deep conversations with the VP of the San Jose Chapter, a brother named, Cole Austin.

"You sure you don't want to wait until Butcher is free, so I only gotta tell this story once?"

Shades growled, "Butcher's got his hands full right now. Shit went down with one of Cole's men while you were gone. In fact, I was worried it was somehow connected with you being MIA."

Ghost frowned. "What shit? With who?"

"Wolf."

"What happened with him?"

"He was sliced up pretty bad. He's in the ICU in Sturgis."

"You're fucking kidding me. What happened?"

"Got jumped by a sick motherfucker. A DK by the name of Taz."

"No shit? We get the motherfucker?"

"Yeah. That's been taken care of, and that is hush-hush."

Griz grinned. "You missed it, bro. We all went and pissed on his grave."

Hammer pointed to a tree on the other side of the campsite with a chuckle. "Using his cut for target practice."

Ghost glanced over. Sure enough, there was a Devil Kings' cut with a bowie knife nailing it to a tree. He whistled and asked, "Do the DKs know Taz was killed? And by us?"

"No, and we're keeping it that way. As far as they know, he took off. He's always been nomad, and those guys don't live by anybody's rules, so it'll take a while before Big Ed realizes he's missing. And that'll be San Jose's headache."

"So the Devil Kings aren't starting shit with us?"

Shades shook his head. "No. Cole claims it was a personal grudge between him and Taz. The fucker's club wasn't involved. Had no clue what he was up to."

"You sure?"

"Well, I was worried when *you* turned up missing, but Cole assures me the grudge went back to some shit that went down between him and Taz years ago. Wolf just got in the way. Guess he was supposed to be some kind of sick message to Cole."

Ghost stared. "That's messed up shit. How's Wolf doing? Hell, I can't fucking believe this. We were just with him at the tattoo shop."

Shades nodded. "I know. We've all been watching our

backs ever since. But Cole says Wolf's gonna pull through. I guess it was touch and go there for a while. He lost a lot of blood, but he's conscious now and stable."

Ghost lifted his chin to all the club chapters that were still there at the campground when most clubs would have pulled out on Sunday. "That why everyone's still here?"

"That and you being missing, asshole."

Ghost grinned. "Sorry about that, man. Couldn't be helped."

"You lose your fuckin' phone?" Griz snapped.

"Battery died."

"You couldn't borrow one to make a fuckin' call into your club?" Shades asked.

Ghost shook his head. "We were holed up in a shed in the middle of nowhere."

Shades gave him a look. "And why was that?"

"It's a long story."

"Then why don't you fuckin' start at the beginning?"

"Like I said, Jessie's got some info that the club's gonna find useful. Butcher's gonna want to hear it."

"Why don't you run it by me first. Then we'll decide whether to bring it to Butcher. I've got my doubts that little girl could possibly have any information that would be significant."

"This is."

Shades brows shot up. "Then fuckin' tell me."

Ghost twisted the bottle cap off his beer and pitched it into the fire. Then he took a long swig before he dropped the bomb.

"Death Heads planted a man inside the DKs Atlanta Chapter."

That got a brows-raised expression from his VP. "You're shittin' me?"

"Nope. They're plannin' to take Georgia. Gonna take the DKs down from the inside out. And get this… Supposedly *we're* next."

"Hell, it's no secret they've been trying to push across the state line. Thought we had that handled."

"Yeah, we did. I guess they decided to change tactics. Swung their focus to Georgia first, but we're next on the agenda. Guaranteed."

"And this all comes from her?" Shades gave a chin lift toward the shed.

"Yup."

"You wanna fill me in on how she obtained this info?" Shades asked.

"She overheard it."

"She *overheard* it?" Shades asked with an incredulous tone.

"Straight from Florida's mouth."

"Florida? Who the hell is Florida?" Hammer asked.

"President of the Death Head's Jacksonville Chapter," Butcher filled him in as he walked up, overhearing the talk.

Ghost's eyes swung to his President. The man had gray hair, a beard, and wire-rimmed glasses. He had always reminded Ghost of Jerry Garcia of the Grateful Dead. Right now the man's eyes were boring into his.

"How in the hell was this girl in any position to *overhear* anything, Son?"

"Wrong place at the right time."

Butcher gave him a long look and raised one brow. "Or wrong place at the *wrong* time for *her.*"

"Yeah," Ghost agreed with him.

"They know she knows?" Butcher asked.

Ghost nodded. "Yup."

"They know she's with you?"

"They saw me, and they'll remember my face. But I don't think they got a look at my cut."

"You don't *think?*"

Ghost lifted his hands, shrugging. It was the best answer he could give. "They ain't showed up here yet, have they?"

Butcher let out an aggravated breath. "Why don't you start at the beginning."

"Picked up a nail in my tire—"

"Yeah, yeah. I know all that part. Get to the part where you hooked up with this chick. The one with all the information and the Death Heads on her ass," Butcher snapped.

Boot and Slick, the chapter's Treasurer and Sargent at Arms walked up. They were two of the older members in the chapter, and two of Butcher's most trusted brothers. Butcher nodded for Ghost to continue.

He explained the whole story from the moment he first saw Jessie until they rolled into the Evil Dead camp.

Butcher shook his head. "What a cluster-fuck." Ghost watched him turn away, run his hand over his beard, and then turn back to snap, "You believe it?"

"Which fuckin' part?" Shades asked Butcher with a huff that showed his exasperation with the whole mess.

Butcher's eyes swung to Shades. "Any of it. All of it."

"She wouldn't lie. Not to me," Ghost bit out.

Butcher's head came up, his brows raised. "You sure about that?"

Ghost nodded once. "Yeah. I'm sure."

"You trust her?" Shades asked.

"Yeah. I do."

"With your life? With the lives of your brothers?" Butcher added, piercing him with a look.

"I do," Ghost replied tersely, his jaw tight. The air was thick with tension until finally Shades broke it. He looked over at Butcher.

"How do you want to handle this?"

Butcher didn't hesitate, his eyes drilling into Ghost's. "We use her and what she knows to make a deal with the DKs."

Ghost knew what that look meant. His loyalties were with the club, and if he had a problem with this, he'd better get "right" with it, because he had no choice.

Shades cut his eyes to Ghost, and Ghost could read what *that* look meant. He was wondering if his brother was going to be okay with it. He wasn't. Not really. But he would have to be. Because when it all came down to it, he and his club were the only thing standing between her and the Death Heads. That deal could be the only way to keep her safe from them, and to get his club behind helping her, she had to be of some use to them. Making that deal would do it.

"We roll out tomorrow, first light. San Jose Chapter is going to wait for their guy to get released. Now that the crowds have left, they're gonna hole up in a motel until he's fit to travel."

"How long's that gonna be?" Griz asked.

Butcher's gaze swung to him. "Couple more days." Then his eyes returned to Shades. "Make sure the boys are ready to roll out in the morning."

Shades nodded. "Will do."

Butcher stalked off with Boot and Slick at his back.

Shades looked to Griz and Hammer. "Give us a minute, boys." After they walked off, Shades' gaze swung to Ghost. "You gonna be good with this?"

"Gonna have to be, won't I?"

Shades nodded, gazing out over the landscape. "She tell you everything? You got a good feeling about that?"

Ghost stared at his VP. But Shades was much more than just his VP, more than just a brother, he was also a close friend. They'd joined up about the same time and come up through the ranks together. He was closer to Shades than to any of the others.

Shades gaze swung back to his.

It was Ghost's turn to shift his eyes to the horizon. He had to be honest. "Not sure she's tellin' me everything, but I believe the information she's givin' us is true. She wouldn't lie about that."

"Hope not. It won't go well if she is," Shades gave him the warning he didn't need, and then took a swig of his beer. "You want to tell me about her?"

Ghost took a long pull off his own beer. "Not really."

Shades gave him a look.

Ghost grinned. "But I guess I will."

"What I can't figure is why I've never heard about her in all this time. Not once, Brother. What the hell? Thought I knew you."

"You know me, bro."

"Then how is it you have a stepsister I never knew about?"

"My dad's second wife. She had two kids, Jessie and her brother, Tommy. They moved in with us when I was thirteen."

Shades nodded, but remained quiet waiting for Ghost to continue.

"By the time I was hanging around the MC, I'd already moved out of the house. Tommy joined the military. My father divorced Collette not long after that." He took a sip of beer. "Tommy was killed by an IED, and they shipped his body home. I was in lockup awaiting trial on that bullshit assault charge, and I missed the funeral. When I got out, I visited his grave, and Jessie was there. She could barely look at me though."

"Why?"

He shrugged. "She was devastated. Pissed at the world. Next I heard she'd dropped out of school. Two months before graduation, can you believe that? Then she left town with some loser. Anyway, I lost touch with her after that."

Shades studied him, his eyes narrowed. "And?"

"And what?"

"What aren't you tellin' me?"

Ghost blew out a breath and rolled his eyes. "Let it go, man."

Shades grinned. "I see. So that's how it is."

"We had a moment. Once. A long fuckin' time ago. It shouldn't have happened, and it never happened again."

"By 'a long fuckin' time ago' you mean when?"

Ghost tossed his beer bottle in a nearby oil drum. It shattered with a loud crash. "She was sixteen, I was twenty-one. And before you say anything, it wasn't much more than a kiss."

Shades grinned. "I didn't say a word."

"Yeah, but you were thinkin' it."

"She ain't sixteen anymore, bro."

"No, she's not." Ghost sure didn't need Shades to point that out. He was well aware.

"I see you've noticed." Shades chuckled. "Half the club's noticed, too, just so you know."

"Fuck."

"I take it you're putting her off limits."

"Abso-fuckin-lutely."

Shades grinned. "Noted. I'll pass the word."

"I'm gonna take a hot fuckin' shower and hit the sack."

"Enjoy it, bro, cause I see a bunch of cold showers in your future."

Ghost could hear Shades' laughter as he walked away. *Fuck if that wasn't the truth.*

***

Ghost stood beside the empty bunk next to the one

where he'd put Jessie at the end of the row. She was sound asleep. He pulled off his cut and tossed it up on the top bunk. Then he collapsed on the bottom, exhausted. There were a couple of old-timers crashed on the other side, snoring away, but for the most part the shed was empty. And he could see why, with the rain burned off, the shed was hot as hell.

He turned his head and looked over at Jess. She had her back to him, but he could see the outline of her body. She'd kicked off the cover of the sleeping bag in the heat, and his eyes strayed down over the curve of her hip.

Shit.

He turned his head and locked his eyes on the underside of the top bunk. He couldn't allow himself to get any ideas about her and that sweet body of hers. He needed to remember how much she was going to hate him when she found out his club was going to put her in the middle of an alliance with the DKs.

It was a long time before he finally fell asleep.

CHAPTER SIX

Jess awoke when the bunk shook. She opened her eyes to see Ghost standing over her.

"Wake up, Jess. Roll-out's in ten minutes."

She squinted up at him. "Roll-out?"

"The club is pulling out. Heading home."

"What time is it?"

"Seven."

She groaned.

He grinned. "Not a morning person?"

She sat up, rubbing her face. "I need coffee."

He held out a Styrofoam cup. "Saved you the last of it."

She looked up at him as she took it. "Oh, God. Thank you."

He leaned against the top bunk. "We're gonna be ridin' hard today. I want you in the chase van with the prospect."

She looked up at him, wide-eyed. "Why can't I ride with you?"

He shook his head. "Can't take the chance of you being seen on the back of my bike as the club rolls out of town, brat."

Oh. Right.

"You mean by the Death Heads?" For a moment she'd forgotten that just because Ghost made her *feel* safe, it didn't mean she wasn't in danger.

"Exactly. You ridin' in the van is the safest place for you."

She blew out a breath, knowing he was right.

Ghost grinned. "I see you get my point."

"I get it."

"Good, then we won't have any trouble, will we?"

She shook her head. "Nope. You want me in the van, I'm in the van."

"You always this agreeable in the morning?" he asked with a grin.

She rolled her eyes. "No, but you brought me coffee, so I'm being nice."

"Coffee's the golden ticket, huh? I'll have to remember that."

"It is this morning," she murmured against the rim of the cup. She pushed the sleeping bag aside and stood up, catching Ghost's eyes as they swept down the outfit she was wearing the day before. She stood barefoot in her same shorts and his flannel shirt. Her boots sat at the side of the bed.

"Maybe somewhere along the line we can pick you up a pair of jeans."

She nodded. "That would be good."

He rolled his sleeping bag and tied it up, while she drank down the last of the coffee and slid her boots back on. When he was finished tying the last knot, he tucked the roll under his arm.

"Ready?"

She nodded and followed him out.

As they passed the bonfire that one of the men was pouring water on, Jessie noticed a Viking-like biker, who had *California* on his bottom rocker, kick the leg of another who was still snoring away in his bedroll.

The passed out man sat bolt upright, mumbling, "Fuck your mother."

The other biker snorted, "Yeah, in your dreams is the only place that's gonna happen, Green. Get up, bro."

"You save me some coffee, Red Dog?"

"No, I didn't save you any fuckin' coffee, you dumbass. Get up."

Jessie couldn't help but smile at their banter.

"Green?" she asked Ghost as he pulled her along.

He glanced back at the man, and then replied, "He's Irish. It's a long story. Don't ask."

Ghost continued on, pulling her toward the field where lines and lines of motorcycles sat gleaming in the early morning sunlight. He moved through the maze of bikes to his and strapped the sleeping bag onto the back, on top of his pack. Everywhere she looked, men were doing the same thing, some already sitting astride their motorcycles, waiting patiently.

When he was finished, he walked her over to a dark van.

A young guy sat behind the wheel, his window rolled down and his arm hanging out, a cigarette in his hand.

"Yammer, this is Jessie. She'll be riding shotgun with you," Ghost informed the kid. "Jess, Yammer."

"Hey," she said lamely.

The kid was her age, early twenties maybe, with sandy blond hair and an eager-to-please grin. "Climb in, darlin'. Hope you don't mind if I smoke. I'm tryin' to quit, but it's a bitch, ya know? You smoke? Don't matter; I can toss it out if you want me to. I've only got a couple left in the pack, but I'll share if you want one. You want one?"

Jessie's eyes slid to Ghost as she shook her head.

Ghost grinned like he knew her time in the van with Yammer was going to be a trip.

"Don't mind him. He's wired," Ghost said by way of explanation. Then he walked around to the passenger side and opened the door for her. She climbed in, and he braced his hands on the frame and leaned toward Yammer.

"You fix my shifter?"

"Yeah, man. You're good to go. Ingenious temporary fix you came up with, by the way."

"That'd be Jessie who came up with that idea."

The prospect's eyes moved to her. "Really? *Damn.*"

Ghost's expression hardened, not liking the kid's sudden interest. "Keep your hands to yourself, Prospect, you hear me? Or you and I are gonna have a problem."

Yammer nodded, raising his hands in the air. "Hands off. I got it."

Jessie lifted her eyes to Ghost's, and he grinned. "We'll

stop at a truck plaza east of town to gas up. I'll try to get you something else to wear there. And maybe, just maybe, you can get back on my bike there."

She nodded, making a silly face she hoped told him how thrilled she was to be stuck in the van with a wired-up prospect. "Gee, thanks, that would be lovely."

He made a face back at her, then reached in and ruffled her hair, before slamming the door and walking off toward his bike.

The sound of a hundred bikes roaring to life reverberated across the field.

Yammer sat forward with his forearms resting on the top of the steering wheel watching as the bikes all lined up and rolled out, two by two.

"It's a sight, ain't it?"

Jessie had to admit, it *was* quite a sight.

She noticed several different states listed on the bottom rockers that passed them by: *Alabama, Louisiana, Mississippi, Missouri, California,* and *Nebraska.*

"All the state chapters travel together?"

"Yup. Except for the California brothers. They got a man in the hospital they're waitin' on. So they'll be breaking off and relocating to a motel in town, way I heard it."

When the end of the line passed by, Yammer put the van in gear and pulled out onto the blacktop behind them. It was then that Jessie noticed two guys, their bikes parked on the shoulder, holding up traffic so the entire MC could pull out together in one unbroken line. After Yammer pulled out, she saw one of the guys run back and lock a swinging iron gate with a chain as big around as her wrist, effectively closing up the property until the next rally, she supposed.

She watched in her side mirror as the man ran to his bike, and he and the other biker gunned their throttles speeding to catch up with the line. A moment later they zoomed around them to take their places up ahead.

As they rolled over hills and valleys, Jessie could see the long line of bikes riding two-by-two strung out at least a mile long. As their speed picked up, she was amazed at how perfectly they rode, in such tight formation, mere feet behind the back tire of the bike in front of them.

"They ride so close together," she couldn't help observing.

Yammer responded, glancing over to her, "Yeah, yeah, I know, right? MCs know how to ride, and they ride together in pack formation daily. These guys know their brother's riding style better than they know their own."

"It's amazing."

"Yeah, pretty cool, right? They know what they're doin', know exactly how to approach a corner or dodge a vehicle while remaining only a foot or two of distance from each other. Each of 'em watches the riders five rows ahead. You smash into your brother's bike, you're gonna meet his fist personally."

He glanced over at her, his wrist resting on the top of the steering wheel; he lifted just his finger to point to the bikes. "Ridin' shoulder to shoulder like that, darlin', it's an intimate thing. Mastering tight turns in formation like that, it's a rush.

"The bikes up in the front are really starting to pull

away."

"Yeah, those are the club's officers up there. Those guys at the front and the ones right behind them, they're some of the best riders in the club."

Jessie nodded, taking it all in.

"Yeah, when you're riding in a pack, there's nothing like it. You don't worry about those guys hauling ass in the front of the pack."

"How do they know when the front is stopping or someone's having trouble with their bike?"

"We got our own form of sign language. Different signals for a lot of different shit like if they point at the gas tank, it means they're low on gas. If they tap the top of their helmet it means slow the fuck down. Signals for if the law's up ahead or if there's debris in the road. Shit like that."

"Fascinating."

"You gotta make sure your bike is dialed in and can take the abuse of the pack ride, too. One thing you don't want to be is *that guy*.

"That guy?"

"The guy who slows the pack up because his bike is running like shit. Nobody wants to be *that guy*, least of all a prospect."

***

About an hour later, they followed the line of bikes taking an exit ramp that led to a big truck plaza. The roar of bikes was tremendous as the multitude jockeyed for position to form a dozen lines at the various pumps. Yammer pulled off to the side, parking behind a blue pickup truck. He looked through the windshield and chuckled. Jess turned to see what it was he found so funny. She saw a bumper sticker in the back window of the cab that read, *Foreplay in Texas: Get in the truck.*

"That's a good one. You like cowboys? What is it with women and cowboys?"

Jessie just gave him a mystified shrug, hoping he wasn't actually expecting her to explain it to him.

He just grinned and winked. "Bikers are better."

He might be right about that, she had to admit silently in her head.

The van rocked as Yammer climbed out to fill the tank. She heard him unscrew the gas cap and then the nozzle clank as he jammed it into the tank.

Jess slowly undid her seatbelt and climbed out looking around, trying to find Ghost in all the bikes. She needed to go inside and pee.

She told Yammer where she was going, then headed across the lot. Halfway to the building she heard a sharp piercing whistle and looked to the right.

Ghost waved his arm in the air, motioning her over. She felt the eyes of a dozens bikers follow her as she made her way to him, still wearing her leather shorts and high-heeled ankle boots. She heard some catcalls and whistles, but she ignored them.

Ghost's eyes skated down her as she reached him. He pushed his shades up on his head.

"Already checked inside. Only option in there are some pink sweatpants with *Bootylicious* written across the ass." He shrugged with a grin. "Your call."

She rolled her eyes. "Uh, no."

"Yeah, I didn't think so." He glanced around at the area. "Maybe there's a Farm and Fleet around we could check out."

Shades, who was one pump over, hung his nozzle up and recapped his tank. "Not happening, bro. We're not holding up a hundred bikes while you take your girl shopping."

"She needs some jeans, Shades," Ghost replied.

Shades eyes skated down her bare legs. "It's seventy degrees. She'll be fine. Won't ya, darlin'?"

"I guess," she answered.

"That's the spirit," Shades replied with a grin as he passed them on his way inside.

Ghost looked at her with a resigned expression. "Guess it's back in the chaps for you."

"I need to pee."

He lifted his chin toward the building. "Make it quick, brat."

She hurried inside.

When she came back out he held the chaps out to her and waited while she put them on, then he tossed her his leather jacket and a pair of riding glasses. "Here, take my extra pair. The jacket will keep the wind off you if you need it or I can put it back in the saddlebag. But we probably won't stop again for hours. Up to you."

"I'll take it."

"You should probably braid your hair," he suggested, holding out a hair tie that he'd pulled off his handle bar.

She took it, shoved the arm of the sunglasses between her teeth, and began to braid her hair while he stood there patiently waiting. When she was finished, he handed her a spare helmet he'd pulled out of his saddlebag and strapped it on her head.

"All set?"

She nodded.

He swung his leg over the bike, lifted it off its kickstand and fired it up. Then he motioned her to climb on behind him. When she was on, he rolled over and got in the line next to one of his brothers, who looked over and nodded to him, then smiled at her and winked.

She grinned back.

He revved his throttle and turned his attention to the line waiting to pull out. A moment later, the bikes roared to life as the line began to move. When Ghost hit the on-ramp, he twisted his head and yelled over his shoulder, "Hold the fuck on."

She tightened her arms around his waist, and he gunned the throttle. She felt the bike surge forward beneath her. When they reached the top of the ramp, Ghost and the brother to his left eased over in synchronization as if they'd been doing this maneuver for years. She supposed they had.

The wind surged over her, and she watched the landscape soar by.

It was the most thrilling experience of her life. She'd never been on a bike before, except for one time when she'd begged her brother, Tommy, to give her a ride on his dirt bike. He'd refused, but later that afternoon, after her brother had gone to a dentist appointment with their mom, Ghost had sneaked her a ride to the end of the block and back. She remembered holding him tight. He'd been just a boy, then. It was a whole different story holding on to the muscled man he was now.

She smiled, resting her cheek against his back, recalling the memory. A moment later she felt his left hand settle over her thigh just above her knee and give her a reassuring pat and squeeze. It was almost as if he was letting her know he was happy she was on the back of his bike.

She couldn't stop a strange feeling from running through her that maybe, just maybe, this was where she'd always belonged. It had just taken her a long roundabout way to get here. But she was here now. Finally.

***

Five hundred *long* miles later, the club pulled up to the clubhouse of the Omaha, Nebraska Chapter—their hosts for the night. Surprisingly, it was an unassuming, large clapboard two-story building that looked like it was built around the turn of the last century. It was buried back in an old neighborhood on the corner of a tiny side street that ended in a dead-end that butted up against the rail yards. As they rolled up on the corner, Jessie lifted her gaze to the side of the building. There were four windows on the second floor, each one covered with a banner with a different letter that spelled out: E D M C. It didn't take her long to figure out that stood for *Evil Dead Motorcycle Club*.

The windows on the first floor were bricked up with glass blocks. There was one entrance on the side, and some type of warning sign was posted on it, but they rode by too quickly for her to read what it said.

They rolled around the corner, and she got a look at the front of the building. Two narrow windows up top had vertical banners covering them from the inside. One read, *Evil.* The other read, *Dead.*

On the ground floor, on either side of the main entrance were two big windows, each covered with a flag of the Evil Dead logo.

As her eyes scanned the building, she also noticed cameras mounted high in several locations as well as security floodlights. There was a big, newer addition on the right that didn't have a single window, just a door. There was also a six-foot high wooden privacy fence with a gate.

The bikes began backing to the curb and parking in a line that extended all the way to the dead-end and back up the other side of the street. Ghost and the man riding next to him maneuvered into a spot. When he stopped, she scrambled off quickly, and he rested the bike on its kickstand, climbing off himself.

Ghost and his brothers took a moment to stretch, some lighting up smokes before they began to head through the gate into the large compound.

Jessie moaned as she stretched and rubbed her ass.

Ghost grinned. "You sore, brat?"

"Uh, we did just ride all day, so yeah, I'm a little sore."

Ghost chuckled, took her hand and led her inside the compound. She immediately noticed a large group of women waiting to welcome back the Omaha Chapter like conquering heroes.

There was hugging, kissing, and drinks passed around.

She soon found herself pressed against Ghost's side, tucked under his arm, with a beer in her hand, standing among a group of his brothers. There was meat cooking on several grills and tables laden with food. The ol' ladies obviously took care of their men, as well as all the visiting chapters. With no time wasted, the party started cranking up, and even though the men had to be tired from the ride in, it didn't seem to slow them down in the least.

Jessie took it all in, watching the interactions between the men. But, it was the women that fascinated her. Some openly stared at her, some with suspicion that bordered on hostility, some with just curiosity. She couldn't stop herself from asking Ghost about it.

"Why are they staring at me?"

Ghost's eyes followed the direction of her eyes.

"They're wondering who the hell you are, and why you rode in with the club when they all know the annual run to Sturgis is for the club only, no ol' ladies invited."

"Should I be worried? Are they going to hassle me?" She knew they questioned why she was there. But apparently they knew better than to ask.

"Nah, since you didn't show up with anybody from their chapter, they'll pretty much let it go." Ghost nodded in the direction of one of the meaner looking ol' ladies. "Now if you had ridden in on the back of her ol' man's bike it'd be a different story."

Jessie looked up at Ghost and saw the teasing twinkle in

his eyes.

"Good thing I didn't then, huh?"

He grinned. "Yup."

Jessie took a sip of her beer, and then the thought crossed her mind that perhaps Ghost had an ol' lady. Why hadn't she thought of that? She'd never even considered it. Would she have to stand and watch some woman welcome him home with open arms? She felt her stomach drop at the thought.

Even though she was almost afraid to hear the answer, the words came out of her mouth. "Will there be an ol' lady waiting for you when we get back to your clubhouse?"

"You worried about getting beat up?" he asked with a grin, and she couldn't tell if he was joking or not. That wasn't it at all. She *was* afraid of getting hurt, but not in the way he was talking about.

"You didn't answer the question."

"No, Jess, there's no ol' lady waitin' on me."

"Don't let him fool you, darlin'. They'll be women waitin' on him, just no ol' ladies," Shades teased her with a grin, and then held a bottle of Jack Daniels out to her.

"Shut up," Ghost told him as she took it and drank.

She imagined what Shades said was true. Ghost was a very good-looking man. Of course there'd be women, probably a whole line of them. She wasn't sure how she felt about that, but she didn't have time to consider it.

Another one of the members of Ghost's chapter walked up, saying, "I think I'm in love."

"Well, I've got just the cure for that, Hammer," Ghost

said, shoving a bottle of Tequila at him, probably glad for the timely interruption.

Hammer took it, grinning. "I just got a blow job from that cute redhead over there, and now she's off getting me a burger and a beer." He took a bow. "And that, my brothers, is how it's done."

Jessie stared at him with her mouth open.

He looked back at her with a shy grin and lifted his arms, shrugging. "Hey, when you got it, you got it."

Griz pulled a cigarette from his mouth and teased, "Yeah? Well five bucks says she'll change her mind about you by morning."

"Fuck off," Hammer snapped back.

"Yeah, you can always tell how a woman really feels about you by the way she cuts your brake lines," Heavy put in.

The others all turned to look at him.

"Maybe that's just me," he murmured.

Ghost turned to Shades and said, "Bet I stopped listening before you did."

Shades burst out laughing, and Jessie giggled.

Ghost took the bottle out of her hand and handed it back to Shades. "Stop givin' her booze, she's a lightweight."

"I am not," she insisted, staring up at him, and then ruined it by hiccupping.

Shades grinned down at her, then reached up and ruffled her hair. "You tell him, girl."

"I think you've had enough partying, brat," Ghost insisted.

Jessie looked up at Ghost. "Are we staying here tonight?"

"Nah. It's crowded as fuck with all the chapters passing through, even with the Omaha boys crashing at their own cribs, there's not much room. Besides, I figured you'd be more comfortable in a motel." His eyes connected with hers. "Am I right?"

She nodded and yawned.

Ghost smiled as he watched her.

"Aren't you tired?" she asked.

"Yeah, a little. You obviously are."

She hiccupped again, and both Shades and Ghost chuckled.

"Time to go, brat," Ghost insisted, taking her by the arm and steering her through the crowd. He led her out to his bike, and they headed down the road.

Jessie laid her head down on Ghost's back and held on tight. Surprisingly, she dozed off. Also surprisingly, she didn't fall off.

CHAPTER SEVEN

A few miles from the Omaha Clubhouse, Ghost spotted a cheap motel and slowed to turn in. Just as he was making the turn across lanes and into the drive, an old man driving a Cadillac roared out. Ghost swerved to avoid him, but the old man clipped his back tire, and Ghost lost control and laid the bike down. They slid about ten feet across the parking lot.

Jess rolled clear of the bike, but it landed on Ghost's leg. He quickly scrambled to lift the six-hundred pound bike off of where it had his leg pinned. As he did so, he twisted to see where Jess was. He called out to her. "Jessie! You okay?"

She didn't respond right away, but he saw her roll over slowly and sit up. He yanked his leg free and scrambled to his feet, moving quickly to her side, favoring his left leg.

"Babe, are you hurt?" he asked, squatting down next to her.

She leaned to one side, her hand going to her hip, and winced. "My side."

Ghost rolled her and pulled up her shirt and jacket. The skin was fine there. Then he moved down to her hip and thigh, and he could see that when they slid across the pavement, her shorts had been pushed up and exposed the skin between the bottom hem of her shorts and where the chaps started. There was about a three-inch scrape on her skin.

"Fuck, babe. I'm sorry."

She struggled to sit up.

"You're hurt. Just stay down."

The manager of the motel came running out of the office.

"Are you okay?"

Ghost glanced up at the man. "I'm good. She's hurt."

"Do you want me to call 911?"

"No, please. I'm fine," Jessie begged.

"You sure, babe?" Ghost asked her, frowning.

"It's just a scrape."

"There's a first-aid kit in the office. It really should be cleaned up, ma'am."

Ghost looked up at the man. "Yeah, that'd be good. We were pulling in to get a room. You got one?"

"Yeah, got one left—the handicapped room, first floor. Please, come in the office. Are you sure you don't want to report this?"

"An old man in a Caddy hit us. He's long gone by now. Nothin' the cops can do about it but file a report, and that's a waste of time for all of us."

The man nodded and glanced over to where Ghost's bike

still lay on its side in the middle of the parking lot. "Let's get her inside, and I'll help you with your bike."

"Thanks, man."

Fifteen minutes later, they were checked into a nearby ground floor room, Ghost's bike parked outside the door. Luckily, the accident had just bent the passenger foot peg, scraped some paint, and damaged his taillight. Yeah, he was pissed, but those were easy fixes. He was just thankful Jessie hadn't been hurt more seriously. Especially when he noticed the scratches on her helmet as he removed it and set it on the dresser.

He guided her to the bed and tossed the first-aid kit that the manager had given him next to her. The man had offered to help, but Ghost had declined. No way in hell was he letting the man put his hands on Jess, especially given that the area that needed attention happened to be on her lower hip.

She shrugged out of the jacket Ghost had given her, dropping it on the mattress. Ghost grabbed it and tossed it aside, thankful she'd had it on. It had saved her from a far worse injury, protecting her tender skin from the asphalt.

He knelt down in front of her and began removing her boots, cursing silently to himself that he should have seen the Cadillac sooner. She moaned as he pulled off her left boot. His eyes flashed up to hers. "Jess, are you hurt worse than you're lettin' on?"

"I'm okay, just banged up a bit. That's all, I swear."

He took her small foot in his hand and rotated her ankle gently, watching for any sign in her reaction that maybe she'd broken it. "Does that hurt?"

She shook her head. "No. I'm fine, Ghost."

He nodded, pulled off the other boot, and then rose to his feet awkwardly. When she saw him favoring his leg, she asked, "Ghost, you're the one that's hurt. Your leg—"

"I'm okay. Just got it hung up under the bike. It's fine."

"Are you sure?"

"Yeah, now let's get these chaps off you, darlin'," he said in a low voice, his hands already moving to the zippers that ran up the outside of each leg. He gently removed them, taking care not to brush against the scraped area. "We need to get you out of those shorts, too. Lay back."

She did, giving him no lip for once. He unzipped the shorts and carefully eased them down, studying her face and watching for pain as he did so. He could tell the effects of the alcohol she'd drunk at the clubhouse were still dulling her senses, and he was glad for it. It may actually have done some good, keeping her body loose when the bike went down. Otherwise, if she'd tensed up, she may have hurt herself worse, perhaps even broken a bone.

Shit, he'd like to catch up with that old man and kick his motherfucking car door in. He blew out a breath, letting go of the anger. It wouldn't do her any good for him to get riled up right now.

She lay back against the pillows in nothing but his flannel shirt, her bra, and panties. Ghost swallowed and reached for the first-aid kit as he sat on the bed next to her.

"Roll on your side, Jessie. Let me have a look," he instructed softly. She complied, rolling to face him. He examined the scrape. It was bleeding a bit, but not too badly.

"How much does it hurt?"

"It stings a little."

He grinned. "I'll bet. Don't worry; I'll fix you up. Stay right there while I go wash my hands first."

"Okay, Doc," she teased. He smiled and headed into the bathroom to scrub his hands. When he returned, her eyes were closed.

"You with me, brat?" he asked as he opened the kit and dug around for an antiseptic wipe. Her eyes opened, and she tried to smile.

"I'm still here."

"I know you've had a lot to drink, but stay with me, okay?" He tore open the packet and took out the wipe. "This may sting a little, sweetheart."

She hissed when he gently cleaned the area.

"Sorry, Jess. I'm trying to be careful."

"I know. It's okay," she whispered.

His eyes flicked up to hers, and he winked at her. "Your first case of road rash."

"Is this some type of rite of passage?"

Ghost chuckled. "Maybe. But I didn't lay the bike down on purpose."

"I guess I dozed off. Last I remember we were pulling away from the clubhouse. I'm lucky you didn't lose me on the road somewhere."

"I felt your weight against my back, and I had one hand clamped around your forearm. I wouldn't have let you fall, brat."

"What happened?"

"Guy almost hit us. Old man in a Caddy. He came barreling out and clipped the back of my tire as we pulled in the lot. I'm just glad you weren't hurt more seriously." He shook his head. "I'd have never forgiven myself if something had happened to you."

"I'm okay, Ghost. It's just a scrape."

"You were on the back of my bike. I take that shit seriously, Jess."

"I know you do."

He tossed the antiseptic wipe in the trash and dug out an ointment packet. He squeezed some onto his finger, dabbed it tenderly across her scrape, and watched her for signs that he was hurting her. "This has an analgesic in it, so it should help with the pain."

She nodded, closing her eyes as he finished.

"Okay, babe. I'm done. You can open your eyes again." He grinned when they fluttered open. "I think you'll survive. You want me to cover it with a bandage or let it air out?"

"Leave it."

"Okay, but you'll need to sleep on your side."

She nodded. "I'll be fine."

He dug some pain meds out of the kit and moved to the dresser. Picking up one of the plastic cups next to the ice bucket, he pulled the paper wrapping off, and then he moved to the bathroom to fill it with water. He returned to the bed and held the pills and glass out to her.

"Here, take these."

She went up on an elbow and tossed the pills back. She gave him the glass when she was through, and he set it down on the nightstand

It was then he realized that the room only had one bed. *Fuck.*

She lifted her hand to him. "Lay down with me."

He shrugged off his cut, tossed it over a chair, and then sat on the side of the bed to pull his boots off. They landed with a thud on the carpet. "I'm gonna take a shower. Wash some of this road grime off."

She nodded. "Okay."

His eyes slid over her bare legs, and he swallowed, thinking he might make that a cold shower.

***

Fifteen minutes later, he stepped out of the bathroom, his jeans pulled back on, the top button undone.

His eyes swept over Jessie as he moved toward the bed. Her eyes were closed, her hands tucked under her cheek. He smiled. In sleep, she looked like the young girl he remembered. He slid on the bed next to her, his back to the pillow and headboard, and he put his arm around her. She snuggled closer, her head moving onto his chest and her leg sliding over his thighs. Her arm stole across his bare abs.

He kissed the top of her head while his fingers slid through her hair. His eyes couldn't help but drift down to her ass that was revealed as the flannel shirt rode up. He fought the urge to take his hand from where it played with her hair and move it down to stroke and squeeze that cute ass cheek. His jaw clenched as he tried to tamp down his swelling desire. He couldn't have thoughts like that. Not about her. Then his eyes moved along her hip to the red scraped skin, and he closed them, thanking God that things hadn't been worse.

He'd promised Tommy he'd look out for her, take care of her if something ever happened to him. It was a promise he intended to keep. She hadn't made it easy, running off like she had, disappearing from his life. But he'd understood why. And, with the way things had been before he'd moved out, maybe distance was the best thing between them.

But now she'd come back into his life, in typical Jess fashion, bursting upon him with all the drama of a chase scene. Jess couldn't do anything simple. No, it always came with drama and flair.

Question was, what the hell was he going to do with her? When they got back to Birmingham, the trouble she was running from would follow. Which meant he'd need to keep her safe, and that meant he'd need to keep her close.

There was the rub of it—the two of them together. How long would it be before he couldn't fight the attraction that flared up every time he was near her, the desire that clawed at his gut, even now?

As if she read his thoughts or maybe felt the sexual energy vibrating through his body, her hand began to move across his abs, her palm gliding over his skin, lighting him up like a fucking Christmas tree, a trail of static electricity shooting straight to his groin.

The hand that still toyed with her hair froze. Her head lifted, her big eyes coming to his before dropping to his mouth. *Ah, hell. Don't look at me like that, babe.*

She only had to move a couple of inches, sliding up ever

so slightly, and their lips met. It was soft at first, just a touch, and then her mouth opened, and the tip of her tongue traced along his lips.

And fuck, that's all it took.

His hand in her hair tightened, holding her head as his tipped to the side to fit their mouths together. He opened and took her kiss, taking over control, taking the lead. His other palm came up and cupped her face, holding her head immobile as his tongue swept inside her mouth.

Jesus Christ, he'd forgotten how sweet her kiss was. No, that was wrong. He remembered. He remembered every blessed moment of that kiss they'd shared so long ago. But she wasn't sixteen anymore. She was a woman, and her half naked body was pressed against his in a soft, warm bed. A situation that could test the will of a saint, and he was no saint.

He couldn't stop his hand from straying down her throat to the opening of that soft flannel shirt of his she still wore, his fingers curling around the first button, popping it free, then the second, which was all she had done up. The edges fell free, and his hand slid inside. He'd been expecting to find her lacy bra underneath, but when his hand closed over warm silky skin, he broke the kiss, staring down at her.

"Where's your bra?"

She looked up at him dazed and confused, a little frown creasing her brow as she answered, "I took it off."

He hadn't meant to go this far, hell he hadn't meant to do any of this. He could tell, looking down into her eyes, that she was still a little tipsy. He pulled his hand away, but not before realizing just how perfect her breasts were, soft and warm in his hand, how perfectly they fit. He gritted his teeth, pushing her away, his hand closing over her upper arm to do so.

"Jess, you should get some sleep."

She looked up at him with those big eyes, confused again. Then her gaze dropped to his mouth and apparently she'd thought better of that idea, deciding she didn't want to sleep, because she moved in to take his mouth again.

He pushed her back.

"Jess, stop it. We can't do this."

"Why not?"

He shook his head. "You know why."

"Don't you want me?"

Right, like that was the problem. "You know that's not it."

"Then kiss me."

"Jess."

She curled further into him, that thigh of hers sliding back and forth across his crotch driving him to distraction. Fuck, did she even know what she was doing to him? *Of course she did.* "Brat, we can't do this."

His use of the nickname he'd always called her must have gotten to her.

"I'm not a child anymore, Ghost."

He huffed out a laugh. "Yeah, no shit. That's part of the problem."

Her hands slid up his chest, cupping his neck, his jaw. "We're both adults. We both want this. I know you want me."

His hands clamped over her wrists, pulling her hands off him before he succumbed to her touch. "Jess, we can't. Not you and me. That's not what we have. We can't ever go there."

"Why not?"

"Because it's you. I can't go there with you and then…"

"And then what?"

He shook his head. He couldn't have a fling with her. It couldn't lead anywhere—not with the life he led, not with the things he'd done. There were things he knew, the moment she found out, she'd be done with him. She walk out that door so fast, it'd make his head spin. Then where would he be? How could he have her, taste her, take everything she had to give, and then let her go? He couldn't. He knew himself well enough to know that it would be the straw that broke him. After losing Tommy, after pulling away from her because he knew it was what was best, only to have to let her go all over again? No way. He couldn't do it.

It gave him the strength to push her back.

"Not gonna happen, brat. Now go to fucking sleep." His voice came out harsher than he'd intended, probably because of all that pent-up desire surging through his body. She looked hurt, but maybe that was for the best. It would probably be enough to keep her from pulling this shit again. She'd be mortified in the morning, embarrassed she'd come on to him and he'd rejected her flat.

She pulled away, moving across the bed, putting a good foot between them. She flounced onto her stomach, turning her face to the opposite wall, her back rigid. His eyes stayed on her. Hell, he hated hurting her like that, especially when it was all bullshit lies. *He wanted her*. Hell, he'd wanted her since she'd come of age, maybe even before that. But he couldn't go there. Not with her. That was a line he couldn't allow himself to cross. She trusted him, she always had. She'd always looked up to him with big eyes filled with worship. He'd seen it, right from the beginning. With Jess it was hard to miss. But his job had always been to protect her. A job he took seriously. And he'd do that now, even if it meant protecting her from himself.

He turned his head, his eyes to the ceiling. Fuck, it was gonna be a long night and an even longer trip. They had another stop before they got home. Another night of this torture—trapped in a room with her and forced to keep his hands to himself. His jaw tightened. And then what? What the fuck was he going to do with her when they got back home? Her mom was living in Daytona now, Death Head territory. He sure as hell couldn't ship her off there, not that Butcher would let him. Not with what she knew. Nope, Butcher would use her to make a deal with the DKs—a deal the club needed. Butcher wanted an alliance with them. *Needed* one to keep the Death Heads from pushing into both their territories. Hell, it was an alliance that benefited both clubs. It was just a matter of talking the DKs into seeing it that way that was the problem. But with the information Jessie had, it could make the difference.

Fuck, he was exhausted. He felt the long miles of road they'd traveled catching up with him, and his eyes slid closed. He'd worry about dealing with a pissed off Jess tomorrow. Tonight he just needed sleep.

CHAPTER EIGHT

Jessie felt the bed move and cracked one bloodshot eye open. Ghost got up and went into the bathroom. When the door shut, she rolled to her back and squinted at the crack of light coming in the curtains, groaning as a hangover headache throbbed in her temples. Swinging her legs over the side of the bed, she slowly sat up. Her tongue was thick with cottonmouth, and her body ached from yesterday's long ride.

The sound of the toilet flushing carried through the door, drawing her eyes to it. A moment later, Ghost walked out. He stopped when he saw she was awake.

"Morning," she whispered. She watched his eyes sweep down her and stop on her chest. She glanced down and realized the flannel shirt was unbuttoned and hung open, exposing a three-inch wide gap from her throat to her panties. She quickly pulled the plackets together and buttoned two buttons.

"Morning," he said, finally finding his voice.

She watched him move to the nightstand and pick up his cell phone, glancing at it. She stood and moved toward the bathroom, but he caught her hand. She turned to find him shoving his phone in his pocket, his eyes on her.

"How's your hip?" he asked, lifting his chin toward it.

"It's fine," she replied, her eyes cast down, embarrassed that she'd gotten drunk last night, mortified that not only had she come on to him, but that he'd rejected her attempt.

"Let me see."

"It's fine."

His brows rose, and his voice deepened. "Let me see."

She exhaled a breath and gave in, knowing he'd insist anyway. Turning, she pulled the tail of the shirt up, exposing the scrape.

"Satisfied?" she bit out in a sharp voice.

Ignoring her snarky attitude, he dipped his head and examined the wound. She also dipped to look, bringing their heads close together. When she did, his eyes lifted and connected with hers. For a long moment neither said anything.

Finally Ghost broke the spell, straightening.

"Were you wanting to take a shower?"

"I'd planned on it, yes. If that's okay with you?" she ground out. God, why were these antagonistic words just jumping out of her mouth? Because she was hung-over, and more likely because she was embarrassed and humiliated over what had happened between them last night. Or correction, what *hadn't* happened. She watched his jaw tick as he appeared to hold back a retort.

"That's fine with me, brat. I was just going to suggest we coat it in ointment again first to protect it from the water. *That okay with you?*"

"Fine," she snapped.

"Fine," he snapped back, lifting his chin toward the bed. "Sit down."

She flounced down on the bed like a recalcitrant child, crossing her arms and sticking out her chin. She was fully aware she was being a bitch, but something in her couldn't help it. She could cut the tension smoldering between them with a knife, and she knew it was sexual tension. And damn him for not admitting it.

He moved to the dresser to get another packet of ointment out of the first-aid kit. Then he squatted down in front of her, tearing it open. Squeezing some out, he smeared it over her skin, covering the wound completely.

His touch was gentle, even though she knew he had to be a little irked with her right now. And with the tender way he ministered to her wound, another little piece of her heart became his. It took her right back to when she was a child, and he would wipe her tears and tell her she was okay.

Damn him. Why did she have to be so attracted to him and yet he seemed to be able to put her aside, to walk away from any desire he might feel for her? Was it just that easy for him?

"That should help." His eyes trailed up her body to her face before he slowly rose.

She nodded. "Thanks." Then she moved to the bathroom, closing the door and leaning against it. Oh God.

Could he see what he did to her written on her face? Could he tell how her pulse quickened whenever he looked at her like that? How her breathing accelerated?

Was it obvious how she felt about him? Mortification washed over her knowing he didn't return the feeling. Yes, he'd kissed her last night, touched her, but then he'd stopped, *pushed* her away actually. So he couldn't possibly feel what she felt. How pathetic could she be? She'd practically thrown herself at him last night.

Pushing away from the door, she turned the shower on. She couldn't think about that now, not with her head pounding like it was. She crossed to the door, opened it a crack to call out to Ghost, "Hey, are there any more painkillers in that kit?"

A moment later, he was passing a packet to her along with the cup she'd used last night.

"Thanks."

"No problem, brat. Headache?"

"Yes, a doozy."

He nodded, as if that explained her foul mood. "I'm gonna run out for a couple minutes. When I get back, we'll grab some breakfast, okay?"

She nodded, wondering where he was going. Perhaps it was club business. She watched his retreating back a moment before closing the door and climbing in the shower.

***

Twenty minutes later, she had a towel wrapped around her and was finishing applying her eye makeup using the mirror over the sink, when she heard the motel room door.

Setting the eyeliner on the counter, she opened the bathroom door to see Ghost tossing a plastic bag on the bed. His eyes lifted, sweeping over her body to take in the towel.

"You're back," she said, clutching it around her.

He jerked his chin toward the bag. "Picked you up a change of clothes."

Her mouth parted. She'd had no idea that his errand involved shopping. For *her*, no less. She frowned, her curiosity drawing her out of the bathroom toward the bag. She hesitated, torn between excitement to have some different clothes and fear over what he'd picked out. What the hell did men know about these things?

"You...got me clothes?" She stared at the bag like it contained a snake.

The corner of his mouth pulled up. "You *did* need some, right?"

Her eyes rose to his, and she bit her lip, nodding. "Yes."

"We should bandage your scrape before you put 'em on."

Her eyes moved to the first-aid kit. "Right."

"Sit." He gestured toward the bed and dug out a large square bandage.

She sat and carefully raised the edge of the towel at her hip, embarrassingly aware that she was completely naked underneath. He squatted down in front of her, their eyes level, connecting momentarily before his fell to her skin. She leaned to the opposite side so he would have better access.

"Looks better. Ointment seems to be working."

She nodded, her voice deserting her as his hand slid

gently up her thigh as he examined it, his light touch sending tingles skittering across her skin.

Did he even have a clue how much his slightest touch affected her?

His eyes briefly connected with hers before he pressed the large square bandage over the spot. He used a tender touch to press around the adhesive edges, securing it in place.

She watched as his palm softly cupped the bandage and applied light pressure.

"You gonna be able to stand sliding pants on over it?"

Her eyes connected with his. "I think it'll be fine."

He nodded, reached for the bag, and handed it to her. "Go get dressed then, brat. Guys are already at the diner. We hurry, we'll have time to eat before they're ready to roll out."

She stood, but then stared at him as if in a trance.

He nodded toward the bathroom. "As much as I'm enjoyin' the sight of you in nothin' but a towel, we need to get a move on."

She blinked.

Right. He was waiting for her to move, and here she stood like a complete moron.

She hurried to the bathroom, closing the door. Then she tore into the bag, setting the items down beside the sink. She pulled out a pair of low-rider jeans. They were a no-name brand, but she was surprised to find when she glanced at the tag that they were the correct size. Then she pulled out the rest: one black tank top, one white tank, and two pairs of lace panties—one black and one red.

She stared at the lacy scraps of fabric in her hand and

couldn't help but wonder what had gone through his mind as he'd picked these out.

She shook her head, telling herself not to read anything into it, and hurried to dress.

***

Fifteen minutes later they pulled up at a tiny brick storefront diner down on Fortieth Street. The sign read Pearl's. There was already a line of shiny black bikes parked at the curb, their chrome pipes gleaming in the early morning light. Ghost backed into a spot and shut his bike off.

As Jessie slowly climbed off, the muscles in her thighs and ass screamed in pain, reminding her of the hours of abuse they'd taken on the long ride yesterday. Between that and the still dull hangover headache, she whimpered.

Ghost looked over at her as he unbuckled his helmet. His white teeth flashed with his grin, but his eyes remained hidden behind dark shades. "You sore, brat?"

She couldn't help but run her hands over her ass. "Yeah, a little."

He took her helmet from her and hung it on the handgrip next to his. "How's your head?"

She pulled her riding glasses off, immediately squinting into the glaring sun. "Beating like a drum. It'd be helpful if it wasn't so bright."

He grinned and took her hand, stepping onto the sidewalk. "Maybe you'll feel better with some food in your stomach."

As they moved toward the door, she saw one of his club brothers standing at a nearby car parked at the end of the line of bikes. The hood was up, and he was tinkering under it. Two young, pretty girls stood by watching. It was obvious to Jessie that it was their car. The man had a beard and black wraparound glasses that made him look like a member of ZZTop. Full sleeves of tattoos decorated both arms. He glanced over and nodded to Ghost, who gave him a chin lift as they walked by.

Then Ghost held the door open for her, and she stepped inside.

It was a small place with a cozy down-home feel. The floors were linoleum, the ceilings were pressed tin, and vinyl-coated green-checkered cloths covered the tables. Jessie couldn't help smiling. It was a greasy spoon with *old-school cool*. She loved the place already and murmured, "This place is totally sweet."

The corner of Ghost's mouth pulled up at her remark as he led her to some tables in the back that his leather-clad brothers had taken up. The men looked up at they approached.

She recognized faces from the run and from the Omaha Clubhouse. As they walked up, she noticed a couple of the patches. Some read Louisiana, some Alabama, and some Nebraska.

Ghost glanced around the table, his eyes skating over every man. "A bunch of badasses." He paused, his eyes landing on the last man. "And their friend, Sandman."

The men at the table chuckled at Ghost's joke.

The man he teased slumped his shoulders. "Aw, come on, man. Why you gotta be like that?"

Ghost's eyes moved from Sandman to the man in the chair in front of them and greeted him by name. "Blood."

Jessie watched the man as he twisted to look over his shoulder. He was good-looking, with dark hair and a close beard. But it was his eyes that were stunning. The kind of eyes that could root you to the floor, gazing all the way down to your soul. Those eyes skated past Ghost to her, and then ran down over her body slowly. "Heard you had some new pussy. This her?"

Before she realized what she was doing, she slapped him. *Crack*, right across the face.

The table suddenly got deadly quiet.

He rose to his feet, staring down at her. "Is that all you got, pussycat?"

"Blood," Shades growled in a warning tone.

She felt a hand clamp around her upper arm, and Ghost pulled her behind him as he stepped nose to nose with the man.

"We gonna have a problem, Blood?"

The corner of Blood's mouth pulled up in what she supposed could pass for a grin. "Nope. I like a woman with spunk and sass."

Ghost nodded with a brow raised. "Good to know. 'Cause she's got plenty of that."

Blood's teeth flashed as his smile widened. A second later those eyes shifted from him to her. "Sorry, sweetness. No offense meant." He pulled his chair out and waved her into it with a flourish.

She stared at him suspiciously, as if he might just pull it

out from under her to have her land on the floor on her ass.

His brow arched. "What? Chivalry isn't dead."

She bit her lip and moved cautiously to sit on it.

He scooted the chair in a few inches causing her to grab at its base nervously, and he leaned in close, his hands still gripping tightly on the back of her chair and added, "Guys just get tired of ungrateful bitches."

She sucked in a breath and felt Ghost sit in the chair next to her, squeezing her between him and Shades. He leaned over and half-whispered, "That's code for 'say thank you', sweetheart."

She glanced up at Blood who still stood over her. "Thank you."

"You're welcome."

"I'm not an ungrateful bitch."

"Good to know." And she swore the man almost smiled before moving to a seat on the other side of the table.

Ghost leaned forward on his elbows, his eyes hitting one of the men from the Omaha Chapter that sat the end of the table. "Heard you were knee deep in some sexcapades last night, Skunk."

The man grinned back. "You know my motto: two blondes are better than one."

Ghost grinned. "Were they twins? You workin' through some kind of sexual bucket list?"

"Nope. Had twins, never triplets, though. That's the holy grail."

"You got that list all printed up and everything, Skunk?"

He grinned as he lifted his coffee mug to his mouth.

"There's an app on my phone."

"You're not right in the head, dude."

"It's an interesting list. I've seen it," another man at the table added.

"Want to see it?" Skunk offered.

"Does it include farm animals?" Ghost asked with a grin.

One of the brothers almost spewed coffee all over the table.

Shades looked over at Ghost. "You missed all the fun last night. Cops came and everything."

"Really."

One of the Omaha men added, "Well, hell, it ain't a party till there's gunfire, right?"

More chuckles.

"Absolutely."

"Marlene gave me the third degree last night about who the new girl was." His eyes slid to Jessie for a moment.

"A jealous woman does better research than the FBI, man," the brother next to him added, forking food into his mouth.

"You got that right."

The man that had been outside helping the women with their car ambled in. He glanced over at a nearby tableful of young teenage boys and tossed them a nugget of advice as he made his way to the table. "Fellas, learn how to fix shit. It will get you blowjobs. You're welcome."

His brothers all grinned as he yanked out a chair and sat down.

"I take it that went well," one of them commented,

chuckling.

"Absolutely."

A waitress arrived, passing out plates of food to the men who had ordered earlier. Jessie's eyes swept around the table, taking in the various plates of heaping food. They were all piled high with different items that all smelled terrific. She looked over at Shades' plate. It was a smothered rib-eye, and she practically drooled. "Sweet merciful mother of…"

Shades grinned over at her. "Get you one."

"No way. I couldn't eat all that."

He nodded toward the man across from him. "How about that?"

She looked over to see a stack of pancakes that took up the entire plate. Her eyes got big as she looked back at a grinning Shades. "That pancake is the size of my face."

"You're a goof," he replied.

Ghost handed her a menu.

Mugs of piping hot coffee were brought out quickly and set in front of the two new arrivals.

One of the guys looked over at her. "If you're one of those hippy-dippy coffee snobs, this ain't the place for you."

"I'm not," she replied. But she had spent the last few years in Seattle, the coffee mecca of the world, so, yes, she was spoiled with some superb product. She sipped the coffee, surprised to find it was really good.

Sandman's plate was set before him, and he immediately reached for packets of grape jelly, mixing them in with his scrambled eggs and making a big purple, mucky mess.

Jessie arched a brow. "That's grape jelly."

He looked over at her with a conspiratorial look and put the side of his index finger to his lips. "Shh. There's not enough for everybody."

"You're weird," she replied, grinning at him.

"What? That's normal."

Ghost chuckled. "Normal is a destination you ain't ever gonna reach, bro."

Sandman shoveled a big forkful into his mouth and spoke around it. "Ask me if I give a fuck."

One of the men, who she recognized as one of the Omaha Chapter members looked up from his plate. "Menu has all the good stuff. This is our go-to place the morning after a night of general debauchery. Nothing fancy about the place, just good comfort food. You name it, they got it, and the best part? It won't break the bank."

"Home-style on the cheap, bro," Shades said over her head to Ghost.

Sandman shoved a forkful into his mouth and spoke around it. "Food's nothing to complain about."

The man across from him snorted. "You always got something to complain about, Sandman."

Sandman spoke around his mouthful, "Not this, bro. It's as if some wizard cast a spell and created a singularly awesome breakfast."

"Don't mind him. He's stoned," Blood teased.

"I am not," Sandman insisted. "Just hungry."

Jessie couldn't help but giggle.

The waitress came to stand behind her and Ghost. "What'll you two have?"

Jessie looked up to find the woman's eyes on her. She quickly glanced down at the menu and picked something. "Um, toast, bacon, and fresh fruit.

Ghost grabbed it out of her hand and handed it to the waitress. "She'll have the stuffed French toast. I'll have the chicken fried steak."

After the waitress walked away, Jessie turned to Ghost. "Why did you do that? I'm not that hungry."

"You need to eat. We got a long day of riding ahead of us. And I seem to recall you love strawberries," he added with a grin.

He remembered! Why did that make her want to grin from ear to ear? She sucked her lips into her mouth to keep from doing just that and having the whole table see her reaction.

Shades grinned. "Strawberries, huh?"

She rolled her eyes, but couldn't help grinning back. "I like strawberries. What of it?"

His brows shot up, and he looked over her head to Ghost. "She's a feisty one, ain't she?"

"Yup," she heard Ghost reply, and her head whipped around to him.

"I am not!"

"Oh hell yeah, you are." He grinned, taking a sip of his coffee.

The men continued shoveling food in their faces, occasionally pausing long enough to talk, or, more accurately, make smartass comments back and forth to each other.

It wasn't long before their plates arrived. Her eyes got big when her order was plopped down in front of her. French toast stuffed with strawberries, topped with whipped cream and powdered sugar.

She didn't waste anytime digging in. At the first bite, she moaned in delight. "Hmm. It's super yummy."

"Did she just say 'super yummy'?" Hammer asked.

"Why yes she did, and I agree," Shades replied with a grin.

When they'd finished with their food and were relaxing over cups of coffee, Ghost turned to her. "Maybe you should ride in the chase van with the prospect."

"I'm fine."

"Bullshit. You're hung over, scraped, and your ass is sore."

That brought grins out all around the table.

"Oh, *really?* Why's her ass sore?" Blood asked.

"Yeah, what'd you do to her last night?" Sandman added.

"Shut the fuck up." Ghost swung his gaze back to her. "You're in the van."

She huffed out a breath.

"Ooo, the 'woman huff'. Which, in my experience, is never a good thing," Griz teased.

Ghost arched a brow at her, ignoring his brother. "Don't give me any lip."

"Fine," she snapped.

"Ooo, that's even worse. When a chick says 'fine', ain't nobody gonna be fine."

Shades got up, chuckling. "Let's go, boys."

They all moved out to the bikes at the curb. The men started mounting up. Ghost stopped next to his bike and held her helmet out to her. She took it, staring up at him.

"Do I have to ride with Yammer again? He talked my ear off the other day."

"How do you think he got his name? Because he won't shut up. Yammer, yammer, yammer. I seriously have my doubts if the brothers are gonna to be able to get past that when it comes time to vote him in."

"Please don't make me ride with him again," she whined pathetically.

Ghost grinned and reached an arm around her, his hand slapping down and grabbing her ass cheek for a squeeze.

"Oww," she moaned at the reminder of how sore she was.

"You need more convincing than this?" He gave another squeeze.

"Okay, okay. I give. I'll ride in the bloody van with Chatty Cathy."

Ghost grinned even bigger. "Thought you'd see it my way."

"Do you always get your way?"

"Yup. And don't you forget it, pretty girl." He released her ass cheek, but smacked it one last time, before stepping away.

"Oww. You sadist!" She rubbed her ass and glared at him.

He threw his leg over his bike, lifted it off the kickstand,

and patted the seat behind him, still grinning. "Climb on, brat."

They rode back to the Omaha Clubhouse where the men formed up to roll out. Good to his word, Ghost deposited her in the van with Yammer.

She leaned back, folded her arms, and wished she had her headphones. But no, she had to listen to the prospect drone on for five hundred miles about anything and everything that popped into his mind.

CHAPTER NINE

They arrived after dark at their second stop. Jessie gazed up at the building. The Saint Louis, Missouri Chapter's Clubhouse. It was a medium-sized brick building on the edge of an industrial neighborhood, west of the old brewery section. It looked like, in a past life, it may have been a corner tavern. But any welcoming feeling was long gone. It was now marked with *Keep Out*, *Private Property,* and an assortment of MC signage. There was a parking lot that had been fenced off and gated with chain link that was filled in with diagonal black and white security strips—the Evil Dead colors.

Some members rolled through the gates and into the compound, while the overflow, Ghost included, parked out on the street in a long line of bikes backed to the curb.

Yammer found a spot half a block down and parked, then walked her down to where Ghost was waiting. He took her by the hand and led her through the gate.

It was pretty much a repeat of the previous night, with ol' ladies and other clubwomen there to welcome the men like conquering heroes. There was food and booze, and once again it didn't take long for the party to crank up into high gear.

Ghost didn't spend too much time before he led Jessie by the hand through the crowd, back out to his bike, and to a motel.

This one was much the same as the last one, except this time she noticed he'd made sure there were two beds.

She watched as he tossed his pack on the bed nearest the door.

She noticed he always put himself between her and the door. That was just his way. Always had been. He always put himself between her and any possible threat.

"I'll take that one. You can have the one closest to the bathroom," she offered mostly just to see if he'd do it.

"Not happening, sweetheart."

"Why?" she asked, just to see if he would confirm her theory.

"Anyone tries to come through that door, they have to go through me to get to you."

"Oh." Then she remembered the very real threat that someone might just want her dead, and she realized this wasn't a joke. There really was danger out there.

Ghost studied her face. "Yeah, *oh*."

She bit her lip. "You really think the Death Heads followed us?"

"Doubt it. Just bein' safe."

She looked worriedly toward the window, and he must have seen her reaction because a moment later he was standing in front of her, drawing her attention away.

"Hey."

She looked up at him, the worry still plain on her face, she was sure.

"Nothing's gonna happen. I'm right here, Jess. Not gonna let anybody hurt you. You're safe with me." He stared into her eyes, and she felt a calm come over her. A calm she always felt when she was with him. A calm no one else had ever made her feel.

She believed him. Every word.

His eyes searched hers, waiting, so she nodded. "I know."

He stood there another moment longer, studying her. Then he, too, nodded once and stepped away.

"I notice we didn't stay long at the clubhouse," she commented to his back as he dug around in his pack. He glanced over his shoulder.

"Figured you were tired, and the boys get a little wild. I sure as hell didn't want a repeat of this morning."

"This morning?" She frowned, not sure what he was referring to.

He turned back to her, his brows raised. "You. Slapping Blood."

She bit her lip. "Oh. That."

"Yeah. *That.*"

"Well, he deserved it."

"Ain't sayin' he didn't. But, brat, you have to

understand, shit like that is not tolerated. No woman disrespects a brother like that. Ever. We clear?"

"Whatever."

"No, babe. Not *whatever.* You need to understand that. Down to your bones. I'm lucky Blood was in a good mood this morning, or he and I would've been punching it out in the street over you."

"*Good mood?* You're joking, right?"

"Nope."

She raised her brows.

Ghost continued on. "So, next time you feel the need to react or feel an impulse like that, you better squash it down. It's that kind of shit that'll force me to cut you loose."

"Maybe I am impulsive. I suppose I get it from my mother."

"You definitely are impulsive. I'll testify to that. Not always the best trait to have, though, babe."

"Like mother, like daughter, huh?"

"Don't talk bad about your mom, Jess. She did the best she could by you. And she tried with me, she really did. Hell, I'm sure I was a handful. But she did try. Much as I didn't like her, I have to give her that."

"Do you know why she moved us out?"

***

Ghost stared at Jessie wondering where she was going with this, how their conversation had taken such a turn. But he also felt she had the need to talk. One thing Ghost knew about women, when they needed to talk, you'd best let them. Otherwise they bottled that shit up, and it was bound to explode all over you when you least expected it.

He shook his head, watching her closely.

"She read my diary."

"And?" *Why did his chest suddenly feel tight?*

"And she found out about…you know…us."

"Us? There was no 'us', Jess," he stated emphatically. *Jesus Christ what the hell was in that diary?*

"There was that kiss."

His brows rose. "You wrote about that in your diary?"

"Of course."

"What *exactly* did you write?"

She flushed.

Fuck, that wasn't good. "Jess?"

She shrugged. "Just that we kissed."

"And?"

"She blew up at your father. Told him to keep you away from me."

"I'd already moved out by then."

"I know. But you still came around."

"She didn't have anything to worry about. I told her that."

It was her turn to frown. "You did? When?"

"She confronted me. Did you really think she wouldn't?" He watched her jaw tighten.

"I hated her for moving us out."

"Don't be like that."

"I wish they hadn't divorced."

"It must have been hard on her. Losing Tommy, then the split, and you running off." When he saw her blanch at his words, he closed his eyes. *Fuck.* He shook his head, running a hand over the back of his neck. "I shouldn't have said that. I didn't mean it was your fault. You were grieving, too."

"I know. It's okay."

"She reached out to me. Did you know that?"

She shook her head, frowning. "No."

"I just couldn't be there for her, you know? Couldn't be what she needed. Couldn't be Tommy for her."

"I'm sure that's not what she wanted."

"Maybe not. But I let her down, just the same."

"Why do you say that?"

He shook his head. *Christ, he needed to shut up before he said too much.* "Never mind."

At his curt words, she let it drop, and he was thankful for that. He was beat from the ride and put his palm on his back, stretching and groaning as his tight muscles flared in pain.

"Long trip, huh?" she asked.

"Yeah," he gritted out, trying to smile. "Don't get me wrong, I love to ride, but fucking hell, this trip is motherfucking long."

"What a mouth you have on you now," she teased.

"Lotta shit about me has changed. Not the boy you used to know," he bit out a little harsher than he intended, his exhaustion stringing his nerves out.

"Yes you are," she countered quietly.

"No, I'm not. And you need to understand that, babe, right now." Perhaps his exhaustion was putting him in a mood. Didn't excuse him taking that shit out on her. He knew she didn't deserve to have him snap at her. Still, he couldn't seem to stop. Shit just spilled out of his mouth, shit he hadn't intended to say.

"Ghost—"

"I've done a lot of shit, Jess. Things you'd never understand. Things you'd never get past if you knew. Maybe I'll tell you one day. And when I do, you'll walk out that door, sure as shit."

"That's not true."

"Yeah, *it is*, Jess."

"Ghost—"

"You lookin' to start a fight? That's where we're goin' with this. So just drop it."

"Okay, fine. It's dropped." She raised her hands.

He ran a frustrated hand down his face. "Sorry, brat. Didn't mean to snap at you. I'm just tired." He sat on the end of the bed. "Fuck, my back hurts."

She moved to sit behind him.

"Maybe I can help you feel better."

"Don't think so."

She slid her hands on his shoulders, squeezing the muscles. *Fuck, that felt good.* His eyes slid closed and he moaned, rolling with her motions, allowing her to manipulate some of the tightness out.

"Well, it *is* what I do for a living." *What the fuck?* He was off the bed like a shot, spinning to look down at her. She stared up at him, confusion written on her face. "What's wrong?"

"You make men *feel good* for a living?"

"What? No! Jesus, Ghost, get your head out of the

gutter!'"

"What the hell did you just mean?"

"Are you saying you think I'm a…a…streetwalker or prostitute or…whatever?" She was at a loss for words.

"What are *you* saying?" he snapped right back. "You get paid to do *what* exactly?"

She surged to her feet. "I'm a massage therapist, you moron!"

His chin pulled back. "Massage therapist?"

"Yes. Trained and everything."

He frowned, wondering when the hell that had happened. "Seriously?"

Her hands landed on her hips. "Yes, Ghost. *Seriously.* And I'm good at it. I can work the tightness out of your back if you'll let me. But after that remark, I'm not so sure I want to anymore."

"Brat, you gotta see where I was confused. When you said—"

"Just shut up before you dig a deeper hole."

Good fucking advice. He knew enough to know when a woman told you to shut up, you best shut up. So he nodded and kept his mouth closed.

She huffed out a breath. "Fine. Lay back down."

He eyed the bed. "Maybe this isn't such a good idea."

"Your back hurts, doesn't it? Or don't you think I know what I'm doing?"

Okay, now she was getting offended again. Fuck.

"Take off your shirt. I'll get my oil."

"Your *oil?*"

"Yes, massage oil."

"Oh." He watched as she crossed the room to the dresser and dug through her cross-bag, coming back with a small bottle. He hadn't moved, so she lifted her brows.

"Well?"

He found his hands going to his shirt and yanking it over his head, and then he moved to his stomach.

"Other way."

He looked at her.

"With your head at the foot. Makes it easier to reach your neck and shoulders."

He complied, and she moved to stand over him at the foot. Then she uncapped the bottle and poured a small amount of oil in her hand. He watched as she rubbed them together to warm the oil before she touched him. A moment later, he felt her small hands settle on his shoulders. She smoothed the oil over his skin with long gliding strokes. God, it felt wonderful.

"Take slow, even breaths. Try to relax," she ordered, and he found himself complying willingly as she began working the tension out of his muscles. "It helps if you visualize something calming and soothing."

"Got any suggestions?" he asked, not sure how relaxed he was going to be able to stay with her hands on him.

"I use the ocean. I imagine myself lying on the beach just in the surf line, feeling the waves wash over me, gently lifting me, the warmth of the sand and the sun, the sensation of floating in the water."

"Sounds nice," he murmured as her hands glided over

his skin.

She leaned over and started at the bottom of his back, moving upward, applying pressure, then bringing her hands down his sides with a light touch. She maintained contact, without applying pressure, as she brought her hands back down. She repeated this technique for about five minutes while gradually increasing from light to medium pressure and warming up his back, neck, and shoulder muscles.

Then she began shorter, circular strokes with more pressure, kneading, rolling, and pressing. She alternated between using her palm, fingertips, and even her knuckles. She did this for several long minutes.

Next she worked her way outward down his arms and back again. Then she worked his spine, kneading the muscles on either side of it, and he fought the urge to groan aloud in pleasure.

Every time she leaned over him to work the tightness out of his lower back, her scent would envelope him. It was heaven and hell all rolled into one.

He felt the tension easing out of his muscles as she worked her magic. At the same time, he felt himself getting hard in a different location.

"How's the pressure?"

"Harder would be good."

"All right. It would help if I straddled you, is that okay? I can get better leverage that way."

Seriously? Hell, yeah.

"Climb on," he found himself answering. A moment later, the bed shifted under him as she kneeled, and then she threw a leg over and settled on his ass. Using her body weight, she was able to lean over and do a better job of applying deep pressure. It felt phenomenal.

This time he did groan aloud.

"Am I hurting you?" she immediately asked.

"No. Don't stop. It feels fucking fantastic."

He could hear the grin in her voice as she replied, "So that was a good groan, then?"

"Abso-*fucking*-lutely."

Her ministrations went on until he felt all the tightness from the road slip away.

"Damn, this feels good."

"Just relax and enjoy it."

"Oh, I am. Definitely. Maybe too much."

"Too much. What does that mean?"

Well hell, she asked.

He flipped over underneath her until he was on his back, staring up at her with his hands gripping her hips. He saw the look of surprise on her face as he applied slight pressure of his own, pulling her crotch against his and watched her mouth fall open in realization as she felt his all-too-obvious erection.

"Oh," she said breathlessly.

"Exactly." He stared up at her, watching every subtle expression cross her face. Surprise. Uncertainty. And then something else, something he hadn't expected.

He watched as one small palm settled on his stomach and slide up his chest as she bent to lean over him, planting the other hand in the bed near his head. Her eyes connected with his.

"I could help you with that, too, if you want."

Before he even gave himself time to consider how stupid it was, he rolled, taking her to her back on the bed. She gasped with the quickness of his movement and the shock of finding herself under him.

At that moment, getting her under him was the only thought that had permeated his brain. Well, that and sinking into her warm welcoming heat. *Jesus Christ, what the hell was she doing to him?*

He stared down at her and watched as her eyes fell to his mouth, and that sealed the deal. He dipped in, his mouth settling over hers before he thought better of it. She opened for him, eagerly, freely, like he knew she would. It was just as sweet as he remembered, her little tongue sliding forward to tangle with his, her lips soft beneath his. He ate at her, turning his head from side to side, changing his angle, going back again and again for more, until finally he broke off, pressing his forehead to hers for a moment, his breathing heavy as he rasped out the question on his mind.

"Black or red?"

"What?" The word came out breathlessly as she frowned up at him.

He pulled back, lifting up off her a few inches as his big palm slid down over her ass cheek to cup, squeeze, and pull her against him. "Black or red?"

And then she knew what he was referring to. He could read it in her face as it dawned on her. The panties he'd bought her.

"Been wonderin' all damn day." His brown eyes, molten with heat, bore into hers.

"Oh, God. You thought about my panties *all day?*"

"Yeah, brat. All damn day. You gonna tell me?"

She swallowed, and he could read her mind. She was trying to decide if she should admit it or let him wonder. Or just maybe let him discover for himself. Hell, he was up for that.

"That's for me to know and you to find out."

His chin moved to the side a fraction of an inch. "Not a good idea to give out a challenge like that, not to a man like me."

She stared back at him, not giving an inch. *Well, goddamn.*

He held her eyes as desire coursed through him. No, not desire... unbridled *lust*... pure and simple, and stronger than he'd felt for any woman in a long fucking time. Maybe lust wasn't the right word either. It was *need* that burned through him, *need* that clawed at him to take her fast and hard.

Fuck, what was wrong with him? This was Jess he was on top of.

Suddenly he found himself vaulting off the bed. She looked up at him with obvious confusion, and he answered that look with a fierce one of his own.

"You better think long and hard on what the hell it is you want from me, Jess. You need my protection you got it. This doesn't have to be part of the deal. Some fucked up payment for helping you."

She came up on her elbows, her eyes wide.

"It's not, Ghost. I swear."

"You better mean that. You don't barter your body with me. Fuck, you don't barter your body with *any* man. You understand me?"

He paused as she flushed from his words that sounded too close to an accusation.

"I'm not a whore."

He ran a hand over his mouth. "I know that, Jess. I'm just sayin' this"—he paused, gesturing between them—"this can't be that. I don't want you wantin' me 'cause you're grateful or some shit."

"That's not what this is, Ghost," she whispered in a voice so soft he barely heard the words.

Jesus Christ. Could she really want him? His eyes strayed down her body as it lay on the bed before lifting to meet hers, with a piercing gaze. "This what you want, Jess? Really want? 'Cause once we cross that line, there's no goin' back. You know that, don't you?"

She nodded. "I know."

"And you're gonna be able to handle it? Handle me?"

That gave her pause. He could see it flicker in her eyes.

"What do you mean?"

"I'm not that boy you remember, the one who let you walk out of that garage that afternoon."

"I know you're not."

"Do you?"

She nodded.

Just the same, he felt the need to clarify, to make sure she understood. "I take what I want. When I want a woman, I take her. And she doesn't walk out that door again until I'm through with her. You up for that, Jess? Because you better be damned clear on just what it is you're signing up for. I get what I want. And right now, I fuckin' want *you*."

"I want you, too. So what's the problem?"

"What's the problem?" He ran a frustrated hand through his hair, turning away from her, and then, just as fast, spinning back to pin her with his eyes. "And tomorrow? If this all goes to shit, you gonna be okay with that? You gonna be okay with me? Havin' that between us and then goin' our separate ways?"

"You're already so sure it won't last." It was a statement, not a question, but he answered it just the same.

"Yeah, I am. I *know* so. Guaranteed. We got no future, Jess. All we got is now. You up for that? Think you can handle that?"

He saw the disappointment weigh in her eyes. *Fuck.* She had some kind of knight-in-shining-armor fantasy going on in her head, still just as in awe of him as she'd been as a kid. But he was no one's hero. He couldn't be that for her. He would *never* be that for her. She just didn't know how wrong she was. But she'd find out the truth. Sooner or later, she'd see him for what he was.

He shook his head. "Jess."

"Ghost, it's okay. Whatever you're willing to give, I'll take, and I promise I won't ask for more." She extended her hand toward him. "Please."

Fuck. She was like Eve holding out the apple. An apple he wanted to take. He needed to turn her down. Knew he should. Knew it'd be best for both of them in the long run. But right now, havin' her look at him that way, like he hung the fuckin' moon, *Christ*, he couldn't stop the swelling in his chest. He wanted that. Craved it. To have a woman look at him the way she was right now? Christ, it was everything.

He found himself taking a step toward the bed, his hand lifting to grasp hers, their fingers intertwining, lacing together. And then he was moving over her again, his weight settling back on top of her, pinning that hand to the bed near her head.

The time for excuses was over. His mouth took hers again and she welcomed him, her free hand coming up to clutch at him, pulling him closer. He loved the way she made him feel like she couldn't get close enough. His free hand slid into her hair, his fist tightening as he took control of the kiss.

He kissed her a long time, taking his time with her, enjoying every moment. He'd wanted this for a long time, fantasized about it a million times, jerked off to the image of her in his head more times over the years than he wanted to admit.

His mind went back to that moment they'd shared in the garage so many years ago. She'd been just sixteen then, she was a woman now. Her kiss proved that. She matched his hunger, kiss for kiss, and he ate it up, giving back as much as he took. Until eventually kissing wasn't enough, for either of them.

He lifted, straddling her and pulling her upright. Then he reached for the hem of her shirt, pulling it up and over her head, and tossing it to the floor. His eyes moved over the lacy black bra she wore, the one he'd first seen in that bathroom in Sturgis when he'd bent her over that counter and pretended to fuck her. That was another vision that had tortured his dreams the last few nights.

He'd pictured himself doing that to her for real, and it got him rock hard.

He reached around and undid the fastener, then pulled it off, tossing the bra on the floor with her shirt. Her breasts fell free, soft and round and the perfect size as his hand closed over one He leaned forward, taking her down flat on her back. His mouth trailed from her throat to her breast as he squeezed with his hand. Then his mouth was at her nipple, sucking so hard that her back arched off the bed. That only drove him on further, sending an urgent, instinctive need to take her. He'd never felt it this badly before.

But he fought it, beat it down, refusing to rush this, wanting to take his time with her—to savor every inch of her incredibly soft skin.

She moaned and writhed beneath him. He slid to the bottom of the bed and stood, yanking her boots off, and then his hands were at the waist of her jeans, undoing them and yanking them down her legs.

Red lace hit his eyes, and he paused, staring. Goddamn, she was beautiful, lying there almost naked, nothing but that scrap of barely-there red lace.

Prettiest thing he'd ever seen.

He stripped his own clothes off, and then stood at the foot of the bed, just looking at her. His eyes finally made it all the way up to her face to see that her gaze was trailing down his body, taking him in.

She writhed on the bed, one knee bending. The bottom of her foot teased over the bedspread in a seductive way that had the blood rushing from his head.

***

Jessie stared up at Ghost, taking in all the beautiful, muscled body that had just been revealed to her. He was gorgeous. He stood there just taking her in, and her body ached for his touch, wanted his warmth stretched back on top of her, skin on skin.

She slid her foot along the bed, trying to entice him back.

A moment later, she gasped as his hands closed around her ankles, and he pulled her across the bedspread to him. Then he was kneeling, his hands going to her lace panties and pulling them down her legs and off.

His warm hands landed on the inside of both thighs, just above her knees, parting her legs to him, and then those hands slowly slid upward, his eyes boring into hers.

Her breathing accelerated as she lay before him, open and vulnerable. Her chest rose and fell, her breasts quivering with the movement, and he didn't miss it.

"You scared, Jess?"

She shook her head, rolling it on the bedspread.

"I don't want you to be scared of me, sweetheart."

"I'm not."

His palms reached the apex of her thighs, and then his thumbs were brushing over her. At the first soft graze, her back arched, her hips lifting in offering, wanting more.

He stroked over her again, a barely-there touch that drove her insane.

"Ghost," she moaned.

"You like that?"

She nodded. "God, yes."

"Touch your breasts for me," he ordered, his voice deep.

She lifted her hands to squeeze them in a kneading motion.

He kept stroking her. "Play with your nipples. Pinch them."

She did, moaning, her head going back. Then his mouth was on her, his tongue driving her insane as he lapped and sucked until she was thrashing on the bed. He didn't let up; he held her thighs wide as he tortured her over and over with his mouth until she couldn't take it anymore.

"Please, baby. Please."

Then he really got serious, toying with her clit in a rapid-fire motion that had her crashing over into a huge orgasm.

She'd barely recovered before he moved over her, bracing up on the palms of his hands. His hips pressed against hers, pushing her legs apart. One hand moved between her legs, his fingers separating her a moment before she felt the head of his cock press against her, seeking entry. Their eyes locked the whole time, and then he speared inside her with one powerful thrust. Her body clamped down, her muscles tightening, and he stopped, having only gained entry halfway.

He held himself poised above her, his muscles rigid. He

dipped his head, his nose skating along her cheek, his mouth coming to her ear to whisper, "Relax for me, sweetheart. Let me in."

His words were like some magic entreaty, unlocking the doors, and she felt her body tingle, her muscles relaxing, and a new rush of lubrication flowed from her. He eased in, pressing deep.

"That's my girl. Take it all." His voice was sweet, soft, and seductive. She knew right then that he had the power to coax any response from her that he wanted.

He lowered to his elbows, his weight coming down on her as he moved inside her, advancing, retreating, and dragging along a thousand nerve endings with every smooth stroke.

She moaned.

"I should have taken more time with you. Made you come over and over before I took you. I was just so goddamned impatient to be inside you, but I'll make it up to you, baby. I swear. The rest of the night will be all about you. But right now, I need this, okay? I need to just take. And I need you to give."

She nodded, her hands sliding over the warm, smooth skin of his back, down to his ass. Her hands tightened, and she pulled him against her and heard him moan in response.

That deep, low, masculine moan was the sexiest thing she'd ever heard.

"Oh, fuck, baby. Do that again. Show me you want me just as bad."

She did, pulling him tight with an urgency that surprised

and thrilled her just as much as it did him. He grabbed her wrists, threading their fingers together as he pressed her hands to the bed beside her head.

"Wrap your legs around me." He growled the command, his voice rough with need. His control was breaking; she could see it as she looked up at him. He watched her eyes as he began to pound into her, his whole body tight, every muscle flexing with his exertions as he took control of her, of this. His mouth came down on hers, his tongue delving inside, demanding everything, and she gave, taking him deep. He kissed her until he had to break away so they both could breathe.

He released one of her hands, and she felt his palm closing around one breast, lifting it as he dipped his head, his mouth latching onto her nipple. With the deep, pulling tug, her head went back into the pillow and her back arched, offering her breast up for more. He moaned against it, sucking long and hard, giving her exactly what her body silently begged him for. A jolt shot through her, straight between her legs, and she undulated, her hips lifting to meet his.

His mouth broke free of her nipple with a pop. He shoved up on his knees, his hands locked around her thighs, and he pulled her up against him. Her ass dragged up his thighs as he began to pound into her with everything he had. His eyes locked with hers a moment before they broke free to watch her breasts bounce with his assault. That only drove him on to a more furious pummeling.

She took it, reveled in it, watching a sheen of sweat form

on his flexing muscles, taking in the glory of his masculine power and this deeply primal act. He growled as his control broke and he found his release, his body going solid and still, as he poured into her.

His breathing sawed in and out, and he released his grip on her thighs. He planted one palm in the mattress next to her, bringing his slick, sweat-covered body down on top of her.

Her arms and legs immediately wrapped around him, enfolding him in her embrace. She held him as his breathing slowed, and his body melted deep against hers, every muscle relaxing. One of her hands drifted up, her fingers threading through the hair at the base of his neck. His head turned, his mouth nuzzling just behind her ear to press kisses along her neck. She turned her head, her mouth seeking out his, and he gave it to her, kissing her deeply. He lifted a hand to her face, his palm stroking her cheek.

And then he smiled, and it was the most beautiful thing she'd ever seen.

CHAPTER TEN

Ghost awoke to the sound of his phone vibrating on the nightstand. He cracked an eye open. The room was dark, but soft morning light filtered in around the window curtain. Picking up his phone, he squinted at the time. *8:00.* Groaning, he swiped the alarm off and set the phone back down.

When he moved his hand back to his waist, he felt the small hand on his abs, the soft skin of the arm around his ribs, and the warmth snuggled to his back.

He closed his eyes. *Christ, he'd fucked up.*

Last night had been amazing. Phenomenal. Best he'd ever had. *No fucking lie*. But today he had to shut it down and tell her they couldn't do this. Last night had been a huge mistake.

She was going to end up hating him. He could only hope that by nipping this in the bud, they would avoid the worst of it. Maybe, by some miracle, they could go back to the way it was. Maybe one taste would be enough for her. Maybe it had all just been curiosity on her part. Maybe she'd always wondered at roads not taken, and all that bullshit.

Hell, he knew he had.

He'd wondered about the what-ifs for years. Wondered what would've happened had they crossed the line back then. What if they'd run off together? Left it all behind?

But that wasn't the way the world worked. Shit like that never worked out. Not that society's mores had ever meant that much to him, but she'd always been a line to him—a line he knew he shouldn't cross.

But that wasn't what had him second-guessing what they'd done last night, now as he lay next to her sweet body. No, it was much more than that. It was the secret he carried. The shit she didn't know about.

The one thing he knew she'd never be able to forgive.

He rolled to his back, and she tucked up under his arm, her head landing on his chest.

"Jess." He rubbed her back, shaking her gently. "Jess, wake up."

She groaned, her hand sliding across his belly.

Fuck, that hand dipped any lower and they were gonna have a totally different wake-up call.

"Jess." His hand clamped over her wrist, keeping hers from straying any further south.

"Hmm," she groaned.

He moved to slide out from under her, swinging his legs over the side of the bed as he glanced back to find her blinking her pretty sleepy eyes at him. And then she smiled, and it took his breath.

"Good morning," she murmured.

"Mornin'," he grunted back.

Her hand slid across the sheet and up his back. When she spoke, her voice came out breathy, low, and sexy as hell.

"Come back to bed."

Tempting. Very tempting. Eve holding out that apple again.

He stood and yanked his jeans on, needing to put some distance between them before he could look at her again.

Confusion. That's what he saw on her face. Better than the hatred that someday would replace it.

"Time to roll, baby doll." He lifted his chin toward the bathroom. "You want to go first?"

She shook her head, clutching the sheet to her chest as if she were now unsure of herself. Fuck, he hated doing that to her—making her feel insecure in her own sexuality. He suddenly felt the need to say something.

"Look, Jess, last night…" He broke off. How the hell should he say this?

She looked up at him then, meeting his eyes with a wariness that he hated seeing there.

Fuck, just say it, you pussy.

"It shouldn't have happened. I shouldn't have let it go that far." He watched her face harden, and her jaw tighten.

"Please, spare me the blow-off speech like I'm some…some piece of club ass you picked up for the night."

That got his anger up, and he gritted his own teeth. "Didn't say you were. And for your information, I don't give *club ass* a blow-off speech. I don't have to. They know the score. They know what this shit is."

"This *shit?*"

Goddamn. The look on her face tore at him. He hadn't meant to snap at her like that.

"Jess—"

Her palm came up. "Don't. Just *don't*, okay? I don't need your damn excuses, or your—"

Oh, *fuck* this shit. He grabbed her hand, jerking her closer. "Just fucking listen to me a minute, will you?"

That shut her up.

"You said you'd be okay with this. You said you could handle this."

She tried to pull her hand free, but he held tight. She glared up at him as she ground out her answer. "That's because I didn't think you'd be regretting having sex with me before the sheets were even cold!"

He let her go then, staring down at her, stunned. "I don't regret the sex, Jess. Christ, is that what you think?"

"What the hell am I suppose to think?" she bit out.

He pointed a finger at the bed, his motion jerking with anger. "That was the best fuck of my life, sweetheart. Off the charts amazing."

She slumped back, confused, but still fucking pissed. "The best?"

"Yes, Jess. The best. By a long shot. That what you wanted to hear?"

"But, how…" He watched a frown form on her pretty face.

"How could it be the best? Easy. Sex is a whole different ballgame when it's with someone you care about."

Why did she look shocked? She had to know he cared about her.

"Then I don't see why we can't—"

He cut her off. "Don't, Jess. Okay? I thought I could do this. But I can't. Not with you."

"Ghost, please don't be like this."

He grabbed a clean shirt from his pack, moved to the bathroom, and slammed the door. Leaning on the sink, he stared in the mirror.

Shit. He'd fucked up.

She was going to be much more difficult to let go than he'd ever imagined. He knew there'd always been something between them, something smoldering just below the surface. But now? Now that he'd had a taste of just how fucking good it could be between them, how in the hell was he going to let her go when this was all over? And how in the hell was he going to handle the look on her face when she found out his club was going to *use* her to make a deal?

Christ, he was fucked.

***

Jessie stared at the closed bathroom door.

What just happened? Everything had been so perfect last night. She'd always suspected Ghost would be good in bed, but the reality was so much better than she could have ever imagined. They had something together. Chemistry, magnetism… whatever it was called, it was there, burning hot between them. One look. One touch. Hell, he just had to walk into a room and she felt it, felt *him*, felt his presence, undeniable and strong. He was the magnetic pole that drew her like a compass.

She knew he felt it, too. So why was he fighting it?

Goddamn, he could be stubborn. She remembered that about him.

Newsflash... she could be just as stubborn.

And she wasn't going to let this go.

Jessie wasn't normally one to throw herself at someone or to court rejection. With Ghost, however, she'd found something she'd never found with anyone else. She'd be damned if she was going to watch it all slip away, and she sure as hell wasn't about to let *him* throw it away, or make that decision for the both of them.

It was worth fighting for. *This* was worth fighting for. She knew it, down to her soul. And before she was through, he'd know it, too.

She smiled at the closed door.

Challenge accepted, big boy.

***

After they'd both showered, they once again met up with some of Ghost's brothers for breakfast. The tiny diner they pulled up to was not as cool as the one they'd eaten at the previous morning, but the aromas that assaulted them as they walked in promised the food was good.

Jessie followed behind Ghost's broad shoulders as he made his way toward several booths along the front windows. They squeezed in with Shades and Hammer, Ghost nodding for her to sit next to Hammer, while he sat next to

Shades.

Her eyes skated over Hammer's big tattoo-covered biceps as she scooted in, and a smile pulled at the corner of her mouth. This could work perfectly into her plan to get Ghost to realize the error of his decision to keep things platonic between them. *Well, Mr. I-can't-go-there, let's see how you like this action.*

"My, my, you're a big one. You must lift weights," she purred as she gently ran a finger over Hammer's bicep. He sat with his forearms on the table, a fork in one hand and a piece of toast in the other. Turning his head, his eyes fell to where she touched him. Then he lifted his eyes to hers and grinned.

"Mornin', Sunshine."

"Good morning," she murmured back with a smile. Her eyes dropped to his plate. "How's the food?"

"Food's great. Want a bite?" he offered, holding his fork out to her.

"Sure," she purred.

He put the fork to her mouth, and she opened, taking the bite of the omelet he offered.

"Mmm," she moaned around the mouthful, and his grin got bigger as he winked.

"Okay, enough flirting, Hammer," Ghost growled as he reached across Shades for two of the plastic menus jammed behind the napkin dispenser. He passed one to Jessie with a look that told her to behave.

She smiled, still chewing. Seems her plan was working already. *Behave? Not on your life, lover boy.* "So, Hammer, is it? How did you get that name?" She smiled up at him, shamelessly flirting as she scooted closer.

Shades answered for him. "We call him Hammer because he nails anything with tits." Shades shrugged at the glare Ghost gave him. "What? She asked."

Ignoring them both, she turned her attention back to Hammer, running her hand up his bicep again. "Is that really how you got your name?"

Hammer's eyes moved from her to connect with Ghost's as if he was on to her plan. Instead of answering her question, he asked Ghost, "She's your stepsister, right? You're not claimin' her?"

"She's off limits, Hammer."

Hammer's brows rose. "You're shittin' me."

"Ain't shittin' you, bro. Leave her be."

What the hell?

"What do you mean I'm off limits?" Jessie snapped at Ghost.

She didn't get an answer because the waitress appeared at the booth. She held a thermal carafe of coffee and two clunky white mugs, which she plopped down in front of them and began filling without even asking if they wanted any.

"What'll you have?" she asked Ghost, barely giving Jessie a glance.

He grabbed the menu out of Jessie's hand and shoved them both back behind the napkin dispenser, saying, "We'll both have the special."

She nodded and walked away.

Jessie glared at him as she reached for her coffee. What

was with him and ordering for her all the time? "Would you stop doing that?"

Ghost reached for his coffee. "Nope."

***

After they ate, Ghost studied Jessie, who'd barely spoken to him throughout the meal. Instead, she lavished all her attention on Hammer, who enjoyed it way too much for Ghost's liking. Nodding toward the back hall, he snapped, "You need to use the restroom, better hit it now, Jess."

He watched her get up and head to the back, his eyes following her ass as she walked away. When he turned back, both Shades and Hammer had their necks twisted to watch her ass, too.

They both grinned at his glare when he caught them.

"What? That's a damn fine ass, my man. Be a crime not to look," Hammer answered with a tormenting grin.

"Shut the fuck up, and keep your eyes on your own paper."

Shades chuckled, downing the dregs of his coffee. "You're a bit cranky this morning. Something happen?"

Ghost cut his eyes to him. "Not your business."

"Somebody needs to get laid," Shades teased.

Hammer eyed Ghost, running a hand slowly over his beard, his white teeth flashing. "I'm thinking somebody did, and it didn't go too well."

Shades almost choked on his coffee, his wide eyes flashing to Ghost. "That true, bro? You hit that?"

Ghost glared at them both, but finally came clean, nodding once.

"Fucking-A, man," Hammer said with a grin before he turned and shouted across to another table. "You owe me ten bucks, Griz!"

Griz glanced over, pulling a red plastic stir-stick from his mouth that he'd been chewing on. "No way! Are you shittin' me?"

Hammer grinned at Shades as he raised his hand. "High-five, bro."

Ghost stared in stunned disbelief as they slapped palms, then he glared at Shades. "You *both* bet on this shit? Hammer, I'm not surprised. But, you?"

Shades just grinned. "Easiest ten bucks I ever made."

Griz ambled over to their booth and leaned his palms on the table, his eyes on Ghost. "Dude." He shook his head. "You let me down, man."

Shades lifted his hand palm up, two fingers waggling. "Pay up, Griz."

Griz straightened, pulled his wallet out of his back pocket, and glared at Ghost as he pulled two tens out and slapped them on the table. "Shoulda known *Romeo*, here, couldn't keep it in his pants."

Just then Jessie walked up, and Ghost straightened in his seat, running his hand over his mouth. *Fucking hell.*

Griz glared at her. "You just cost me twenty bucks, sweet cheeks." Then he strolled back to his table.

"What was that about?" she asked, eyeing the money.

"Nothing," Ghost snapped, rising from his seat and grabbing her by the upper arm. He turned her toward the door. "Let's go."

"Hey, your bill," Hammer said.

Ghost turned his head, not stopping. "You can pick up this one, Mr. Moneybags."

"Fucking hell."

***

Once they were back at the Saint Louis clubhouse, the different chapters took a few moments to say goodbye to each other. At each stop, the line of bikes got shorter as the various chapters broke off. Now, some were splitting off toward Memphis, some toward Louisiana.

They posed to take a photo—a bunch of leather-clad men with beards and dark shades, all grinning at the camera. Jessie noticed they all held their arms crossed over their chests, five fingers extended on one hand and four on the other. She frowned, wondering what that meant. She'd seen the number fifty-four on the wall here and also at the clubhouse in Omaha, now that she thought about it. What was up with that?

After they were finished and said their goodbyes, pounding each other's backs the way men do, Jessie asked Ghost about it.

"Why did everyone hold up nine fingers like that?"

Ghost grinned. "Not nine. Five and four."

She shook her head. "Okay, so, what does that mean?"

"It means Evil Dead. E is the fifth letter in the alphabet and D is the fourth. So, five and four, or fifty-four."

"Oh, I see."

"You ready, pretty girl?"

She grinned at the endearment. Apparently his earlier

surly mood had shifted back to his usual happy self. "I'm ready. Am I on the back of your bike today?"

His eyes searched hers, his smile fading. "That where you want to be?"

She nodded, mesmerized by the way he looked at her, like there wasn't anyone else around. "Yes."

"Because you want on the back of my bike? Or because you want out of that van?"

She bit her lip, trying not to grin. "Maybe a little of both."

The corner of his mouth pulled up. "Least you're honest. Okay, brat, let's rock and roll."

She rolled her eyes at the nickname, but couldn't help the smile that lit up her face. *Yes! She was going to get to ride today!*

CHAPTER ELEVEN

The line of bikes roared southbound on I-65, eventually rolling down through Nashville, and then crossing the Alabama border an hour after that. They continued past Huntsville and ultimately hit the exit, rolling through Birmingham toward the clubhouse.

Jessie took in the sights of the hometown she'd left years ago when she'd run away at the age of seventeen. Some things had changed, but the feeling was the same. This was home—always had been, always would be.

Her arms tightened around Ghost, and she felt his hand drop to her forearm, giving it a pat and a squeeze. He understood what she was feeling. Somehow he had always been able to tap into her moods. Sometimes, it was a good thing. Other times, not so much. She'd never been able to bullshit him.

It worried her, because that was exactly what she was doing now. She hadn't been completely honest with him, and she was afraid she wouldn't be able to keep up the lies for long before he saw right through them.

And she couldn't help but worry about what would happen when he learned the truth.

***

Twenty minutes later, they rolled up to the clubhouse of the Birmingham Chapter of the Evil Dead MC. It was buried back in the poor neighborhoods that bordered the old U.S. Steel plant. They rolled up several side streets coming to a huge old two-story clapboard house that sat on a big corner lot. Next to it was an empty lot with overgrown grass. The two properties consumed the entire short block that ran between a couple of side streets. The back of the clubhouse was surrounded by a six-foot privacy fence and backed up to an alley that faced a junkyard on the other side. Across the street was a burned out house and, next to that, an abandoned house. Obviously, the neighborhood was not primo real estate, and Jessie imagined they liked it that way. The fewer people and neighbors to fuck with them, the better.

The front yard was overgrown, the sides overrun with tall bamboo and kudzu vines. There was a waist-high chain link fence around the front yard and a rusty gate no one ever used. The metal mailbox out on the street was painted black with *Evil Dead MC* in white stencil across it. Up on the front porch, in a chair by the door, sat a skeleton holding a scythe like some leftover Halloween decoration, except for the Evil Dead support t-shirt it wore.

The bikes turned the corner and circled around back to the alley, which led to the only entrance members used.

There was a double wooden gate with the club name, *Evil Dead,* painted, top-rocker style, across it. Up on the backside of the house was a painted, winged skeleton holding a scythe, looking down at the back of the property as if guarding it.

They rolled through the back gate and into a large gravel lot that took up over an acre.

As they climbed off the bike, Jessie glanced at all the women waiting to greet the men. Even though Ghost had assured her there was no ol' lady waiting for him, she couldn't help it when her gaze moved over each and every woman there.

Shades pulled in next to them, and he didn't get two steps from his bike before a gorgeous girl with long dark hair jumped into his arms. He laughed, catching her ass as her legs wrapped around his waist. They kissed passionately like newlyweds.

"Are they married?" she whispered to Ghost.

"Nah, not yet. But she's wearin' his ring. Don't think they've set a date."

When they finally broke apart, Jessie saw the love in Shades' eyes as he looked at his woman. He set her down reluctantly, and she turned her eyes on Ghost and Jessie.

"Who's your friend, Ghost?" she asked.

"Don't I get a hug?" Ghost asked her, ignoring her question.

She went into his arms, and he briefly lifted her feet off the ground before setting her back down.

"How you doin', Hotrod?"

She grinned up at him before shaking her head. "Nuh-uh,

no avoiding the question. Introduce us."

Ghost grabbed Jessie by the hand and pulled her forward. "Skylar, this is Jessie. Jessie, this is Skylar, Shades' ol' lady."

The pretty woman extended her hand, and Jessie took it, shaking it warmly. "Hi, nice to meet you." Jessie couldn't help but notice Skylar's eyes. They were the most beautiful blue she'd ever seen—a light crystal blue that stood out starkly against her dark hair.

She turned her electric gaze to Ghost, her brows raised. "And you two know each other how?"

"He picked up a souvenir in Sturgis." Shades filled his woman in with a teasing smile and a wink at Jessie.

Skylar's brows shot up, and she giggled. "Is that so?"

Ghost let out a slight chuckle. "Something like that, yeah."

"Interesting." She eyed Jessie up and down, and then her eyes swung to Ghost in a considering, analyzing way.

As if Ghost could read her mind, he replied, "Don't even go there, Sky."

Her eyes got big, but her knowing grin stayed. "What? I didn't say a word."

Shades pulled her away, remarking, "I'll fill you in later."

"Oh, yes you most definitely will."

Jessie watched them walk off, and then she turned on Ghost. "What was that about?"

He shook his head about to answer when another girl walked up, plastering herself against him. "I missed you, baby," she purred.

Jessie's eyes swept over her. She was a stacked blonde with a catty look on her face, her hands sliding up and down Ghost's cut like she owned him. It had Jessie's spine straightening as jealousy flared to life inside her.

Ghost took her by the upper arms and set her aside. "Quit, Ash."

"Who's this?" she asked, her eyes on Jessie and venom in her voice.

"Not your concern," Ghost snapped, clamping his hand firmly around Jessie's. Then before Jessie could do much more than turn to watch the girl over her shoulder, Ghost dragged her off through the crowd.

"Who was she?" she asked him quietly, her eyes still on the girl.

"That's Ashley. Nobody for you to worry about."

Jessie couldn't help the feeling that crept up her spine and told her the exact opposite.

Ghost led her inside his clubhouse, and Jessie forgot all about Ashley as her eyes moved around the place. There were flags, pictures, and club memorabilia all over the walls, even hanging from the ceiling. The place was crowded with the returning brothers, and Ghost shouldered his way through the leather-clad men, leading her to a bar against the back wall.

He jockeyed a position and leaned on his elbows, calling to a short woman behind the bar serving up drinks. She was petite, with white-blonde hair in a cute, super-short, spikey cut. It accented her long slender neck and slanted green eyes.

"Hey, Tink. Be a sweetheart and grab me a couple bottles."

The woman turned, her face lighting up as she saw him. "Sure thing, Ghost. Welcome home!"

"Good to be back, darlin'."

A moment later she set two ice-cold bottles of beer in front of them. Her eyes briefly touched on Jessie as she gave her a slight nod.

"Seen Hammer, yet?" Ghost asked her with a grin.

She rolled her eyes. "No, and don't start, Ghost. I was in a good mood."

Ghost chuckled, putting the bottle to his mouth and taking a long drink.

The girl was soon called away to serve up the crowd, and Ghost twisted, leaning against the bar to face Jessie.

"Tink?" she asked.

"Short for Tinker Bell." He shrugged. "I think the nickname is self-explanatory."

Jessie's eyes moved back to the pretty, petite woman. She supposed it was.

"Why did you ask her about Hammer?"

He eyed her, his smile fading slightly. "Why? Jealous you might have some competition for your new boyfriend?"

"Stop teasing me. You know that was all just fun."

"Um hmm. It better have been."

"So, what's the deal with them? She his ol' lady?"

Ghost snorted. "Not hardly, but it ain't from lack of tryin' on his part. She won't have anything to do with him, though."

"Why's that?"

He shrugged, grinning. "'Cause she's a smart girl. Hell, I don't know, why don't you ask her?"

Her chin came up. "Maybe I will."

"Oh, Lord." He rolled his eyes.

"So, tell me more about this Ashley chick."

Ghost took a hit off his beer bottle, his eyes on her. "Told you, nothin' to tell."

"She said she missed you. That's not nothing, Ghost."

He shook his head. "Drop it, Jess. She's nothing. Don't worry about it."

"I'm not worried."

"Good. Then we can stop talking about her."

Jessie rolled her eyes. If only it were that easy. Is that really how men thought women's minds worked? *Nope. Not even a little.*

One of his brothers walked up and leaned into Ghost's ear, telling him something she couldn't hear. He listened intently, their eyes connecting as the man pulled back. Ghost nodded, and the guy glanced to her before walking away.

When he was gone, Jess asked, "What was that about?"

Ghost looked at her and shook his head. "You don't get to question everything, Jess. Not anything that has to do with the club. Understand?"

"Fine. Whatever."

It was Ghost's turn to roll his eyes. "There's that word again."

"Well, what do you want me to say? It's not fine? Is that what you want to hear?"

"Just shut up and let's go."

"Fine," she bit out just to be antagonistic.

Of course it didn't work with Ghost. He just huffed out a laugh and led her out the door.

"Where are we going?"

"My place. You're tired, right?"

She nodded. "Where's your place? I thought maybe you stayed here."

"At the clubhouse? Hell no. I'd never get any sleep. I got a place over near the airport."

At that, she frowned. "The airport?"

"Yeah, the airport, Jess. Why?"

She shook her head. "Nothing."

They mounted up and pulled out.

Twenty minutes later, true to his word, Ghost rolled down some backstreets near the airport. They were over on the southeast side, off to the side of the end of one of the runways. He turned down an old driveway that was overgrown with shrubbery. It looked as if at one time it had been the entrance to some type of restaurant, judging by the signs that were now partially grown over with vines.

It was back in an area that obviously got very little traffic; in fact, it was the last place on the dead end. The drive in was maybe a hundred yards in from the turn off. It opened to what once must have been the parking lot, but grass and vegetation were now starting to break through. The place looked like it could have been the setting for a scene from a zombie apocalypse movie—that's how abandoned and deserted it felt.

Ghost pulled to a stop, and they both climbed off. Once her helmet was off, Jessie got her first close look at the building, glooming in the dark of night.

It looked like an old French farmhouse, from the turn of the century, with white stonewalls and turret towers with shingled, conical tops.

She noticed an old WWII era jeep parked in the overgrown grass at the front like some kind of weird statue.

"What is this place?"

Ghost paused beside her, one booted foot up on the curb. He tipped his head back, admiring the place with her. "It used to be a themed restaurant. It was designed as a replica of a 1917 French farmhouse. It was called Flying Aces for the fighter pilots that flew in WWI and WWII. It was filled with tons of military and aviation memorabilia. Some of it was left behind."

"Left behind?"

"The place never really took off, and the owner died of a heart attack. It sat empty for years. His widow finally put it up for sale for what was owed in back taxes. I happened to have an in with someone in the family, and she sold it to me."

"No other restaurant company wanted it?"

"Nah. The location was great for the idea, letting customers look out over the airport, watch planes land, but the neighborhoods you have to drive through to get here are not the best, and it kept a lot of people away. It was a cool idea, though. You want to see inside?"

"Yes, but, you bought this place? You own it?"

"Yes, ma'am."

"But, why?"

He shrugged. "At first I thought it would be a cool place to live. I got it dirt cheap. But times have changed, and the neighborhoods around here aren't as bad as they once were. I think it might just make it as a nightclub or an event location." He shrugged again. "Just a dream, really. Come on, I'll show you the inside."

He led her through massive double wooden doors. They entered an area she supposed was once the hostess station. The walls were made to look like plaster, with areas showing the exposed stone beneath. He led her up a set of winding stairs, only they were lined with faux sandbags, designed to look like it was a bomb shelter or something.

When they got upstairs, there was a set of coat hooks on the wall with old vintage WWII bomber jackets, aviator caps, and goggles hanging on them. To the left was a bar with a large mirror backing it and shelving with more memorabilia. To the right was what must have been the dining room with a bank of plate glass windows that overlooked the most amazing view. She could see the runway landing lights and the control tower off in the distance.

The ceiling had exposed beams, and there was a huge stone fireplace anchoring the other side of the room. In between, where she supposed all the tables had once been, was now some living room furniture.

"So…you live here?"

"Yup. Come on, I'll show you the rest." He walked her through the room to a doorway on the other side. It must have been a private event room. It also had windows overlooking the view, and he'd turned it into a bedroom with a bed facing that view.

"Oh my God!"

He grinned. "Like it?"

"It's amazing. You wake up to that view every morning?"

"Yes, ma'am."

She frowned. "But what about the noise from the airplanes landing and taking off?"

He shrugged. "You'd think they'd be a problem, but they soundproofed the place pretty good. Come on, I want to show you my favorite part of the whole place."

He grabbed two bottles of beer from a cooler behind the bar, and then led her down another staircase. This one brought them to an outdoor courtyard setup to look like a bombed-out section of the building—the roof was missing, leaving only the rafters and a few exposed beams. A stone fireplace sat on the far side, opening toward the airport.

"Pretty cool, huh?"

"It feels like I'm in some World War ruins. It's amazing. God, you could have some awesome parties and events in a place like this. I can just imagine the place cleaned up and with strings of lights…"

He took her hand. "Well, there's still a lot of work to do before I start planning any parties." He led her toward the side that faced the airport. There was a stone terrace with a circular fire pit and some Adirondack chairs sitting around it.

They both sat, and he handed her a bottle. The night air

was the perfect temperature, warm with a cooling breeze. She could smell honeysuckle blooming nearby, but couldn't see it in the dark.

The lights of the runway flickered in the distance.

They sat for a few minutes, enjoying the quiet night. A plane came in on its final approach in the distance, and they both watched it land and taxi toward the terminal.

She felt Ghost turn his head and could feel him studying her for a long moment until finally he spoke.

"Tell me why you ran away."

She noticed it wasn't really a question. She turned and looked at him, his eyes were clear, intent, and brooked no nonsense. He wanted an answer, a serious one, not some flippant joke. She took a sip of beer, her eyes going back to the lights of the airport.

"Everything just fell apart."

"I want to know all of it, Jess."

She rolled her head on the back of the seat. "Tommy died."

He nodded. "Before that. Something happened before that, didn't it?"

She looked away, unable to continue to meet his probing stare. Yes, something had happened before that—Ghost had removed himself from her life. She swallowed, unsure she'd be able to admit the effect it'd had on her.

"Tell me." His voice was low and deep, yet insistent.

She set her bottle down on the stone and rubbed her arms. "It's getting kind of chilly out here."

"Jess—"

He was on to her stalling tactic.

She turned on him, her voice sharp. "You were gone. Is that what you wanted to hear? You left. And then Tommy left."

He looked a little stunned, and she suddenly felt a little sick to her stomach, but she kept going, knowing she needed to get it all out or she never would.

"I started hanging with the wrong people."

He nodded. "Yeah, you did. But what I don't understand is why."

She shrugged again.

"Jess, talk to me."

She stood, walking a few feet, hugging herself. With her back to him, she admitted quietly, "It broke my heart when you stopped coming around. It was like you cut me out of your life."

It was quiet for a long moment, the silence only broken when she heard his chair creak. She felt him come up behind her, his arms wrapping around her waist as he pulled her against him. He pressed a kiss to the side of her head, and then moved his lips to her ear.

"Never meant to do that, brat. Never meant to hurt you like that. Never."

Oh, God. She'd break down if he went all sweet on her. She could handle an argument easier than she could handle sweetness from him. "Ghost, don't."

"You didn't understand why I left, did you?"

She shook her head.

He tightened his arms. "I thought I was doing what was

best for you. You had a bright future, Jess. College…
everything. I would have sidetracked all of that. I couldn't do
that."

"I needed you," she admitted in a whisper.

She felt him dip his head to her shoulder, pressing a kiss
to the curve of her neck. "I'm sorry. I couldn't come around
you then. Not with how things were between us."

"I thought things were good."

"Jess, you know what I mean. I gotta spell it out? You
were growing up, and I was taking notice in a way I
shouldn't have."

She shook her head. "It hurt, Ghost. You just cutting me
out like that."

He exhaled deeply, and his tone hardened "What do you
want me to say? The things I started to feel, the things I
started to want…" He broke off releasing her and stepping
away.

She turned to him. "Say it. I need you to say it."

He whirled back on her. "I wanted you. But I couldn't
have you, Jess. You know that. Leaving was the best thing I
could do for you."

"Doesn't feel like it turned out that way."

He slammed a fist into his chest. "And that's my fault?
You runnin' off with that loser? That's *my* fault?"

She looked down.

"You were supposed to go to college, Jess. You were
smart. You could have done anything. Hell, you had your
whole life ahead of you." He paused, running his hand
through his hair. "And what do you do? Run off with that

little fucker, following him clear across the country."

"Stop!"

"No, Jess. *You* fucked up. *You!* Don't try and put that on me."

She turned from him, brushing away the sudden tears that burned her eyes. She *had* fucked up. Every word he said was true. But he just didn't understand. She'd been in such a dark place then.

"Look, I'm sorry," he said. "I didn't ask you about this shit to start a fight."

"Then why did you ask?"

"Tryin' to understand, I guess."

"Understand what?"

"Why you went off with that guy. Hell, if you were going to throw it all away, you could've done that with me."

She turned her head to the side, just far enough to see him out of the corner of her eye. "You were jealous?"

She saw him stiffen.

"Was he better for you than I would have been?" he growled.

She swallowed. No, he wasn't even in the same league. He'd been okay to her at first, but things had soon gone downhill. She'd stayed with him because she'd been ashamed to admit she'd made a mistake. Pride had made her stick with him longer than she should have. *Way* longer. And when it'd turned physical, she'd been even more ashamed. She'd left with no plans, no possessions, just the clothes on her back. She was even more embarrassed that she'd allowed it to escalate that far. When she reached that final straw and had nowhere else to turn, she went looking for the one man who made her feel safe.

"Was he, Jess?"

She shook her head, replying quietly, "You know he wasn't."

"You left Seattle with no car, no bags, barely any money. What happened?"

She shook her head again. "Nothing. I'd just had enough."

"What aren't you tellin' me, Jess?"

"Stop, Ghost, please."

"He hurt you?"

Yes, badly. But she couldn't tell Ghost that. He'd go off the deep end. So, instead she shook her head.

"Jess, tell me. Say the word, and I'm on my bike headed to fucking Seattle to beat that motherfucker's ass."

She didn't want Ghost to commit a felony for her, and the last thing she wanted was to ever have anything to do with Kyle again.

She pasted on a bright smile and turned to face Ghost. "Gonna play the Big Bad Brother, huh?"

"If that's what you need me to do, absolutely."

She laughed and rolled her eyes. "Not necessary. No ass-beating required. I promise."

His eyes searched hers, and she was sure he could read the lies on her face.

"Someday you're gonna tell me all of it. *That's* a promise."

She went to him, pressing her head into his chest, her

arms hugging him tight. "Bu not tonight, Ghost. Please."

His arms closed around her, and his lips brushed her forehead.

"Okay, brat. Not tonight."

Her eyes closed, and she breathed in his scent, soaking up his warmth. She felt safe from all of it: Kyle and the Death Heads.

What little energy she had drained right out of her. Ghost held her a few moments longer, somehow sensing she needed it. Then his hold loosened.

"Come on, brat. Let's get you to bed.

He took her inside and set her up in his bed, taking the couch for himself.

This time, she didn't try to persuade him to join her, the wounds of his rejection still smarting. It didn't make the long night alone in his big bed any easier, especially since she was surrounded by the scent of him lingering on his sheets. She curled up, inhaling deeply from the fistful she pulled to her face, and fell asleep, wishing things were different.

CHAPTER TWELVE

Ghost woke to the smell of bacon. He pushed the throw blanket off him and glanced around, finding it strange to be waking on his couch for a split second before it all came rushing back.

Jessie was in his bed. Only she wasn't. She was, apparently, making bacon.

He walked into the tiny room around the corner behind the bar that he'd converted into his kitchen, leaving the industrial kitchen alone until he decided what to do with the place.

He leaned against the doorframe, folding his arms and took in the sight before him. Jessie was standing at the stove adding a sprinkle of cheese to some scrambled eggs cooking in a pan.

His eyes skated down her. She had on one of his flannel shirts, her legs bare underneath, and he couldn't help but wonder what else she'd left bare. As he leisurely took in the sight, she lifted one foot to rub it against the back of her calf, and hell, if that wasn't the sexiest thing he'd ever seen.

"Mornin', brat."

Her head swiveled, and her startled eyes took him in—the bare chest, the sweats hanging low on his hips. He watched, amused, as she flushed and swallowed.

"You're up."

"To a man, the smell of bacon cookin' is better than any alarm clock."

She grinned. "I'll have to remember that. I hope you're hungry."

He moved to the stove, his eyes to a pot. "Are those grits?"

"Um hmm. And fried potatoes, and there are cheese biscuits in the oven. I didn't make gravy—I know how you love biscuits and gravy—but I couldn't find—"

He cut her off by pulling her into his arms, his mouth coming down on hers with a smack.

She looked up at him, startled. "What was that for?"

"You cooked for me. I haven't had anybody cook for me, hell, probably since you and your mom. At least not a good southern breakfast like this."

She pushed out of his arms, grinning, and he watched her blush. With embarrassment or happiness that she'd pleased him, he couldn't be sure.

"Well, go sit down, and I'll bring you a plate."

He walked to the bar, taking a seat on one of the stools.

A moment later, she carried out two plates, setting one heaping helping in front of him. It smelled amazing. He dug in and groaned around the mouthful. "Damn, baby. This is delicious." He looked where she sat beside him. "I forgot how good you could cook."

She gave him a shy smile and shrugged. "Its just breakfast. Anybody could do it."

"Uh, no. In my experience not just *anybody* can do it. Some people can't even scramble an egg, let alone cook all of this." He waved his fork over his plate.

"Mama taught me."

He nodded. "Whatever else you say about her, she was a phenomenal cook." He grinned. "Probably how she hooked my old man."

She looked down at her plate and replied quietly, "Yeah, maybe."

He bit into a strip of bacon and studied her suddenly sad expression. Was it the mention of her mother that made her sad, or the mention of his father? "Jess?"

"I miss him, you know."

He frowned, chewing. "Who?"

She turned suddenly glassy eyes on him. "Tommy."

He swallowed at that, the food suddenly feeling like a rock in his throat. He looked down at his plate. "I know, brat. I miss him, too."

When she was quiet, he reached over and took her hand, giving it a squeeze. "Remember that time he tried to sneak into the pool of the apartment complex down the street? He climbed on the little storage shed and fell through the roof."

That got a smile out of her. She looked over at him, a tinkle of laughter escaping.

"Funniest thing I ever saw," he admitted, grinning.

"Me, too."

"Management chased him through the whole complex, remember?"

"You hid me behind the dumpsters while they chased him."

"Couldn't let you go down for our crime."

They finished the rest of their breakfast in happy chatter, reminiscing about days gone by.

"You cooked, so I'll clean up," he said, reaching for both their plates.

"You remember that rule, huh?"

"Your momma taught me well. I do my share." He stood with the plates in his hands and nodded toward the bedroom. "Go take a shower. I got this."

She jumped off her stool. "Sounds good to me."

He grinned, watching her walk off, his eyes right where they shouldn't be—her ass. He blew out a breath and headed into the kitchen to clean up.

About ten minutes later, as he was starting to cover up the leftovers, he heard the rumble of some bikes pulling up. He tossed the dishtowel over his shoulder and headed downstairs.

Ghost opened the door, his eyes sweeping over five of his brothers, and he blocked the entrance. "What the fuck do you want?"

"We're selling magazines to support our meth addiction. Can I interest you in a subscription, sir?" Griz joked with a straight face. "Or a donation?"

"I gave at the office."

Griz pushed past him. "You ain't got an office."

In trooped Hammer, JJ, Heavy, and lastly, Shades.

"To what do I owe this visit?" he asked, folding his arms.

Shades tossed a bag to Ghost. "Skylar sent over a few things."

Ghost caught it to his chest, looking down at it. "Why'd she do that?"

"I told her about the "bootylicious sweats" incident at the truck stop. She offered to take your girl to the mall later. Sent a few things to tide her over till then." Shades tugged on the dishcloth on his shoulder with a grin as he made to move past Ghost and head up the stairs. "We need to talk, Betty Crocker. Come on."

Ghost's brows rose as he watched his brothers all head up the stairs, and he called after them in a sarcastic tone, "Well, come on in and make yourselves at home, why doncha?"

"Thanks, we will," Hammer replied, his voice echoing down the stairs.

"Son-of-a-bitch," Ghost grumbled beneath his breath as he locked the door, and then followed them up the stairs.

They were all sitting at the bar, except for Griz, who emerged from the kitchen with a plateful of Jessie's cheese biscuits, munching on a piece of bacon.

"You make these?" he asked.

"Don't be an idiot," Shades replied. "He couldn't make a biscuit if his life depended on it."

"Gimme one," Hammer demanded, already reaching toward the plate.

They all grabbed one.

JJ pulled his apart. "It's like a fluffy cloud of magical goodness."

Ghost rolled his eyes.

Griz sat on a stool, groaning and reaching for his back. "Christ, it'll take me days to recover from that fucking ride home."

"Your back hurt?" Ghost asked.

"'Course it does. Doesn't yours?" he growled back.

"Nope. I had the most phenomenal massage the other night." Ghost grinned like the Cheshire cat.

Shades looked over at him with brows raised, his mouth full of biscuit. "Oh, is that so? Do tell."

Hammer leaned forward to look around Shades. "You sayin' she can cook like this, looks like she does, and gives backrubs, too? Hell, you don't marry her, I will, Son."

Ghost's eyes moved from Shades to Hammer. "You ain't touchin' her, bro."

Just then, their heads all swiveled as the woman in question walked out of the bedroom, wrapped in a towel. Her head was bent as she rubbed a second towel on her wet hair.

JJ let out a wolf whistle that brought her head up, and she stopped dead in her tracks.

Ghost's arm swung out, smacking JJ in the side of the head.

"Oww. Son-of-a—"

"Watch your mouth," Ghost snapped.

"Oh! I didn't know you had company," Jessie stuttered out, looking stricken with embarrassment.

Ghost tossed her the bag Shades had given him. "Here, Shades' ol' lady sent some clothes over for you."

Jessie scrambled to grab up the bag, almost dropping the towel. She clutched it to her chest. "Thank you. That was nice of her."

Shades gave her a smile, nodding. "She's a good woman."

"Thank her for me, will you?"

"Will do," Shades replied.

"Well, don't just stand there, brat, go put some clothes on," Ghost ordered with brows raised.

"Hell, let her stand there in just a towel. I ain't complainin'," Hammer put in.

Ghost smacked Hammer in the back of the head, barking to Jessie, "Move."

"Oww. Fuck," Hammer bitched, yanking his head away.

When she was gone, Ghost moved around the back of the bar, pulled the carafe from the coffee maker, and poured himself a mug.

"You're not going to offer us any?" Shades asked with lifted brow.

Ghost brought the mug to his lips, replying in a growl, "No, 'cause you ain't stayin' that long."

"We interrupt something, bro?" Hammer asked with a smirk.

"Yeah... breakfast, fuckface."

A few minutes later, Jessie returned in a pair of jeans

and tank top. She moved behind the bar and got herself a cup of coffee.

"Good morning," she said, eyeing the men.

Heavy replied, "What's good about it?"

"What's wrong with you?" she asked him.

"Ignore him. He ain't a mornin' person," Ghost informed her.

Heavy looked up at her with a surly face. "There are only two kinds of people in my book. Morning people." He paused, one brow lifting as he looked at her threateningly. "And the people who want to kill them."

"All righty, then." She got in his face, showing no fear. "So, just coffee, then?"

He glared at her.

"Warning, bro. She's got an attitude and she knows how to use it."

Heavy's eyes cut to a grinning Ghost, and then back to her. "Coffee would be good. I wouldn't say no to a cup of Joe."

Her brow rose, and she waited.

"What?" he asked, staring at her.

"Pretty sure you didn't use the magic word, Heavy," Ghost offered helpfully.

Heavy cut his eyes to him, frowning. "You fucking serious?"

Ghost folded his arms.

Heavy let out a long exasperated breath. "Fine. May I please have a cup of coffee, ma'am?"

She grinned. "Why yes, of course, sugar-pie. You want it

black?"

Heavy frowned over at Ghost. "Sugar-pie? Did she just call me sugar-pie?"

"Yup," Shades replied with a grin. Then he looked over at Jessie and added, "He loves it when women call him butterbean."

Heavy pointed a finger at Ghost and warned, "She calls me butterbean and I'm leaving. Just sayin'."

"Hmm. Butterbean. I'll remember that in case I ever want to get rid of you," Jessie teased, and then poured him some coffee.

Shades grabbed the last biscuit from Griz's hand and shoved it in his mouth.

Griz looked like a kid who'd just had his candy taken from him. He glared over at his VP. "Sometimes you really kill my joy, you know that?"

Shades grinned around the mouthful of cheesy biscuit. "Mmm. Soooo good!"

"You suck."

Shades just licked his lips in response.

"Karma has no expiration date," Griz warned. "Just sayin."

"I'm shaking in my boots."

"You will be when I tell Skylar you're eating biscuits when she's got you eating low carb."

"You fuckin' tell her, and you'll be eating through a straw for the next three months."

"Ooww, I'm shakin' in *my* boots, now."

"And why aren't you home fucking your ol' lady?"

Ghost teased Shades.

"'Cause his future father-in-law is stayin' in town," Hammer offered with a chuckle.

Ghost's eyes cut to Shades, and he grinned big. "That true, bro?"

"Motherfucking yes."

"Got you a little on edge, does he?" Ghost teased.

Shades glared at him and snapped, "You'd be on edge too if the fucking New Orleans Chapter President was taking over your house."

"Sucks to be you. But you're the one who had to go and pick his daughter to make your ol' lady," Griz teased.

"Like I need you to remind me."

"I'm sure Undertaker reminds you all the time," Hammer added, grinning big.

"You two want to cut the shit long enough to tell me why you're here?" Ghost asked.

"Let's go outside. I need a smoke," Shades growled.

They all headed to the terrace and kicked back in the chairs.

Shades and Ghost both dipped their heads, cupping their hands around their lighters as they lit up. Then they both tipped their heads back, exhaling long plumes of smoke in the air.

Ghost tossed his lighter on a glass side table with a clatter. "So, what's up?"

"Butcher called a meeting," Shades said, pulling his phone out and glancing at the time. "We got about half an hour before we need to head out."

"And?"

"He wants us to bring your girl."

"What the fuck for?" Ghost frowned.

"Wants her kept under lock and key until we get this meet set with the DKs."

"Why?"

Shades shrugged. "Just coverin' our bases, bro. You know we got a lot ridin' on this deal."

"She's not goin' anywhere, Shades," Ghost growled. This was bullshit.

Shades nodded. "I know she's not. That's why he wants her in lockdown at the clubhouse."

"Are you shittin' me?"

"Nope."

"What the hell for? Does he think I can't keep her safe?"

"Ain't about you keepin' her safe. It's about you controlling her."

"Say what?"

"The woman's headstrong. We've all seen it. Hell, I gotta remind you that she slapped fucking Blood, of all people? Not a lot of chicks I know would dare to slap Blood."

Ghost ran a frustrated hand down his face. "That doesn't mean shit."

"Look, Butcher's afraid she'll decide she doesn't need you watchin' out for her now that she's back in her hometown." Shades shrugged. "Just playin' it safe. Makin' sure she doesn't... *run off.*"

"Are you fuckin' serious?"

"As a heart attack, bro."

Ghost surged to his feet and walked a few feet away, violently flinging his cigarette in the distance.

Shades moved to stand with him.

"I want to serve my club, Shades. But using her to do it—" He broke off shaking his head.

"You gonna be able to keep your head on straight about this girl? You gonna be able to use her for the benefit of your club? You good with that?"

"Club first, right?"

"Right. You made that decision the day you put that cut on your back."

Ghost nodded.

Shades slapped him on the back. "Maybe you don't want any part of this, but you're a loyal brother, so you better fall in line like the rest of us."

Ghost shrugged off his arm and headed back inside.

"Where you goin'?" Shades asked.

"To tell Jessie we're ridin' out in a few minutes. That okay with you? You *do* know how long it takes chicks to get ready, right?"

Shades grinned. "Right."

***

Half an hour later, Jessie was standing on the curb outside with Ghost's brothers. He had paused at the door to lock up, and Shades was up there talking to him, but she was too far away to hear any of it. Whatever it was, it made Ghost smile, which was good because ever since the guys got there, he'd been in a surly mood.

Griz leaned over to half-whisper in her ear. "Ten bucks says you can't get him to break formation on the way over to the clubhouse."

Jessie frowned at him, wondering if this was some type of test to see if she could hold her own with them. Never one to back down from a challenge, she knew she had to accept. If he thought she'd punk out, he didn't know what she was made of. *Well, bring it on, big guy.* She smiled up at him. "You're on, old man."

Hammer just shook his head. "Didn't you lose enough money already on this trip, Griz?"

Griz didn't break eye contact with Jessie as he answered Hammer. "You stay outta this, this doesn't concern you."

"It's your funeral," Hammer replied.

"Wait, what?" Jess broke eye contact with Griz to look over at Hammer. She was beginning to doubt the wisdom of this whole idea. Griz put his arm around her and turned her away.

"Don't you pay no mind to him. You got this, girl. I got faith in you."

"What's the purpose of this again?"

He shrugged. "No purpose. Why has there gotta be a purpose? This is just you takin' a bet. No harm in that. It's all good, doll. Just havin' a little fun."

Jessie's eyes narrowed as she eyed him, considering. "Twenty."

Griz grinned. "Ooo. The girl's confident. I like it. Okay, girly. You're on."

"Okay, wait. Let's clarify. What exactly counts as

breaking formation?"

"You get his bike to wobble. Better yet, you get him to cross the centerline. I'll pay double for that."

"The center line? But couldn't that kill us?"

"You don't do it when there's oncoming traffic, missy. Ya gotta time this shit *just* right." He paused, considering her slowly as if he was rethinking the bet. "You sure you're up for this?"

Her spine straightened. *Of course* she was up for this— she'd never turned down a bet in her life. "I've got it."

He ruffled her hair. "I like you. You're gonna fit right in. Give ol' Ghost a run for his money. He needs someone like you to shake him up."

She couldn't help the smile that lit up her face. *God, she hoped those words were true, because she definitely needed Ghost.*

"Hey, doll?" Griz stopped her.

She turned back.

"Here's a little hint, 'cause I like ya."

"Okay."

He lifted his chin toward Ghost. "Put your hands anywhere they want to go. He likes when girls do that."

"Why do I get the feeling you're trying to get me in trouble?"

"Hell, gal, I'm trying to help you win." He shrugged. "But suit yourself. I'm only a guy, what do I know about how we men like to be touched?"

"Right." She rolled her eyes at his sarcasm. "Thanks."

***

Twenty minutes later, they were walking into the clubhouse. Jessie had a crisp new twenty tucked in her pocket. She was relieved that Ghost had taken it all in stride, laughing at the bet they'd made and being the fun-loving guy she remembered.

He had a tight grip on her hand as he led her to the bar, sat her on a stool, and ordered her a drink.

He pressed a kiss to her forehead. "Sit tight, brat. This shouldn't take too long, okay?"

She looked up at him and made a silly face. "Okie-dokie."

He rolled his eyes. "Goofball." Then his gaze connected with the prospect behind the bar. Thankfully, it wasn't Yammer. Ghost lifted his chin at the man. "Yo, keep an eye on her."

The man nodded. "Sure thing, Ghost."

Jessie watched Ghost head down a hallway with the other patched members and disappear out of sight.

The prospect set a glass filled with cola in front of her. He held up a bottle of rum. "You want me to add a little something to that, darlin'?"

She smiled and pushed her drink forward. "God, yes."

He chuckled. "That's the spirit."

She glanced around. With all the men in the meeting, there were only a few people in the room. An old Rolling Stones song played quietly in the background—Mick declaring he can't get no satisfaction.

Two drinks later, Jessie felt a presence at her side and turned to see little Ashley scooting onto the stool next to her, dropping a pack of cigarettes and a pink rhinestone-covered cell phone on the bar.

The prospect came over, his palms on the bar top. "Ashley. You want a drink?"

She nodded over at Jessie's drink and gave the prospect a big smile. "I'll have what she's having."

He set a glass in front of her, filled it with cola and rum. Jessie sat quietly next to her, sipping her third drink, now listening to the muted sounds of Eric Clapton and Cream's *Layla* coming through the speakers. She found herself wishing the club's meeting would wrap up soon.

Ashley shook a cigarette from her pack. "You got a light, Boo?"

The prospect dug a silver Zippo out of his hip pocket and extended his tattoo-covered arm, flicking the cover open.

Ashley stood on the foot-rung and perched over, her ass in the air as she dipped her head toward the flame. She sucked on the smoke until it flared to life, the smell of tobacco drifting out.

"Thanks, doll." She winked at the man named Boo, who flipped his Zippo closed, shoved it back in his pocket, and then moved off to stock a cooler with cases of beer.

Ashley turned toward Jessie, offering her pack of smokes. "You want one, honey?"

"No, thanks. I quit."

Ashley nodded, tossing them on the bar top. "I tried that once." She blew out a stream of smoke toward the nicotine-stained ceiling tiles. "I lasted about a week."

She smiled over at Jessie, who nodded, not really in the

mood to make friendly chitchat with the girl who'd been so cozy with Ghost.

She could feel Ashley's eyes studying her.

"You don't like me, do you?" she asked.

Jessie turned toward her, shrugging. "Not particularly."

"That's okay. We don't have to be friends. Just so you understand your place."

"My place?" Jessie repeated, giving Ashley a look that could kill.

Ashley grinned. "I'm not trying to be mean. I just want you to know the way things are here."

"And how is that?"

"Never mind. You'll be gone soon anyway," Ashley commented, her eyes on the mirror behind the bar.

Jessie met her eyes in the reflection. "What makes you think I'm going anywhere?"

Ashley tapped her cigarette in the ashtray. "Way I heard it, sweetie, they're taking you to the DKs. Making some deal."

Jessie's brows shot up. "Excuse me?"

Ashley shrugged. "You're part of the deal, least that's what JJ told me last night in bed."

Jessie felt a chill run down her skin. Her mind racing with thoughts, she lifted her glass and drained it. Ghost wasn't going to turn her over to the DKs. It wasn't possible. He wouldn't let his club do that, would he? But if that was their plan, could he stop them? If they did hand her over to the DKs, there'd be only one reason for it: so she could be handed over to the Death Heads. She felt her stomach drop, the rum roiling as panic overwhelmed her. She flicked her gaze to the prospect keeping an eye on her. He was busy stacking cases, and then her eyes moved to the entrance reflected in the mirror.

And she wondered if she could make it out the door without him seeing.

CHAPTER THIRTEEN

Ghost sat at the table with his club. He looked toward the head, where his chapter President sat, eying him.

"Talked to the DKs last night." Butcher's voice was gruff. "They want her brought to the meet. Want to hear it straight from her mouth."

"No way." Ghost's voice was firm as he shook his head.

"Afraid so, Ghost. They insisted. Those are serious accusations she's makin'. They're not turnin' their club inside out lookin' for some rat unless they believe this ain't a bunch of bullshit some chick made up to get a ride across country."

"You know that's not true."

"Maybe I do. What I believe isn't important. We need *them* to believe it. Only way we make this deal."

"Fuck," Ghost murmured, his eyes moving to the scarred wooden table. He felt a tick in his jaw as he gritted his teeth.

"You got a problem with this, you better say so right

now."

Ghost glared at his President, and his VP stepped in. Leaning forward, Shades looked at Ghost.

"You brought this to the club. Coulda kept your mouth shut and put her on a bus."

"I wouldn't keep that from the club." Ghost stared Shades down. "You know that."

Shades nodded. "Damn right. So get right with this, Ghost."

Ghost's eyes moved from Shades back to Butcher. "And if they want more? If they want her?"

His President just stared at him with a cold expression that didn't give Ghost a good feeling.

"Butcher, I gotta draw the line—"

"We draw the line where I say we draw the line," Butcher barked, cutting him off with an arch look that brooked no argument. But Ghost *had* to argue his point.

"I'm not lettin' you turn her over to the DKs. They'll use her to make their own deal with the Death Heads." He shook his head emphatically.

"And maybe we let them think that's a possibility," Butcher growled.

Ghost surged to his feet. "Is it?"

Shades was on his feet just as fast, his fist in Ghost's chest. "Sit the fuck down!"

Ghost fell back in his chair; Hammer grabbing his shoulders to keep him seated.

Butcher remained calm, glaring at Ghost. "You keep your shit straight, Son. And you keep her locked down until the meet. You understand?"

Shades turned to Butcher. "He understands, Prez."

Butcher glared at his VP. "I didn't fuckin' ask you." His eyes moved back to Ghost. "Are we clear?"

"Crystal," Ghost growled back.

Butcher slammed the gavel down. "Meeting fucking adjourned."

Boot and Slick accompanied Butcher down the hall to his office, and the rest of the club all shuffled out. Shades hung back with Ghost, who still sat in his chair, wondering how this had all gotten so fucked up.

Ghost looked over at Shades. "You with him? You afraid she'll run, too?"

Shades stared him in the eyes and asked, "You tell me. Will she?"

Ghost rubbed his face and grudgingly admitted, "There's a damn good possibility."

"Then don't fuckin' tell her. She doesn't need to know shit till we're rollin' toward the Georgia State line."

Ghost rubbed his hand back and forth across his mouth for a long time, then finally looked over at Shades. "How far you think Butcher's gonna take this?"

"What do you mean?"

"You know what I fucking mean, Brother. Do you think he'd actually hand her over?"

Shades shook his head. "No way." His brows rose. "Now, he might let them think that, just like he stood at that back gate with you and me and lied to the DKs about Skylar for *me*. But he ain't gonna hand over your girl. You *know* that, Ghost."

He nodded. He wanted to believe it. But this was Jessie they were talking about, and he just couldn't put her at risk.

Shades patted his shoulder. "Come on, man. It'll be fine."

They both stood and headed down the hall toward the common room.

***

When Ghost entered the room, the first thing he saw was the look on Jessie's face. She was royally pissed off. The second thing he noticed was that the prospect he'd put in charge of keeping an eye on her was now standing behind her, one hand on the bar, one on the back of her barstool.

Ghost slid his gaze down the bar to see Ashley sitting a couple seats over, looking too happy with herself, and a bad feeling snaked down his spine. If he were a betting man, he'd bet that Ashley had something to do with the look on Jessie's face.

He walked up to Boo. The man had a full, dark beard and tattoo sleeves that ran up both arms. He was a man Ghost felt he could count on, having passed every test the club had thrown his way so far.

"Talk," Ghost snapped.

Boo stepped a few paces toward Ghost. He leaned in and said in a low voice, "Ashley said something to her, not sure what, but it rattled her enough to bolt for the door. I caught her in the yard. Been keeping 'em separated."

Ghost nodded, his eyes moving from Jessie's rigid back to Ashley.

"Who'd she take up with last night?" he asked Boo.

"JJ."

"Thanks, man."

Boo nodded and went back behind the bar.

Shades stepped over to Ghost. "Problem?"

"Apparently. Can you tell JJ to get Ashley out of here?"

"I can take care of her. Be my pleasure."

"Let JJ handle her. He fucked her last night."

Shades nodded, and Ghost moved in behind Jessie, taking up the position Boo had been in, one hand on the bar, one on the back of her barstool. "We need to talk."

She whirled on him and bit out, "You're turning me over to them? I'm part of a deal?"

Ghost's eyes lifted over Jessie's head for a split second to touch on Ashley. Just then JJ walked past, and Ghost knew he'd heard what Jessie had just said. Hell, half the damn room had heard her.

And Ghost knew exactly where that shit had come from. That fucking pillow talk was going to get JJ's ass beat. But Ghost couldn't deal with him now. He had a pissed off woman he was supposed to get under control and locked down.

Fucking hell.

Ghost grabbed her by the upper arm and pulled her off the stool. "Let's go."

"Let me go. I'm not going anywhere with you. Go to hell."

Too late, sweetheart, he was already there.

She tried to pull back, but that barely slowed him as he

hauled her down the hall. He threw open the second door on the right and shoved her inside.

It was a room he sometimes used on his rare stays at the clubhouse. It was barebones, with just a twin bed against the wall and a small table hosting a lamp and a half empty bottle of Jack.

There was one window, and the decorating consisted of one lone, framed photo of himself and Tommy. It was a shot he'd always liked, from back when they were in High School. They'd both had their arms around each other, laughing.

Jessie whirled to look at him as he slammed the door.

"You're going to turn me over to them, aren't you?"

"Shut up, and listen to me for one goddamned minute!"

"You're just using me. How could you? I came to you for *help*. God, I never should have trusted you!"

That cut him deeper than he cared to admit.

"Yeah, Jess, you came to me for help. And you were dragging a shit-ton of trouble with you. And I took that on with *no fucking hesitation*. I said I'd help you. I told you I'd keep you safe. But you don't get a say in how I do that or how that happens."

"I don't have to listen to you. You're not the man I thought you were."

"You're right, babe. I'm not. Maybe I never was. But it's time to grow up, little girl. And that means you're going to do whatever the fuck I tell you."

"I don't have to stay and listen to this. I'm leaving. I'm going to my mom's." She made to move past him to the door.

He yanked her back with a hand clamped around her arm.

"Your mom lives in fucking Daytona, Jess. That's Death Head territory. That's the last fucking place you're going."

"You can't stop me."

"*Wanna bet?*"

***

Ghost strode out into the common room and took a seat at the bar next to Shades.

Shades brows rose as he looked over at Ghost. "Everything okay?"

"Yup."

They could hear screaming and yelling coming from down the hall.

"Don't sound like it."

Ghost dipped his head to light up a smoke, then he tossed the lighter on the bar, blew out a pissed off stream of smoke and admitted, "I cuffed her to the bed."

Shades cocked a brow. "You what?"

"Only way to keep her in the room."

They heard a crash.

"What was that?" Shades asked him.

Ghost took a sip of his drink. "Probably a half empty bottle of Jack."

Shades nodded. "Well, as long as it was half empty and all."

Ghost grinned. "Shut up."

"She scare you, Ghost? 'Cause if she doesn't scare the hell out of you a little, she's not the one."

"She scares the shit out of me."

Shades laughed.

"Skylar scare you?"

"Every damn day."

"Women."

"We got some business to take care of. You gonna leave her in there?"

"Yup."

Shades laughed. "Somehow I don't think Butcher's gonna like hearing all that caterwaulin' going on all day."

"Guess it sucks to be him. He wanted her locked down. She's locked down."

"Okay, then. Let's roll."

CHAPTER FOURTEEN

Hours passed as Jessie lay on the bed silently fuming with one wrist cuffed to the bedpost. She'd broken just about everything in sight: The bottle of booze she'd smashed against the door. The lamp, she'd thrown at the window, cracking it. She'd even flung the rickety table across the room. The only thing she hadn't smashed was the framed photo of Ghost and Tommy. Partly because she couldn't reach it and partly because she wasn't sure she could bring herself to destroy it.

She stared at it now as she lay there. It must have been taken back in high school. They looked so happy, the best of buds.

She was shaken from her musing by the sound of the doorknob rattling. A moment later, it was flung open, and there stood Blood, of all people.

Jessie instinctively shrank against the headboard as fear shot through her. She watched as he folded his arms and leaned against the doorframe, his eyes scanning the room, taking in the carnage.

"Heard you were raisin' all kinds of hell. Thought I'd come see for myself."

"I was pissed." She found herself making the lame excuse.

"I've known lots of pissed off women. They go shopping and eat ice cream. Ever try that?"

She rattled the handcuff. "Little hard to do mall therapy when I'm cuffed to a bed."

His eyes took in the handcuffs as if he were just noticing them. Then the corner of his mouth pulled up. "I see. All stressed out and no one to choke, huh?"

"Something like that."

"Who cuffed you?"

"Who do you think? Ghost."

A barely-there smile appeared on his face. "So, you're sitting here on death row waiting for him to come back, huh?"

She smirked at him. "If I had something, I'd throw it at you."

"If it's stress relief you need"—he paused, lifting his chin to the destroyed room—"and judging by the destruction, I'd say you do, then I've got just the thing for that."

He pushed off the doorframe and moved toward her.

She shrank back. If he was talking about sex, he'd better think again.

He stopped next to the bed, one hand digging in his hip pocket before pulling out a key ring. Then he was unlocking

GHOST

the handcuffs. A moment later she was free and rubbing her wrist.

"Ghost gave you the key?"

"Ghost doesn't even know I'm here."

"But you have the key."

"A handcuff key works on any set."

"You just happen to have one on your key ring?"

"Yup."

"Why?"

"Comes in handy. More often than you'd think."

"I'll bet."

He chuckled. "Come on, sweet cheeks. Let's go."

"Go where?"

"Gun range for a little firearms therapy. Get all that aggression out. Works like a charm."

That surprisingly sounded like fun, and anything was better than being locked up in this hot room. "Okay."

She followed him out and through the club. It was deserted, but she did hear someone down one of the hallways. They moved outside into the bright sunshine, and she breathed in the fresh air. It was wonderful after spending hours inhaling spilled whiskey.

Blood threw his leg over his bike. "Climb on."

She did, and he handed her a helmet, waiting while she strapped it on. Then he fired up the bike, and they roared off.

Half an hour later, they were riding down a long dirt road back into the woods. Jessie was so lost she doubted she could find this place again even if her life depended on it. Blood pulled up next to several parked bikes and a couple of pickup trucks. As soon as he shut his bike off, she could hear gunshots coming from farther back in the woods somewhere.

They climbed off the bike, and she followed him down a dirt path, over a rise, and through a thicket, until if finally opened up to a clearing.

There, standing in the dirt, were several men, all with guns raised and firing at targets which consisted mostly of bottles and cans.

As they moved down the line, Jessie spotted several guys with Evil Dead cuts on their backs. Three said Alabama. One said Louisiana.

"I see dumb people," Blood teased.

"Ha ha ha, Blood. You're hilarious."

"Why is she here? I thought she was supposed to be on lockdown."

"What's the matter, Slick? Afraid she'll turn out to be a better shot than you?"

"Everybody's a better shot than Slick," one of the others teased.

"Go stand down there by the targets, fuckface. Bet you twenty bucks I hit you."

They all laughed.

"I'll put twenty on that one. Go on, Gator."

"Fuck all you guys."

They laughed harder.

Blood moved to an empty spot at the end, next to the other man from his Louisiana Chapter.

"Will you get in trouble for bringing me here?" Jessie asked Blood.

"Suddenly worried about my well being, sweet cheeks?"

"No. And stop calling me that."

He grinned. "Relax. I do shit like this all the time."

He pulled a gun out from under his cut.

"Let's start with the basics."

"The basics?"

"Ever fire a gun?"

She shook her head.

"Ever hold a gun?"

She shook her head again.

"This is a 9mm. Let's start with how to load it." He pressed a button on the side of the handgrip, ejecting the magazine.

"You insert the ammo one at a time, with the rounded side forward, until the magazine is full. You re-insert it by pushing upward into the handgrip until you hear a clicking noise indicating the magazine has locked in place."

He handed her the gun.

"Now, you try it."

She repeated the steps he'd shown her.

Then he moved behind her, raised her arms toward the targets, and whispered the rest of the instructions in her ear. She couldn't help but be affected by his body pressed up against her back.

"Disengage the safety by pushing down on the safety lever at the top rear of the gun."

"Blood, kiss her neck. Women love when you kiss their necks," Sandman suggested. *Bam. Bam. Bam.* He fired at his target in rapid succession. "Just not when they're driving," he added.

Bam. Bam. Bam.

"And you're in the backseat."

Bam. Bam. Bam.

"And they don't know you."

Bam. Bam.

Jessie tried to hold back the laughter, her body shaking. "He's a good shot, isn't he?"

Blood snorted. "His greatest talent is finding places to sit down."

"Why you gotta be the worm in my tequila?"

"Ignore him. He ate paint chips when he was little," Blood teased.

Sandman lowered his gun, taking offense to that last comment. "My mind is like lightning."

"Yeah, one brilliant flash and it's gone."

Sandman turned, looked at Jessie, and said in a low, conspiratorial voice, "He loves my ass. Don't let him fool you."

"I've stopped listening, why haven't you stopped talking?" Blood asked him.

Jessie was giggling so hard, she could hardly keep her arms up and the gun on the target.

Blood lifted them back up. "There's gonna be plenty of distractions when you're shooting, you can't let them get to you. Pay attention."

She tried to pull it together.

"Chamber a round."

"Do what?"

"Pull back on the slide on top of the barrel to load a bullet into the firing chamber."

She did it.

"Now aim down the sight at the target."

"Okay." She focused in on a blue wine bottle.

"Place your index finger on the trigger when you're sure you're ready to shoot."

"Okay."

"You pull the trigger one time for each shot you fire."

"Okay."

"Breathe in, exhale, and squeeze the trigger, darlin'."

She inhaled, exhaled, then squeezed. She wasn't ready for the deafening sound nor the recoil the gun made when it went off. Luckily, Blood was there, still at her back, steadying her. When she saw that the bottle was still there, her shoulders slumped.

"I missed."

"First time you've ever held a gun. Did you think you'd be Annie Oakley with the first shot?"

"I hate failing. In anything."

"Competitive bitch, are you?"

"I suppose."

"Good. That I can work with. You're high and to the right. Try again."

She aimed at the target, breathed in, exhaled, and fired. Nothing.

"Again."

She repeated her steps.

And missed.

"Again."

She missed again.

"Focus, babe. We'll be here all day if we have to, till you hit the damn thing."

He knew just what buttons to push to incite her determination to make the shot. She steadied her arm, breathed in, exhaled, and squeezed the trigger.

This time the bottle exploded.

Blood grabbed the gun from her hand as she swung around, excitedly.

"I hit it!"

"Yes, ma'am."

She jumped up and down.

"Good job. Now shoot the shit out of those cans like they're Ashley."

"How do you know about Ashley?"

"Lucky guess."

He handed the gun back to her. She took aim and fired.

Bam. Bam. Bam. Bam. Bam.

When she was empty, he took the gun from her as she turned to him.

"Thank you. That felt so good."

"You're welcome. So, what'd Ashley do this time?"

She hesitated to tell him all of the reasons she disliked the girl, so she just shrugged. "I just find it hard to be nice to her, and I'm a nice person."

"Yeah, well, some people suck the nice right out of you."

"How do *you* know Ashley?"

"For about five minutes, I thought about fucking her. Thankfully, I had the good sense to drown that kitten in the river."

That brought a smile to Jessie's face. "Well, thank you for this. I needed it."

"I could tell."

"Now what?"

He nodded toward the targets. "Now you practice until it comes natural and easy. Never know when trouble might come callin', sweet cheeks, and you need to be able to defend yourself."

She knew right then that he must have heard all about the danger she was in, and she wondered if the reason he'd brought her out here had less to do with "stress relief," and more to do with the trouble that followed her. It spoke volumes about the man; he cared enough to take his time with her like this, preparing her like he was.

"Why are you being nice to me?" she blurted out.

He studied her a long moment, and then began reloading his gun. "Let me put it to you this way: I'll try being nicer, if you try being smarter."

She frowned. "What do you mean?"

His eyes met hers.

"Look, I know Ghost. He's a good guy. And for reasons I haven't figured out yet, unless it's your sweet ass, he's taken on your shit. All of it. And from what I hear, it's a lot."

Jessie swallowed. She couldn't deny any of it.

Blood continued, "He's taken your back. That means something. You need to trust he's got this. That he isn't going to let anything happen to you. So, I guess what I'm saying is, wise up and quit giving him grief. Deal?"

She looked off at the horizon, contemplating his words. Everything he said was true. So she did the only thing she could do. She nodded. "Deal."

He handed her back the gun, his chin lifting toward the targets. "Have at it, Annie Oakley."

She grinned and took aim.

***

An hour later, they pulled back up at the clubhouse. Blood led her through the common room, catching the eye of Boo, who was mopping behind the bar. His mouth dropped open when he saw she wasn't still in the room that he and everyone else knew she was supposed to be locked in. But apparently he knew better than to question a full-patched member, so his mouth clamped shut.

Blood led her down the hall and deposited her in the room, sitting her on the bed. He reached for the handcuff still hanging from the bedpost and held out his hand, waggling two fingers for her to lift her wrist.

"Please, Blood. Don't handcuff me. I promise I won't go anywhere."

"I know it. 'Cause you'll be *cuffed to the bed*."

"Blood, please, don't."

"Stop whining. I'd hate to leave duct tape marks on your face, but I will."

She thought he was joking, but with Blood, she couldn't be sure. She didn't know what his limits were, and she didn't want to cross them. So she lifted her hand, holding it out to him.

"Good girl." He clamped the handcuff around her wrist. Then ruffled the top of her head and headed for the door.

"Blood?"

He paused with his hand on the knob and turned back to her.

"Are you going back to New Orleans? Will I see you again?"

"I'll be around for a while longer. You'll see me again, sweet cheeks."

Then he walked out.

She yelled through the closed door, "Quit calling me that!"

She heard a fist hit against the wall of the hallway, and she smiled.

***

About an hour after Blood left her, Boo came in with a fast food bag. He stepped over the broken glass and approached the bed.

"I brought you a hamburger. Ghost called and said it'd be another hour before they get back, and he thought you might be hungry." He set the bag on the bed and handed her the drink. He righted the table she'd thrown across the room and set it next to the bed so she could put her drink down.

"Thank you. Can you let me go to the bathroom?" She lifted her wrist and rattled the handcuffs.

He eyed them. "Um, yeah, sure. Let me get the key."

A couple minutes later he returned with the key, released and escorted her down the hall to the bathroom.

When she was finished he took her back and allowed her to finish eating before he put the cuff back on her.

"I'll get one of the girls in here to clean up the mess."

"Thank you, Boo. I'm sorry about that. I was a little upset."

He just nodded without comment, then slid out the door.

About five minutes later, there was a tap on the door, and Ashley stepped in, holding a broom.

"Boo sent me in to sweep up the glass." She looked anything but happy about it.

He couldn't have sent anyone else? She supposed the girl was going to rub her nose in it now. Ashley began sweeping the glass in a pile.

"Guess you were pretty pissed off. I would have been pissed, too. I don't blame you for smashing up everything in sight. I'd have done the same thing." When Jessie just glared at her without commenting, Ashley's eyes lifted. "I told you the truth, you know."

Jessie turned her head away, trying to fold her arms, but the handcuff prevented her from doing so, and it rattled with the attempt.

Ashley's eyes dropped to the cuffs, then she put her finger to her mouth, as if warning Jessie to stay quiet.

Jessie frowned as she watched Ashley peek down the hall, wondering what on earth she was doing. She quietly closed the door, and then approached Jessie. Her hand slid into the hip pocket of her jeans and pulled out a key ring, holding it up.

"I was at the bar when Boo grabbed the key, so I saw

where he kept it. When he told me to come in here and clean up, I went behind the bar when he wasn't looking and snatched it."

"And? Are you going to let me out of these?" She rattled the cuffs.

Again Ashley shushed her and hissed quietly, "Do you want us to get caught?"

Jessie shut her mouth.

"It's no secret I want you gone, but I wasn't lying to you. I told you what JJ told me. Now, it's up to you if you want to believe it or not." She shrugged. "Maybe Ghost will let them turn you over, maybe he won't. But is that a chance you want to take?"

"Are you going to release me or not?"

Ashley crossed her arms. "If I do, you better never rat that it was me who let you go."

"Who do you think they'll blame it on?"

She shrugged. "Boo, I guess."

"Fine. I won't rat you out."

"Can I trust you?"

"Can I trust *you?*" Jessie quirked a brow at her. "Besides, how will I get out of here without being seen?"

"Climb out the window." Ashley gestured to the only window in the room. "It faces the side of the clubhouse. No one will see you, but if you're going, you'd better hurry. The guys could come back any minute now."

Jessie held her arm up. "Okay, quick, unlock these."

Ashley tossed her the keys, and they landed on the bed next to her. "Here, do it yourself. Just wait until I sweep up this glass and leave the room."

"Fine, but hurry."

CHAPTER FIFTEEN

Ghost strode into the clubhouse, Shades, Griz, Hammer, and JJ with him. The club business had taken way longer than any of them had expected. He'd never meant to leave Jessie cuffed to that bed for most of the day, and it was late afternoon now.

He made a beeline to the bar and moved behind it, squatting down next to the lower shelf where he'd left the key for Boo. When it wasn't there, he looked over to where the man was standing at the other end of the bar.

"Boo, where's the key?"

Boo looked over at him. "Where you left it."

"It's not here."

Boo frowned and checked his pockets. "I'm sure I put it back."

Ghost stood, his jaw ticking impatiently as he waited for Boo to check all his pockets twice.

"I swear to God, Ghost, I remember putting it back.

Maybe it fell on the floor."

"Find it," Ghost snapped. "I'll be in the room with Jessie."

Boo nodded.

Ghost moved around the bar and down the hall. He opened the door, took one step in, and froze in his tracks. The bed was empty, the handcuffs were hanging from the bedpost, and the fucking window was wide open, the curtain blowing in the breeze.

God*fucking*dammit!

Ghost strode over to the window and leaned out, looking both ways on the sliver of a chance she'd just climbed out. Nothing.

He straightened and slammed his palm against the window frame causing the already cracked window to shatter and smash to the floor at his feet. A moment later he was storming down the hall.

"She's fucking gone!"

Everyone in the room turned to look, stunned at his outburst, but he only had eyes for one man—Boo. He marched straight to him, grabbed a fistful of his shirt, and slammed him up against the wall.

"I left you with one fucking task! Keep an eye on her, and you fucked that up! Where the hell is she?" He slammed him against the wall a second time.

"I swear to God, Ghost. She was in there when I brought her the food."

"When was that?"

"Right after you called."

"Who the hell was in there besides you? 'Cause somebody let her out."

"Ashley swept up the glass. And Blood was in there earlier."

Ghost dropped him in shock. "Blood?"

"I didn't see him take her out, but I saw him bringing her back."

"When the fuck was that?"

"Couple hours ago."

"What the hell was Blood doing in there?"

Boo shook his head. "I don't know. I don't ask patches their business."

"Your fucking business was watching Jessie, fucktard!"

"Sorry, but wherever he took her, he brought her back. She was in there when I brought her the food."

"And you didn't uncuff her?"

"Well…yeah. I mean, she needed to go to the john and to eat. But I locked her back up, I swear."

Shades stepped in. "Ghost, we'll figure out how she got out later. Now, we need to find her."

Ghost whirled on him. "Don't you think I fucking know that?"

"Okay, brother, so where would she go?"

"Hell if I know."

"Think, Ghost."

"I don't know. Her mom is in Daytona. She said she wanted to go there."

"Okay, then let's hit the bus station."

Ghost nodded. "Yeah, okay."

Shades turned to Griz, Hammer, and JJ, who were the only other members in the clubhouse at the moment. "Let's mount up boys."

"I'll put out the word to the rest of the club," Hammer offered.

"No! Let's try and find her before Butcher gets word of this," Shades replied.

They all nodded.

"Let's sweep the neighborhood on the way out, everybody take a different route, we'll rendezvous at the bus station."

They all headed to their bikes.

Shades put a hand on Ghost's shoulder. "We'll find her, man."

Ghost's eyes connected with his best friend's, and he shook his head. "I can't lose her."

Shades nodded. "You won't. We'll turn this fucking city upside down. We'll find her, Ghost. I promise you."

***

An hour later, they had canvassed the neighborhood near the clubhouse, asking anyone they saw if they'd seen her. They'd staked out the bus station to no avail, and they'd even covered the old neighborhood where Ghost's father had lived.

They'd had no luck, and Ghost was running out of places to look. They sat at a stoplight a few blocks from the old neighborhood, their five bikes idling as the sun sank in the west, rapidly taking with it the last traces of daylight. As they waited for the light to change, a hearse drove through the intersection, a small procession of four cars following behind it.

And it suddenly hit Ghost.

One last place she might be.

He motioned to his brothers to make a right turn, and when the light changed, they roared around the corner in a pack. They rumbled through the city streets until finally they reached their destination. Ghost pulled into the entrance to the quiet cemetery and coasted slowly down the long winding lane until he got to the section where Tommy was buried. He saw her in the distance, standing next to the headstone.

She turned when she heard the bikes.

He pulled to a stop, dropping the kickstand and dismounting. His brothers all stopped their bikes, but sat on them, waiting while their brother handled "his woman".

He strode toward her. Relief that he'd found her swamped over him, replacing the fear that had held him in its grip ever since he'd walked into the clubhouse and found her gone. All he'd been able to think about was her falling into the hands of the DKs or Death Heads, or of her leaving town and disappearing, never knowing how he felt about her.

But all that was wrapped up in anger over the hell she'd put him through these last couple of hours.

**

Jessie turned at the sound of the bikes, and she felt her stomach drop. There were five bikes rolling up. She recognized Ghost immediately. He dismounted and headed toward her. For a split second she thought about running, even taking a step back. And she might have had a chance if it was just Ghost, but he had four brothers at his back. They'd corner and surround her. Hell, she wouldn't put it past them to tear through the graves on their bikes to run her down if they had to.

No, the best thing to do was to stand and face him. She was no coward. And besides, as she'd stood at her brother's grave, she'd replayed everything that Blood had told her earlier, and she'd reconsidered her brash decision to run.

She needed to give Ghost the benefit of the doubt. Maybe Ashley was lying to her about everything. As she stood there now, watching Ghost approach, she saw the hardness of his face.

He stopped about four feet from her and just stared. She could feel the anger coming off him in waves, but he didn't yell. In fact, he didn't say a word. Perhaps his silence was more frightening than anything. It was almost as if he'd resolved himself to something. Something she wasn't sure she'd like.

She watched his eyes slide to Tommy's grave, and his jaw ticked. Then his eyes moved back to her.

"You wanted to visit his grave, I would've brought you."

She didn't know what to say to that. She felt the words bubbling up from inside her to tell him she was sorry for running. But then her chin lifted. She'd be damned if she'd apologize.

"You done?" he asked.

She kept quiet.

"Come here."

Her eyes moved past him to the line of bikes. His brothers sat watching them.

"Jess, not a good time to test me."

Her eyes came back to him.

"C'mere."

She moved a step toward him.

He lifted a brow.

She moved a step closer.

He reached out and grabbed her wrist, turning on his heel and pulling her toward his bike.

Twenty minutes later they were back at the clubhouse.

Ghost led her inside, his brothers following, all taking up spots at the bar or the pool table. Ghost looked over at Boo, who stood behind the bar.

"Who's here?" he demanded.

"Nobody but me."

"Butcher?"

"Home with his ol' lady."

"Boot? Slick?"

"Same."

Ghost must have been satisfied with that, because then he was dragging her down the hall to the last door at the end. He pulled her inside, and then slammed and locked the door.

She looked around. This was the infamous chapel—the room where the club held their club meetings. A room she was sure she wasn't supposed to see.

It wasn't all that impressive. Old, scarred paneling covered the walls. A big long table surrounded by a bunch of mismatched chairs took up most of the room. Her eyes were drawn to the opposite wall where several cuts from rival MCs were nailed upside-down.

She turned to find Ghost's eyes on her as he moved around the table, stopping at the head. He leaned his hands on the back of the chair.

"Who let you out of the cuffs?"

She lifted her chin.

His eyes moved over her face, taking in her stubbornness, reading her like a book.

"Was it Blood?"

She looked away, unable to hold his eyes. Damn, how much did he know? Had he spoken with Blood? She didn't want to get caught in a lie, but he wasn't the one who had freed her in the way he meant. And while she didn't like Ashley, and couldn't care less about protecting her, the girl had stuck her neck out for her, and Jessie was no rat.

"I know he took you somewhere earlier today. Where?"

She met his eyes again. "The gun range."

That took him by surprise. She could see the shock written all over his face.

"The gun range?"

She nodded. "Yes."

"Why?"

She shrugged. "Guess you'll have to ask him."

That pissed him off. He shoved the chair and stalked toward her so fast, she barely had time to react before he had her backed against the wall, boxing her in with his arms.

"I'm not your fucking enemy, Jess. No matter what you believe."

Her breathing accelerated as she looked up at him. It was a Ghost she'd only seen a few times before, like when he'd run those bullies off when he was a teenager, or when he'd called her bluff that afternoon in his father's garage. The alpha had come out to play.

"Do you know the fucking hell you've put me through these last few hours? I turned the fucking city upside down looking for you! I was worried sick about you." He slammed his palm into the wall near her head, and she jumped.

Her reaction must have given him pause, for he backed up a step, running a hand through his hair.

"Christ, woman. You're enough to drive a man over the edge."

He shook his head.

She stayed quiet, a little stunned by his reaction. Did she dare to hope it revealed feelings that ran more deeply than perhaps he'd even realized? Was it possible he felt about her the way she felt about him? She had to know. So she pushed.

"Would it have mattered? If I'd gone, Ghost, would it have mattered?"

He looked at her like she'd asked the dumbest question ever.

"Yeah, Jess, it would have mattered."

"To you? Or to your club?"

"I'm not gonna lie to you. The information you have is valuable. My club needs you and that information to make a deal to keep the damn Death Heads from pushing into Alabama. You were right. They want the entire Gulf Coast. And yes, we're takin' you to that meet. I'm not gonna deny it. But I'd never let them have you, Jess. Never."

"How can I believe you?"

"Because you know me, baby. You fucking know me."

"I want to believe you."

"Then do it."

She stared at him.

"I promised your brother I'd take care of you. That I'd watch out for you. I *promised* him."

"When?" She frowned.

"Doesn't matter when. I just did."

"That's why you're helping me? Because of a promise to my brother?" Her heart began to sink. Was she just a debt, a favor owed? Was that all she'd ever be to him?

"Partly."

She started to turn away, her eyes glassing over, but he yanked her back around. "When I'd thought you'd gone…" He broke off, searching her eyes. "The panic I felt had nothing to do with any promise I'd made to Tommy."

She tried to twist free. "I can't do this."

"The hell you can't. You've fucking pushed and pushed. Well, guess what, darlin', you rattled my cage and awoke the bear. No turnin' back. You wanted me. Now you got me."

He yanked her to the head of the table and lifted her ass onto the polished wood.

Her startled eyes widened. "Ghost, what are you doing?"

He pushed between her knees to stand with his hips forcing her thighs wide. His hands cupped her face, pulling her head up to lock gazes with her.

"We gonna do this?"

"Ghost—"

"We gonna do this or not?" he growled.

"Do what, Ghost?"

"Us." And then, without giving her a chance to speak, his mouth came down on hers, his tongue diving inside. He held her head tipped back locked in his hands as he took his fill. When he finally broke away to gasp in a lungful of air, her mind was turned to mush. She couldn't even remember what they'd been talking about; he'd wiped every thought from her brain.

"Ain't playin', Jessie. I want you. Right here. Right now. You want to give us a shot, a real shot, then it starts now. You don't, you say the fuckin' word, and I'm done."

She stared up at him, shocked by his words, but as she read the determined expression on his face, she knew he meant every last word. And the thought of him "being done" with her scared her to death. So she reached up, grabbed his face, and pulled his mouth back down to hers.

A moment later, she was flat on her back on the table as he leaned over her, his mouth devouring hers until that wasn't enough anymore, for either of them. He lifted off her and began fumbling with her pants. Then he pulled off her boots and yanked her jeans down her legs.

His eyes landed on the black lace panties he'd bought her that morning in Omaha, and he hesitated. His palm running over the lace, once, twice, and then he was pulling them off as well.

His eyes locked on her pussy as his hands went to his belt, working the buckle, undoing his jeans.

She knew she was more than ready for him. She'd been soaking wet since the moment he'd backed her against the wall. A second later, he was plunging inside her, his body looming over hers. One hand planted on the table next to her head, while the other stroked over her. His thumb sought out, finding that spot that had her bucking.

"Oh God, baby," she breathed.

"Wrap around me, Jess," he commanded, and she did, wrapping both legs around his waist. "Hold onto me."

He began thrusting, hard and fast, almost as if this was all a dream that would vanish with a poof if he didn't claim her here and now, right this minute.

They stared into each other's eyes, his focused and intent, hers wide with wonder and awe.

"Ain't no goin' back. Ain't no changin' your mind tomorrow," he rasped out.

She shook her head. "No, no going back."

"I'm not gonna let you go, Jess." He stared into her eyes with every thrust underlining his meaning. "Not ever."

"Not ever," she repeated, nodding in agreement.

"You're gonna find shit out about me. Shit that'll make you want to leave."

"No." She shook her head.

He shook his head, too. "Ain't gonna let you go. Not even then."

"I won't leave." She could see the doubt in his eyes, and she stroked his cheek. "I won't."

He turned his head, his mouth kissing her palm, and then he picked up his pace, thrusting into her with the urgency of a man pursued by demons. She wrapped her arms tight around his neck and pulled him close.

"I love you, Ghost. I always have," she whispered in his ear.

A moment later he was pulling out, and she panicked she'd said the wrong thing, until he pulled her off the table only to flip her around and push her face down over it. He slid back into her, pinning her to the surface as he bent over her, his mouth at her ear.

"Been dreamin' about this since that bathroom in Sturgis." He lifted off her, his hands gripping her hips, pulling her back against him. She felt one big palm slide to the small of her back, stroking up her spine almost reverently. "So pretty, baby."

He began moving inside her, and every stroke hit that sweet spot that had her tilting her ass up to meet him.

His thrusts became frantic until he finally went rigid, exploding inside her with a deep male groan that had to be the sexiest sound she'd ever heard.

After several more slow gliding strokes, he collapsed on top of her, his elbow landing on the table to keep from crushing her, but she welcomed his weight, reveling in the feeling of his big body pressed down on top of her.

She reached back, stroking her hand over his ass, and then trailing her fingers up and down his hip.

She heard him moan with delight in her ear, and she smiled.

He finally lifted on his elbows, his palm brushing the hair back from her forehead tenderly. Then he dipped his head to sprinkle kisses all over the side of her face.

"I'm sorry," he murmured.

She frowned. "For what."

"I was a selfish bastard just now. Didn't take my time with you."

"You didn't hear me complaining."

He grinned and kissed her ear. "Still gonna make it up to you when we get home."

"I get to go home? I don't have to stay here on lockdown?"

He pressed his weight down on her again with a grin. "I think I can keep you pinned to the bed for most of the night. Although, we could bring the handcuffs along if you think I'm gonna need 'em."

"You're so bad."

"I think you like bad boys."

"Lucky for you, I do."

He slid out and pulled her up, taking her in his arms. They stared at each other a long moment, and then they both started smiling.

"We're really doing this?" she asked.

"We're really doing this."

***

Jessie threaded her fingers through Ghost's hair, her head pressing back into the pillow as his mouth brought her to another orgasm. She moaned and went limp as he climbed up her body. Good to his word, he was *definitely* making it up to her.

He stared down at her. "I love to watch you come, baby.

The way your breathing changes…" He paused, his eyes skating down her body. "The way you get all flushed. The way you melt like a big ol' pile of mush."

She lay panting, trying to laugh, but she didn't have the energy. A devilish look took over his face.

"Ghost, no."

She could barely move, but it seemed he wasn't done with her yet. His mouth latched onto her nipple as his fingers slid between her legs, thrusting inside to stroke her deep and long until her hips lifted off the bed.

"Ghost, I can't, not again," she pleaded, breathlessly.

He lifted his head, staring at her with determination. "Yes, you can."

She thrashed her head from side to side, moaning, "No."

"Yes," he insisted, increasing the pace of his strokes, his thumb taking up a relentless rhythm over her clit. He brought his mouth down, just bare millimeters from her lips, giving her just enough room to breathe. "Again, Jess," he whispered. "Give it to me again.

She bucked beneath him, and he leaned further over, one leg pinning hers to the bed as he kept at her, and at her, and at her, until she crashed over the edge, giving him what he'd asked for.

When her eyes finally opened, he grinned down at her.

"My beautiful baby. Maybe she can obey me once in a while."

She huffed out a tired laugh and slugged him in the arm.

"Ooow, she wants to play rough, does she?"

Before she knew what he was about, he rolled, going to

his back on the bed and pulling her on top of him. His palm came down with a crack on her ass cheek.

"Ghost!" she shrieked, trying to get away. They wrestled, Ghost pinning her arms behind her, tickling her until she gasped, "I give, I give!"

He quit, and she collapsed panting on top of him. His palms slid to her face, bringing her mouth down to his, and he kissed her long and sweet.

She pulled back, and then it was her turn to grin as she began to slide down his body, keeping her eyes locked on his. It didn't take him two seconds to realize where this was going, and he grinned big, his fingers threading through her hair as he guided her down.

"Mmm, now there's a pretty sight. You between my legs, your hair spread all over me as your mouth takes me deep." He grinned. "If I could only reach my phone, I'd take a picture."

Her mouth popped free. "You'd better not."

His brows rose, the grin still on his face. His hand was already guiding her head back down. "Then you better get back to what you were doin', brat, and take my mind off the idea."

So she got back to what she was doing.

"Damn, that's twice in one night the girl's done what she was told." He grinned. "Miracles *do* happen."

She smacked her palm on his belly, causing his gut to tighten as he burst out laughing.

CHAPTER SIXTEEN

The next day they were back at the clubhouse. There was some type of annual party going on to raise money for some charity that was important to Butcher's ol' lady. Some of the members had taken part in a poker run earlier, but since Ghost was supposed to technically have Jessie on lockdown, they'd slept in.

Now it was late in the afternoon. Most of the club members were sitting around outside, when Butcher's ol' lady approached.

"We're about three hundred dollars short."

"Short of what?" Butcher asked her.

"Our goal."

"Then I guess we're short."

Her hands landed on her hips. "Butcher."

"What do you want me to do about it? I ain't dumping no bucket of ice water over my head, so don't even think it, woman."

Blood, who was kicked back in a chair, asked, "How about we play a little game? I'll show you how we do an ice bucket challenge at the New Orleans clubhouse."

"If it involves me dumpin' a bucket over my head, forget it," Butcher complained.

"Nope. I promise."

Butcher frowned, suspiciously.

"You'll like it, I guarantee." Blood turned and looked at Undertaker. "Am I right?"

He chuckled. "You'll definitely enjoy this game, Butcher."

"Okay, fine. How do we play?"

Blood whistled for one of the prospects and whispered some instructions in his ear. The man trotted off to do his bidding. Then Blood looked around the crowd. When his eyes hit Jessie's, he winked and said, "I'll need a volunteer." He turned and curled a finger at Ashley, who'd been trying to get the good-looking man's attention all week.

She happily skipped over, all smug smiles.

The prospect came back with an empty plastic beer pitcher found in any pizza joint. He tossed what looked like an old purple Crown Royal bag with gold drawstrings on the table, along with three poker chips—one red, one white, one blue.

"Okay, guys, we need the ol' ladies for this one. If you haven't got one, grab a girl." Then he got up and walked over to a big square cooler that was mostly empty now and dunked the plastic pitcher into it coming up with a mix of melting ice and water.

He walked back over to the picnic table they were gathered around, dropped the three poker chips in the bag, and shook them up.

"White is $20, Blue is $50, and Red is $100. Your lady draws a chip, guys. You either have that amount in your pocket to donate, or your lady gets iced." He grabbed Ashley from behind, hooking one arm around her neck to hold her still, and with his other hand he dumped the pitcher of ice down her chest.

She didn't realize what he was about to do until it was too late, and she shrieked, both with the shock of the cold ice water and with rage. To make maters worse, she had a push up bra on, and all that ice got lodged in the cups, so she began jumping around, trying to get it out.

As the rest of the guys were laughing their asses off at Ashley's discomfort, Blood connected eyes with Jessie, and he winked, letting her know he'd just gotten a little payback for her.

She mouthed the words "thank you" to him, and he lifted his chin.

"Hell, I'm in," Butcher declared, grabbing his ol' lady's arm as she tried to make a getaway.

Jessie, who'd been sitting on the ground between Ghost's legs, his hands running through her hair, was suddenly pulled up on his lap.

"You ready for an ice bath?" he teased.

She twisted and whispered in his ear, "You'd better have a hundred bucks in your pocket."

She felt his body shake with his laughter. "I would if you

hadn't wanted that Starbucks on the way over here."

"Damn," she murmured. "I don't want to get wet."

He chuckled. "Then you'd better pray you pick a white or blue chip, babe."

They sat and watched one brother after another either ante up the money or with more gusto, dump ice water on their ol' ladies, until it was Ghost and Jessie's turn. Blood held the bag over her head, grinning down at her. She dug her hand in and pulled out a blue chip.

"Fifty bucks, Ghost," Blood announced.

Ghost dug in his pocket and peeled off a fifty, leaving him about forty remaining. Unfortunately, when Butcher saw money going back into the pockets of some of his men, he insisted they go around the circle one more time.

"Trying to clean us out, Prez?" Shades asked, laughing.

Tink shrieked when Hammer, who'd lassoed her into playing the game with him, dumped ice water down her shirt.

"Hold still, woman. There still more in the pitcher," Hammer teased her.

Ghost bent, whispering in Jessie's ear, "You pick anything other than white, you're getting an ice bath, babe."

She gave him a stricken look.

When it was her turn again, she picked a red chip, and there were hoots and hollers as Ghost stood and grabbed up the pitcher, dunking it in the cooler.

"Come here, babe," he said with a grin crooking his finger at her.

Jessie bit her lip and moved to stand in front of him. He stood against her back, hooking an arm around her shoulders and holding her tight. Then he poured the ice water down her front, taking his sweet time, teasing her until the last drop.

Surprising him, Jessie grabbed some of the ice chunks and whirled around shoving them down his pants.

That got his brothers to roar with laughter. After that, all the other women joined in, and it was soon a big ice water fight. People began slipping on the wet grass, and soon they were all in a big pile on the lawn, laughing hysterically.

***

That night in bed, Ghost held Jessie in his arms. When they'd gotten home they'd taken a hot shower together, warming up after the chilly ride across town.

Ghost rolled over, half on top of Jessie. One leg slid between hers, gliding up and down her inner thigh as he kissed her passionately.

She could feel his erection pressing long and hard against her belly as his mouth moved over her jaw to her neck where he latched on, sucking and making her writhe and moan.

"Ghost?"

"Hmm." He continued sucking, licking and kissing her neck, collarbone, and cleavage.

"When is the meeting with the DKs?"

He lifted his head, studying her eyes. "I'm not gonna let anything happen to you, Jessie. Told you that."

"I know, but when is it?"

The way he studied her, she knew he must have been contemplating whether or not it was wise to tell her or keep her in the dark. In the end, he must have decided he could trust her not to run off.

"Day after tomorrow. Why?"

She shrugged, her hand coming up, her fingers absently twirling a lock of hair. "I just wondered."

He brushed the hair back from her face. "You trust me to keep you safe, don't you?"

"Yes, I trust you, Ghost."

He put his hand over hers, stilling the twirling motion, and kissed the tip of her nose. "Then quit worrying about it. Okay?"

"Okay."

He returned to her neck, picking up where he'd left off. Her arms went around his shoulders, stroking his skin, but her eyes were on the ceiling. She couldn't get the thought out of her head that she needed to tell him the parts she'd left out of her story, and she needed to do it before the meeting. She dreaded it, worrying that his feelings for her would change. At least she had one more day. She'd tell him tomorrow, she promised herself.

She closed her eyes and lost herself to the erotic touch of Ghost's mouth as it moved over her skin.

***

The next morning Ghost got a call. Jessie watched as he walked out to the terrace to take it. When he came back inside, he had a serious expression on his face.

"Get your jacket and boots, Jess. We're leaving in a couple minutes."

"Where are we going?"

"To the clubhouse."

When they got there, Jessie could tell that something was up. All of the club members were there, and it looked like they were all business. No one was drinking. No one was cutting up.

After all of them went off in a huddle, Ghost came back to her side and took her hand. "Come on."

"Where are we going?"

"They moved the meeting up. We're leaving now."

The only thought that ran through Jessie's head was that she still needed to talk to Ghost. She hadn't told him everything yet. And now, as he was pulling her toward his bike, she didn't know if she was going to get the chance.

"Ghost, I need to talk to you."

"Ain't got time now, babe. It'll have to wait."

The group pulled out not five minutes later, heading east toward the Georgia border.

CHAPTER SEVENTEEN

Jessie clung to Ghost's back as the Evil Dead MC rolled up to what looked like an abandoned warehouse in a decaying industrial section of Atlanta. There was a tall chain link fence surrounding the property, and several members of the Devil Kings MC stood guard as the group of five bikes stopped. Shades, Griz, Hammer, and Heavy were with them.

Jessie's eyes moved over the scary men at the gate, as well as the creepy building behind them, and she must have subconsciously tightened her grip on Ghost, because he reached down and rubbed her hand. He was obviously trying to reassure her, and it worked.

They cut the engines, and she climbed off as the men all dropped their kickstands and dismounted.

The DKs approached, and one spoke.

"No weapons."

The guys all held their cuts open, showing their lack of shoulder holsters.

The DK who'd spoken, lifted his chin, and a couple of his guys approached to pat them down. When one of them moved to Jessie, Ghost pushed her behind him.

"You don't fuckin' touch her," he growled.

The man looked back questioningly at the DK who was obviously in charge. After a long tense moment in which he and Ghost stared each other down, he finally relented with a nod.

Ghost took hold of her hand and led her inside the gate with the rest of his brothers. They walked across the lot and into the warehouse.

Jessie's eyes immediately glanced around the big space, with its concrete floor revealed in the dim light from the few skylights high up in the metal ceiling.

There were a group of more men waiting in a half circle, their arms all folded across their chests, and their stances wide, giving them a very intimidating look.

Shades, being the VP, took charge for the Evil Dead, moving to stand in front of the rest of his men, taking up the same posture as the DKs. His eyes moved over the line, past the man with the President's patch, past the man with the VP patch, to land on another man standing to his right. He was younger than both the President and VP, and he was much better looking.

Shades lifted his chin to the man.

"Rusty."

The man lifted his chin in response.

"Shades."

Then Shades eyes moved back to the President.

"Growler."

The President unfolded his arms and stepped forward. "You had some information for us."

Shades nodded once. "We do. First we make a deal."

"First we hear what the bitch has to say," Growler countered.

Shades shook his head. "You hear me out."

Growler stared him down, finally relenting.

"All right. Fucking talk. And it better be something I want to hear."

"You will," Shades assured him. "It'll benefit both our clubs."

"Don't much give a shit if anything benefits *your* club."

A slight grin pulled at the corner of Shades' mouth. "Understood."

"Well?" Growler's brow lifted. "You got somethin' to say, get to it."

"We've got some information for you. Information that you'll find very valuable."

"That remains to be seen," the man countered.

"In exchange for this information, you and I work out an arrangement where both our clubs make an alliance for one purpose and one purpose only. Doesn't affect anything we got now. We keep our own territories, nothing changes."

The President let out a long-suffering breath. "And what exactly is the purpose of this alliance you're askin' for?"

"To keep the Death Heads from pushing into the Gulf Coast. They want Georgia, and they want Alabama. They've got a plan for getting both. You're up first on their list. We're next. The plan to take *you* down is already in motion."

He lifted a brow with a doubtful expression. "Take us down? Really? And what's this fucking plan?"

Shades lifted his chin to the members standing behind the President of the DKs. "These your most trusted guys? 'Cause you've got a rat."

His VP's arms came unfolded. "Who the hell are you to come in here and tell us our fucking business?"

Jessie studied the man. His face was hard and spoke of years of callous violence and disregard for anything that threatened his club. His long scraggly hair and beard were both solid gray. He wore small wire-rimmed glasses on his long thin nose and when he spoke, he revealed teeth yellowed with age.

The President lifted his arm, silencing his VP with no more than that single gesture.

"Tell me what the fuck you *think* you know, before I let Rat run his knife through you," he growled at Shades, his patience obviously dwindling.

Shades held his ground. "We got a deal?"

After a tense moment, the man barked back, "Yeah, we got a fucking deal. Now talk!"

"Death Heads planted a man in your chapter." Shades shrugged. "Possibly a prospect. More likely one of that bunch you just patched over."

Growler's eyes narrowed. "How you know this fucking shit?"

"That's where the girl comes in," Shades replied.

Jessie watched as their President's eyes moved from

Shades to her, sweeping up and down.

"How she know this shit?" He addressed his question to Shades, as if his answer carried more weight than anything that would come out of her mouth.

"She was in Sturgis. Overheard Florida talking to his men."

The President's brows shot up. "Right. She just fucking overheard that, huh? What do you take me for? Do I look stupid to you?"

"She was there, Prez," one of his guys said, and Jessie's eyes moved to the man. He was a big man, six three at least, and muscular. It wasn't just his size that made him stand out; it was his demeanor. He took badass to a whole different level. Aside from the fact that he was a terrifying dude, he was also very good looking, with dark hair that hung past his jaw and brows that slashed low, giving him a stern look. But it was his piercing light eyes that caught one's attention. They practically burned a hole when he turned them on you. And right now, they were turned on her.

Growler looked back at him. "You sure?"

The man nodded, his eyes boring into hers a long moment before they swung to Shades. "You don't know who she is, do you?"

"What the fuck are you talking about, Reno?" his President barked at him.

"She's Florida's."

"The hell she is," Ghost snapped taking a step forward, but Shades' arm came up, holding him back with the silent reprimand.

Reno's eyes swung to Ghost, then ignored him, moving to his President. "Saw her with him. She was cuddled up on his lap all nice and cozy. He was rubbing her ass."

"You saw this where?" Growler snapped.

"Scooter's Bar."

Ghost twisted, his eyes swinging to her with an expression of disbelief. She could tell he wanted to ask her about the startling revelation, but he knew he couldn't look surprised by any of this—not in front of the DKs.

Shades covered for them all, pretending as if he knew.

"Gives what she says that much more credibility. You want to hear what she has to say, or not?"

"Yeah, I want to hear what she fucking has to say," Growler snapped.

Shades' eyes swung to Ghost, and he stared him down until he stepped out of the way, and then Shades lifted his chin at Jessie. "Tell him what happened."

She raised her chin, determined to not cower in front of these men. She met Growler's eyes. "I overheard Florida say they were going to take you down from the inside. He said they'd planted a man in your chapter. Knew your every move. They plan to take Georgia from you."

"How'd you overhear this?" Growler asked.

"I was in a closet. The walls were thin, and they were in an office on the other side talking."

"And what were you doing in the closet?"

"Hiding."

"From who?"

"From the Death Heads."

"Why were you hiding if you were with Florida?"

"I wasn't *with* Florida."

"Bullshit," Reno snapped. "From what I saw, you were definitely with him."

Shades shoved her behind him. "Don't matter what she was doing there. Bottom line, you've got a rat. We've got no reason to come here and tell you this shit if it weren't true. We're up next on their list. We band together now, we save both our states. We don't, you know it's gonna be a fight to the death. The Death Heads can take us down separately. We team up, we got a shot at holding 'em off."

Growler studied Shades, obviously considering his words, and finally, he nodded once.

Shades extended his hand.

Growler looked at it a moment, and then shook it.

Shades nodded back as they released hands. "We need to make a coordinated plan."

"We need to find this rat, first," Growler countered.

Shades nodded. "Give us a call when you find him."

"We done here?" Growler asked.

"Yeah," Shades replied.

Growler lifted his chin. "Then get the fuck out."

Shades grinned, and they all headed to their bikes.

Jessie noticed that Ghost was a little rough as he took not her hand, but her wrist, and pulled her behind him. When they reached his bike, she tried to explain.

"Ghost, it wasn't—"

But he cut her off, shoving her helmet at her and snapping, "Not now."

She looked up at him as she took the helmet. His eyes were cold; his whole demeanor had shifted, like she was a stranger to him. She quietly put the helmet on as he threw his leg over and fired his bike up.

"Get on," he snapped, his eyes full of anger when they met hers.

She did as she was told, and it was a long ride back.

***

When they finally rolled through the gates of the Birmingham clubhouse, Jessie was exhausted, her nerves frayed and shot. She knew a confrontation was forthcoming; Ghost was pissed, but somehow she was going to make him understand. It wasn't what he thought. It wasn't what that man, Reno, made it sound like.

She followed him into the clubhouse, along with the rest of the men.

Boo was behind the bar, and several women were there cleaning up—Skylar, Ashley, Tink and another girl named Sherry. They all looked up when the men trooped in, their smiles of welcome fading as they took in their expressions.

Shades looked at Ghost, lifting his chin toward the hall. "Go, I'll talk to Butcher."

Ghost obviously knew exactly what "go" meant, for a moment later he was tugging her down the hall. He flung the door to his room open and lifted his chin at her.

"Move."

She stepped past him into the room. Before she had a chance to turn around, she heard the door slam, and then he was grabbing her by the upper arm to yank her around.

"What the fuck were you really doing in Sturgis?"

"I told you, Ghost. I was there to find you."

"Bullshit. Tell me about Florida." His eyes searched hers. "What Reno said, is it true?"

She shook her head, "No, Ghost, I swear. Not like he made it sound—"

"Has everything you've told me been a pack of lies? Was any of it fucking true? Can I even trust anything you say?" he snapped, closing in, forcing her to step back.

"Ghost, please, you have to believe me."

"I don't have to do shit."

"Please, Ghost, just listen to me."

"To what? Another pack of lies?" He shook his head. "Don't think you can fuckin' play me, Jess."

"I don't. I'm not."

"You just hung me out to dry in that meeting! I went to bat for you, stuck my neck out for you, and this is how you repay me? You tryin' to make a fool of me in front of my whole fucking club?"

She shook her head. "No, Ghost, of course not. I wanted to tell you. I tried to tell you this morning, but you said there wasn't time, that it'd have to wait."

"Oh, so now it's *my* fault you lied?"

"I didn't lie to you."

His brow shot up. "No? What would you call it then? Seems you neglected to tell me a few key facts." He stalked toward her. "You his ol' lady?"

Jessie frowned, thrown by his question. "Florida's? How could you even think that?"

"How could I fuckin' think that? 'Cause I just heard the man had his hands all over your ass. An ass, I hear, was cuddled up on his fucking lap! Was that a lie?"

"No, Ghost. It wasn't."

"Jesus Christ. Tell me the truth, Jess. All of it!"

"I'm *trying*, if you'd shut up a minute and let me tell you!"

He took a step toward her. "Don't push me, brat. I'm not in the mood."

That was the truth. She blew out a soft breath. "I know, Ghost. Okay? It's just, you're not going to like it."

"Tell me anyway." He gave her one of those looks he was so good at, with his head dipped down, looking at her from under his brow. It was intimidating and badass as hell. He wanted the truth, and she'd better not water it down.

"When I hid in that closet, I wasn't hiding from some random guy. I was hiding from the Death Heads."

He frowned. "Why?"

"I told you I got a ride with a trucker, right?"

"Yeah, so?"

She moved toward the window, fiddling with the curtain. "Well, he didn't take me the whole way to Sturgis."

"So who did?"

She looked back at him. "The Death Heads."

His brows shot up in disbelief, and he barked, "How *the fuck* did that happen?"

"If you'd calm down and stop yelling at me, I'll tell you!"

He ran a frustrated hand through his hair. "I'm trying,

Jess. I'm really fucking trying, but my patience is about at an end."

"They picked me up at a rest stop just west of town. Brought me the rest of the way. I thought…I thought at the time, it was just because I was a girl, you know? But that wasn't it. Turns out they had an ulterior motive." She saw his jaw lock.

"They hurt you?"

She knew what he meant, and she shook her head. "No. Not like that. But I'm sure that was on the menu for later. They just never got that far."

"What fucking happened, Jess? Tell me everything."

She nodded and turned to look out the window, her mind going back to that afternoon that they'd ridden into town.

"It didn't take long after we hit town for me to find out the real reason that they'd agreed to give me a ride. It was the fact that, apparently, I was a dead ringer for the dead wife of the President of the Jacksonville, Florida, Death Heads' Chapter. A man ironically enough called—"

"Florida." Ghost finished her sentence for her.

She nodded, shrugging. "I guess they thought it would earn them some points if they presented me to him like some gift from the great beyond or something. It was sad and ridiculous at the same time. At least I thought so until I met the man. He stared at me, stunned speechless. And then began talking to me as if I actually were his Rose, reincarnated or back from the dead or something. I was terrified, not only by the man himself, but also by the craziness I saw in his eyes. He was definitely less than sane.

"He latched on to me, pulling me onto his lap at the table in the bar they'd dragged me into. That's where I stayed, unable to get away as they drank round after round, and his hands got friendlier and friendlier. I knew I was in trouble, *way* more trouble than I'd ever bargained for, and I didn't have a clue what to do except to brazen it out."

She could see her words were affecting Ghost. He didn't like hearing any of this, especially the part about her being in trouble and helpless against those men. But she had more to tell, so she kept going.

"After a while, it became obvious that they were waiting to meet some other club members, and when they finally showed, Florida got up, telling his men not to take their eyes off me. Apparently, Florida didn't want to let me go, at least not yet."

"He wasn't done playing with you." Ghost said it not as a question, but as a statement.

"No, he wasn't," she confirmed. "I watched him move off toward the back hall, followed by these other men who, judging by their bottom rockers, belonged to the Texas Chapter of the Death Heads.

"After a few minutes, I asked to use the restroom. The two men left in charge of me grudgingly agreed, but watched me like a hawk. I'd hoped there'd be a window in the tiny bathroom that I could climb out of, but no such luck.

"Then, as if fate had given me a second chance, there was some kind of a ruckus in the bar that drew my guards' attention. I peeked out in time to spot them moving off. While they were distracted, I dashed around a corner, hoping to find an exit. What I found instead was a dead end with only one door. When I heard them coming, I ducked inside a utility closet. I pressed to the back in the dark, hoping they wouldn't look for me there.

"That's when I heard voices coming through the wall, and I recognized Florida's. They were having the meeting in the room on the other side, and I overheard every word.

"A moment later, the door was flung open, and they pulled me out of the closet. When they did, they realized they could hear Florida's voice coming through the wall.

"One of them shook his head at me and told me I'd just made the biggest mistake of my life.

"He dragged me into the office, and a pissed-off Florida asked what the hell they'd brought me in there for.

"They told him how I'd tried to run, and that I'd heard every word.

"Florida looked ready to kill his men for the fuck-up. Then his eyes dropped to me, and he growled for them to take me back to the camp so he could deal with me later.

"They dragged me out, forced me on the back of a bike, and drove toward their campsite. As we rode out of town, I knew I had to make a move. I knew once they got me to their campsite, I would never get away. When they stopped at a light, I jumped off, dashing through buildings and alleys until I came to the bar where I found you."

There. That was all of it, the whole story, nothing left out.

"Why didn't you tell me all this shit before?"

"I thought if you knew, you wouldn't help me."

He shook his head.

"I'm sorry."

Ghost sucked in a deep breath and blew it out. He started to walk away, but then turned back to look her in the eyes. "There's one thing you still haven't told me."

"What's that?"

"Why you left Seattle in such a hurry with just the clothes on your back? What really happened, Jess? The truth."

"Things with Kyle were starting to go from bad to worse. His music career wasn't going anywhere, and he was starting to take it out on me. The final straw was when he beat me up."

Ghost looked ready to kill. *"He beat you?"*

"Just once. You know me, Ghost, once was enough. I wasn't about to take that shit." Her chin came up. "Not from anybody."

"What'd you do?"

"He hurt me pretty bad, but when he finally turned his back on me, I hit him in the head with his guitar. He went down like a ton of bricks. Then I got the hell out of there. I wasn't about to stick around and wait to see if he got up. I sure as hell didn't want to be there when he realized what I'd hit him with. That Fender was his prized possession, and I'd busted it clean in two." She couldn't help the smile on her face, but Ghost wasn't smiling.

"Sounds like I gotta make a trip to Seattle."

Her smile faded. "No, Ghost. That's done. He already got what he deserved. Let it go. Please?"

"Not promising you shit on that one."

She could tell he was still pissed. "Are we good now?"

He shook his head. "No, we're not good. How can I help you, Jess, if we don't trust each other?"

She didn't know how to answer that one. When she stayed silent, he turned and stormed out of the room.

She hesitated only a moment before following. If he thought she was going to sit in that room like a chastised child, he had another thing coming. She moved down the hall into the common room. He was standing at the bar talking to Shades, but his eyes lifted as she crossed the room to where Skylar and Tink sat at a table.

"You okay, doll?" Tink asked her.

"I'm fine."

They all watched as the men headed down the hall, probably to have another one of their meetings. Shades patted Ghost's shoulder, nodding for him to follow, while he headed over to the table where the girls sat.

His eyes landed on Skylar's, and his chin lifted toward Jessie.

"Why don't you take her back to our place. We got some shit to sort."

The way he said it made Jessie realize that the shit they had to sort was her. Or at least the fact that she possibly had a closer connection to the Death Heads than any of them had suspected.

Skylar nodded, and Shades bent, catching the back of her neck in his hand. His mouth came down on hers for a brief kiss, and then he was gone.

Skylar turned. "Let's go for a swim, girls."

Jessie frowned at that odd remark, but Tink clarified.

"They have a cabin on Lay Lake."

"Oh," Jessie replied.

"Come on, I'm sure I have a bikini that will fit you. And a swim will get your mind off all of this for a while." She grabbed her purse and keys, and the three of them headed out to her car.

***

Butcher slammed into the meeting room, surveying the men already sitting at the table, as he moved around it to take his position at the head.

"Thought you could trust this bitch?" he snapped, his eyes on Ghost. "Seems she's got some secrets."

"Could she be working with the Death Heads?" Slick asked Ghost.

"No way," he snapped emphatically.

"Seems she's a little cozier with the bastards than you knew, so not sure how good I feel about your answer," Heavy observed.

"If she's workin' with them, she could be feeding them information on us," Boot advised.

"Jesus Christ, she's not working with them!" Ghost slammed his palm on the table. "They picked her up, and she couldn't get away, that's all. Seems Florida took a personal liking to her."

"I can see why," Hammer supplied with a grin.

Ghost glared at him, almost daring the man to make one more remark about how hot Jessie was. Then his eyes returned to Butcher.

"She looks like his dead wife."

"Interesting," Slick said, his hand running over his chin like he was trying to come up with a way to turn that to their benefit.

"So how does her lie affect the deal we just made with the DKs?" Boot asked.

"Is it possible the Death Heads may think she knows who the plant is?" Butcher asked.

"Maybe. Which means they'll be looking to shut her up," Shades told him.

"We make sure they know whatever information she had has already been disclosed. Takes her out of the equation," Ghost insisted.

Slick brought up another point. "We're fighting to keep the coast from the Death Heads. Let's make sure we're not turning it over to the DKs instead."

"Maybe we change up the deal. Turn her over to the Death Heads. Maybe she buys us more from them than the DKs," Butcher suggested.

Ghost surged to his feet. "That was never part of this deal, Butcher. No fucking way."

"Relax, Son. We let them *think* that's what we're going to do. I didn't say we'd actually do it."

Ghost glared at him, standing his ground. "It's not happening. Give me your word, you won't try to pull any shit on this."

***

Two men stood on the banks of the St. Johns River at the

North Florida Shipyards, the lights of the Jacksonville skyline visible in the distance.

"I heard from our plant."

Florida turned to look at his VP, Quill. "Yeah, he got something to report?"

Quill nodded, lighting a cigarette. "They had some interesting visitors."

"Who?"

"Evil Dead. Had a nice little powwow."

"Interesting indeed. You think they're working in collusion on something?"

"I think they know we want their territory. There's more."

Florida turned to look at him. "And what's that?"

"They had a woman with them."

That surprised Florida enough that he pulled the cigar from his mouth. "A woman? At a meet?"

His VP shrugged. "That's what our plant said."

"So what was this meeting about?"

"He wasn't allowed in, but the girl was."

"You're shittin' me?"

"Nope. And that's not everything."

"What else?"

Quill pulled out his cell and swiped his thumb across the screen, opening a photo and holding it up. "He took this picture of her."

Florida looked down at the face of the woman who'd haunted his dreams since Sturgis. "Goddamn it. She's in *Atlanta?*"

"Was. Left with the Dead."

"Which chapter?"

"Birmingham."

Florida stared down at the picture of the only woman who'd ever slipped through his hands. And that wasn't something he took lightly.

"She knows our plans, boss."

"Yeah, she does, and whose fucking fault is that?" Florida snapped, glaring at his man before returning his gaze to the picture. "You think she talked?"

"Must have. There's no other reason for her to be there. Had to be what the meet was about. The Dead found out what she knew and brought her to the DKs, probably to make a deal."

"So, now they know they've got a rat." Florida mulled it over in his head. "But they don't know who it is. Least we still got that goin' for us."

Quill spit on the ground. "Only a matter of time before they figure it out."

"That'd be unfortunate."

"We may still be able to get some useful information out of him before that happens."

"Yeah," Florida replied absently, but it wasn't their plant he was thinking about. He wanted the girl, and he wanted her now. Not only because she looked like Rose, but also because she'd run, and that wasn't to be tolerated. Luckily, they knew where she was. A slight grin pulled at the corner of his mouth. "Bring her to me."

Quill looked over at him, frowning. "What's the point?

She already told what she knew. Be a waste of time."

Florida looked over at him, a little crazy starting to show in his eyes. "Nobody runs out on me."

His VP took in his expression. The man knew better than to question him.

"You want her dead?"

"No. I want her back so *I* can deal with her."

Quill grinned, shaking his head. "I wouldn't want to be that girl when you get her back."

Florida smiled and ordered, "Make it happen. And no fuckups this time."

CHAPTER EIGHTEEN

Jessie, Skylar, and Tink were all stretched out on beach towels on Shades and Skylar's dock. Two empty bottles of wine sat next to them. The lake was quiet, it being the middle of the afternoon on a workday.

Jessie let her head fall back, enjoying the feel of the sun as it soaked into her skin. "God, this feels so good. Thank you. I needed this."

Skylar rolled her head on the wooden dock and pulled her shades up. "No problem, honey. Now, spill. I want to know everything about you and Ghost."

She shook her head. "Where do I even start? It's such a mess."

Skylar went up on her elbow, reached for one of the bottles, and turned it upside down over Jessie's red plastic cup. A tiny bit dribbled out, and she twisted, looking back at a dozing Tink.

"Tink! We're out of wine."

The girl shot straight up, groggily looked around, and said, "Someone mention wine?"

Jessie and Skylar both burst out in giggles.

Tink lay back down on the pier. "You both suck. I was having a fantastic dream."

Skylar looked over at her. "Let me guess. Did it star someone named Hammer?"

"Shut up. Go back to bothering Jessie about her love life. And what do you care about the wine, you're not even drinking it!"

"How am I supposed to get Jessie to spill her guts if I can't get her drunk first?" Skylar replied, and then stuck her tongue out at Tink before turning back to Jessie.

Jessie replied, "Gee, thanks, Tink."

"You're welcome, girlfriend."

"So, are you in love with him?" Skylar asked, getting right down to business.

"You don't beat around the bush, do you?" Jessie asked with a laugh.

"Nope."

"Don't feel like you have to spill your guts to us if you don't want to, Jessie," Tink added.

"Speak for yourself," Skylar insisted. "I want the dirty details!"

"Dirty details?"

"Is he good in bed?" she asked, her brows waggling.

"Oh, Lord," Tink laughed.

"Skylar!" Jessie shrieked.

"What? I've seen his package, so I know he's got to be

good."

This apparently was news to Tink, who shot upright again.

"*What?* You've seen Ghost naked?"

"Only once, just for a brief second, but what I saw was *amazing*." She finished in a high-pitched, singsong voice.

"When?" Tink insisted.

"On that trip to New Orleans, when they took me to meet my father. We all had to share a motel room."

"Wait, the three of you…"

"No! There were two beds, silly. Shades would have flipped his shit if another man even thought about touching me. There's no way in hell he'd share me, let alone with one of his brothers."

"So, Jessie how was he?" Tink teased.

She rolled her eyes. "Amazing, okay? And I'm not giving details."

Skylar giggled. "Okay, fair enough." Then she sat up, her gaze out on the lake. "I've got a secret, and I'm dying to tell someone."

Tink and Jessie both looked at her.

"Ooo, a secret. Do tell," Tink said.

"Can I trust you both not to say a word? I haven't even told Shades."

Jessie looked at Tink, who assured Skylar, "Of course you can trust us. Right, Jessie?"

"Well, according to Ghost I'm pretty good at keeping secrets," she tried to joke, making fun of her own predicament. She wasn't sure why she did it. Maybe it was the suddenly serious and perhaps a bit nervous expression on Skylar's face. She had to admit she didn't know the woman all that well, but what she did know, she liked. She felt like the kind of woman that could become a friend, and a good one at that.

"Skylar, are you okay?" Tink asked, perhaps sensing the same uneasiness. "You're not sick are you? Is that why you're not drinking?"

Skylar shook her head, trying to laugh, but her eyes filled, and she reached up to wipe at them. "No, silly. It's nothing like that."

"Then what is it, honey?" Tink asked, taking her hand.

Skylar laughed away her tears. "Sorry, I guess I'm just really emotional right now."

Tink gasped, sitting up straighter.

Jessie looked at her, wondering what it was she'd suddenly seemed to have figured out. "What?"

"You're pregnant!" Tink guessed.

Jessie's eyes shot to Skylar, who nodded and burst out laughing as Tink was suddenly hugging her neck and squealing in delight.

"Oh, my God! I'm so happy for you!" Tink released the hold she'd had on Skylar's neck to pull away and look at her friend. "My God, you're going to have beautiful babies. Wait. Why haven't you told Shades yet?"

"I'm nervous, I guess." Skylar began fiddling with the engagement ring on her finger. "I know he loves me, and he gave me this ring. But…"

"But what?" Tink gently probed, rubbing Skylar's arm.

"What is it, honey?"

"We've never talked about the actual wedding. He just sort of gave me this ring and moved me in, and we never made any more plans."

"But you know he wants to marry you, right?" Tink asked.

"Yes. I just…I want to be married before the baby comes, and I don't want to be a big pregnant cow walking down the aisle. Now it's too late." She burst out in tears.

Tink hugged her. "Oh, honey. Don't say that. You'll be a beautiful bride, no matter how pregnant you are."

Jessie bit her lip, an idea forming in her head. "Maybe I could help. I mean, I think I have a suggestion."

Both girls turned to look at her.

Skylar wiped her eyes and asked, "What?"

"How about you get married right away, before you start showing? Your father is in town. Now would be the perfect time."

Skylar chuckled, shaking her head. "I don't want to just go down to the courthouse and do it. I want a real wedding, and that takes time. You have to find a venue and—"

"I know a place," Jessie offered.

Skylar frowned. "You do?"

Jessie nodded. "Ghost's. That place he's fixing up? It would be perfect. We could have it in the courtyard."

Tink looked at Skylar. "I've never been out there, so I've never seen the place. Have you?"

"I was there once."

"Do you think it would work?" Tink asked.

"Maybe. It's certainly big enough. I suppose if we decorated—"

"I've got all kinds of ideas! It's got all those exposed beams. We could hang little battery votive candles in glass mason jars from the ceiling, and little twinkling fairy lights! We could make it look magical. And there's that big fireplace. We could set up the altar in front of it. We could have the reception out on the terrace and—"

"Whoa, whoa, girl," Tink cut in, turning to Skylar. "Is this what you want to do? Don't you think you need to talk to Shades first?"

"I say you surprise him," Jessie suggested.

"Surprise him?" Skylar turned to her, frowning.

Jessie grinned big. "Yup. And I know *exactly* how to do it. You know he loves you right?"

Tink cut in, answering that one for her. "He's crazy about her. He'd do anything to make her happy."

"Good. Then it's settled. Tomorrow we go shopping for everything we need," Jessie advised, grinning ear to ear, excited to be involved and building new friendships.

***

An hour later, Jessie was enjoying the warmth of the sun on her skin. It was so soothing that soon it, and the sound of the water lapping against the dock, had almost lulled her to sleep.

Almost.

Until she heard the distant rumble of a couple of motorcycles.

She cracked one eye toward the house, but couldn't see

anything as the drive was on the other side.

"That'll be the boys," Skylar confirmed, never turning her head.

"Great," Jessie mouthed unenthusiastically.

That had Skylar giggling and turning toward her. "Just pretend you're asleep. Maybe he'll leave you alone."

"Right." *Like that had a snowball's chance in hell.*

A few minutes later, the dock shook as some heavy boots clunked down it. They came to a stop just above her head, and she cracked an eye open. Ghost stood over her, his eyes meeting hers before they took a leisurely path down her body, then moved to Skylar.

"Your ol' man wants you up at the house."

Skylar got to her feet.

"Take Tink with you," Ghost added.

Tink got to her feet as well, but not before giving Jessie a look that said, *you're in trouble.*

Oh, hell no. If Ghost thought she was going to sit here and listen to another barrage of how she'd fucked up, what a liar she was, and whatever else he had to throw at her, he had another thing coming. She felt her temper flaring, and that pissed her off even more. She'd been in such a nice Zen state of mind there for a minute.

"You're in my sun," she complained, closing her eyes.

"You've had enough sun from the looks of it."

"You're right. Time to turn over." She flipped to her stomach in a jarred movement, and she knew his eyes were running over her ass. *Good. Let him look.*

"Any longer and that sweet ass of yours is gonna be red

as a lobster. Of course, if that's your goal, I'd be glad to help you out."

"You won't be touching my ass, or any other part of me for that matter."

"Wanna bet?"

She had to laugh at that one. "I remember the last time you said that to me."

"Yeah, you ended up cuffed to my bed."

"And how long did that last?" She smirked, knowing she was rubbing salt in the wound.

"Seems not long enough."

"Bite me."

"Don't tempt me."

A second later he reached down and yanked her to her feet. She pushed him back with a hard shove to his chest, which caught him off guard. He lost his balance and fell off the dock into the lake.

She covered her mouth, not having meant to do *that*, but couldn't help the laughter that squealed out of her as he came up sputtering. Then she hauled ass up the hill toward the house.

"Yeah, you better run, you little brat! Your ass is mine when I catch you!"

She ran shrieking into the house.

"Hide me, quick!" she said, slamming the door behind her.

Skylar and Tink turned with wide eyes.

Shades looked out the wall of windows that faced the lake in time to see Ghost hefting himself up onto the dock, water pouring off him.

"Babe, you pushed him in *the lake?*"

"It was an accident."

Shades burst out laughing. "Yeah, right."

"Quick, lock the doors. He's coming up the hill!" Jessie shrieked.

"I'll do one better than that," Shades suggested, grabbing her by the wrist and pulling her toward the door.

Jessie didn't realize what he was about until he'd shoved her outside and locked the door behind her. She whirled to pound on it, but a moment later Ghost's arms clamped around her waist and lifted her off her feet. He trudged down the hill with her kicking and screaming the whole way and unceremoniously tossed her off the end of the dock.

When she came up, the shock of the cold water taking her breath, all she saw was his back as he strode up to the house.

"I hate you!" she screamed, her voice echoing across the lake.

She heard his laughter echoing back down to her. "You can prove just how much later tonight, brat. I may even let you prove it twice."

"Aaarrr!! I wouldn't touch you again if you were the last man on earth."

"For you, babe, I *am* the last man. So you better fucking get used to it."

***

That night, when they got back to Ghost's place, they were barely speaking. He left her in the living area as he stalked into the bedroom. A moment later, she heard the bathroom door slam. She moved silently into the bedroom, put her ear to the door, and heard the shower come on. She hesitated, wondering how he would react if she joined him. She laid her palm on the door. She'd been wrong to keep things from him. He was right. If she didn't trust him, how were they going to make this work? They didn't stand a chance.

A man like Ghost couldn't have a woman who didn't believe in him. It just wouldn't work. Not a chance in hell. She knew that, she *knew* it. So why had she gone ahead and messed everything up by lying to him? Was she sabotaging her own happiness for some fucked up reason? Deep down, did she think she didn't deserve him? Or did she think she wasn't good enough for him, that she would never be enough to make him happy?

Perhaps that wasn't it at all. Maybe, if she was going to be really honest with herself, she had to admit that she was scared, and a part of her was still all twisted up over him moving out years ago. She was really afraid he'd leave her again. Was this all some fucked up test she'd devised in her subconscious mind to see how far she could push him? To see if this time, nothing would push him away?

She pressed her forehead to the door as it all swamped over her. She had to stop doing this to herself, stop doing this to them, stop sabotaging any shot they had.

She took in a deep breath, and her hand closed over the knob.

The room was already filled with steam.

She pulled her clothes off, dropped them to the floor, and opened the glass door of the shower stall.

He had his back to her, his palms high on the tile, his head dipped as the water pounded down on his shoulders. But he must have heard the door open, or he felt the cooler air roll over him, for his head turned to the side, catching her in his peripheral vision.

Still, he didn't move. He just stood there, motionless, perhaps waiting to see what she would do.

She lightly touched her palm between his shoulder blades and gently stroked upwards toward his neck. Still he was unmoving, so she stepped closer, pressing her smaller body against his muscular one, her arms encircling his waist and her lips brushing a kiss to his back.

"I'm sorry," she whispered.

"Sorry doesn't always cut it, Jess."

"I was wrong. I never should have doubted you. I was afraid."

At that, his palms slid from the tile, and he turned to face her. "Of me?"

She shook her head. "Afraid to be vulnerable. Afraid to be hurt."

"That what you think I'd do?"

She shrugged. "Not intentionally."

He grabbed her face and pushed her back against the tile, boxing her in. "Why can't you trust me, Jess? What do I gotta do to prove it to you?"

She shook her head. "You have nothing to prove to me. I'm the one who has to do that. I want you to trust me,

Ghost."

She watched his jaw tick as he looked down at her. "I wish I could, brat. I do. But it's not that easy."

"What can I do to get your trust back?"

"You want me to trust you, start doin' what I say. Earn it."

She nodded.

They stared at each other a long moment, and then he whirled her around to face the wall, moving in against her. Her hands pressed against the wet tile as he dipped his head to her. His mouth was at her ear, as his hands closed over her hips.

"I'm still pissed at you. That's gonna take a while to work through. You understand?" He squeezed, pulling her against him, and she felt his erection, big and hard press against her hip. She understood completely, and she was okay with that. More than okay. She rubbed the side of her face against his jaw as her ass pressed up against him, and she spread her legs.

"I'm not gonna be gentle," he warned.

She nodded. "Okay."

"You gonna let me take what I want, however I want to take it?"

She nodded again. "Yes."

One hand slipped around her, and she felt his fingers sliding between her legs to separate her folds, opening her to his strokes. It brought her up on her toes, and her head dropped down. Suddenly, his other hand was in her hair, fisting, pulling her head back as two fingers thrust inside her.

She gasped.

"You ready for me?" he asked as he stroked, searching and finding that spot that drove her crazy.

"Yes," she panted, quivering from what he was doing to her with those fingers. "Always."

"Good fucking answer," he growled as he pulled his fingers out, and then replaced them with his dick, burying himself to the hilt in one deep stroke that had her sucking in a deep breath.

One arm locked around her ribs to hold her still, the other hand still buried in her hair, as he twisted her head. He brought his mouth down over hers, stealing what little breath she had left.

Then both arms locked around her hips, and he lifted her, ordering, "Lock your legs around me, hands on the wall."

She pressed her hands to the wall, her heels hooking around his ass, her position almost horizontal as he held her tight and pounded into her from behind.

He went deep, deeper than before, driving into her until she knew her inner thighs would be bruised.

He tightened one arm and released her with the other so he could put his hand to the wall and hold them both up.

It wasn't long before he was grunting, "Fuck."

And then he was pushing her flat against the wall, the tiles cold against her breasts as he slammed into her one last time and came inside her.

His breathing was heavy as he jerked once, twice, and then his muscles went limp as he slid her back to her feet, pressing them both to the wall in exhaustion.

After a moment, he pulled her under the shower spray, soaping her body tenderly, without speaking a word the entire time. While he said no words of love or tenderness, the way he touched her communicated that he cared about her, and that his feelings ran deep, perhaps even more so than words ever could have.

CHAPTER NINETEEN

The next day, the boys had club business to take care of, which worked perfectly into the girls' plans. The only person they confided in, swearing to secrecy, was Skylar's father, Undertaker. She'd called him at the clubhouse before the guys all left and told him their plan. He'd been all for it, but insisted on one thing—that he foot the bill. So he'd left his credit card with Boo and told Skylar to get whatever she needed. He promised he'd get the boys to the event at the arranged time tomorrow.

Next they drafted Sherry, who was as excited as the rest of them to help with the arrangements. They split into two teams. Sherry took Skylar out shopping for a dress and shoes, while Tink and Jessie took care of getting a cake, booze, catering, and some decorations.

Within an hour, they'd pleaded with a local baker to make them a simple two-tiered cake with a pretty dot pattern and some ribbon to adorn it. Their next stop was an amazing barbeque place that did off-site events. Fortunately, they'd been able to squeeze the job in for tomorrow. Then the girls hit the liquor store and bought up cases of booze and a keg of beer.

When they finished their running around town, Tink and Jessie rushed to Ghost's place to start setting up. Luckily, Jessie didn't need the key to access the courtyard they'd be decorating.

***

Three hours later, Jessie climbed back down the ladder and brushed her hands off, surveying all their hard work. They'd strung strands of twinkling lights all around the beams and then used wire to hang dozens of glass mason jars at varying lengths from the ceiling.

They'd decided to have the ceremony at dusk, so that it would be dark enough for the lighting to have its full effect. It was going to be *magical*.

She looked over to the altar, where Tink was putting the finishing touches on two tall candelabras that she'd set up on either side of the fireplace. She'd wrapped trailing flowers all around them.

"Oh, Tink. That looks beautiful."

Tink stepped back. "Are they even with the aisle?"

Jessie surveyed the folding chairs they'd set up in rows. "It's perfect."

"Oh, Jess. The lights look fabulous." Tink pulled out her phone. "It's getting late. We'd better get to Skylar's before the guys get back. I'm dying to see the dress she picked."

Jess folded the ladder and stashed it around the side of

the building where she'd found it. They both jumped in Tink's car and headed out to Lay Lake.

***

Ghost and Shades rolled up just as Skylar was modeling the long gown she'd chosen. When the girls heard the roar of the bikes, they jumped to get her out of the dress.

"Hurry!" Sherry shrieked, grabbing up the garment bag and herding Skylar into the bathroom.

"Stall them," Skylar yelled to Tink and Jessie as she hiked up her dress and dashed out of sight.

Jessie looked at Tink with wide eyes. "What do we do?"

Tink shook her hands in the air, trying to think, then her eyes landed on a glass on the kitchen bar top. Jessie followed her line of sight. The next thing she new, Tink smashed a glass in front of the door.

"What are you doing?" Jessie shrieked.

"You'll see. Quick, grab the broom and dustpan," she hissed in a whisper to Jessie, pointing to the tiny utility closet.

The door rattled and Tink grabbed it, stopping it from swinging open.

Shades stuck his head in, brows pulled together.

"We're sweeping up a broken glass, could you wait outside for just a minute?" Tink asked him with a sweet smile.

"Sure thing, Tink." Shades backed out, and she slammed the door, leaning against it with a relieved look at Jessie. Both girls struggled to muffle their laughter and high-fived each other.

It was the slowest cleanup job on record.

Skylar came out of the bathroom, hopping on one foot as she struggled to slip her shoes back on, while Sherry dashed up the stairs with the garment bag to hide it under the bed.

Then they all looked at each other and burst out laughing, which got frowns from both Shades and Ghost as they walked in.

"What's so funny?" Shades asked.

"Nothing," Skylar replied.

His eyes narrowed. "You're up to something."

She rolled her eyes. "You really want to hear about Tink's time of the month?"

That shut him up. "Uh, no, not really."

The guys walked over to the living room and switched on the game, while Tink gave Skylar the look of death for using her as a diversion.

"My time of the month?" she hissed under her breath as the girl's moved into the kitchen. Skylar tried to hide her grin as she grabbed a package of ground beef from the refrigerator, ignoring her.

"Who wants burgers on the grill?"

***

Two hours later, after they'd grilled out and ate, Ghost stood from the chair he'd been leaning in on the deck.

Jessie sipped her drink, studying him. He was still pissed at her. He was being civil, but the anger simmered just under the surface. She knew it would take time for him to let it go. She'd lied to him, misled him, and not just about what happened in Sturgis, but about Kyle, too. Perhaps the worst of it was what those lies represented in his eyes—that she didn't trust him. That was the biggest wound she'd caused.

She had a lot of work to do to rebuild his trust.

"You ready to go?"

She got to her feet and nodded. "Thank you for dinner," she said to Skylar and Shades.

"Our pleasure," Shades replied, and she knew he sensed the tension between her and Ghost, and he knew she was the cause of it. The look in his eyes told her so. He didn't like his brother being hurt or made a fool, but he'd stay out of it, letting Ghost handle his own business however he saw fit.

"Let's go," Ghost said to her.

Shades stood and embraced his brother, slapping him on the back.

"Thanks, man," Ghost told him.

"Anytime, bro."

They turned to leave, but Shades stopped them.

"Hold up."

When Ghost turned back to look at him, he pulled an envelope from his back pocket and passed it to Ghost. "Can you drop that by the clubhouse on your way home? Butcher's waiting for it. Save me the trip."

Ghost took it. "Yeah, sure."

Jessie and Ghost moved down the stairs, around the house, and climbed on Ghost's bike.

***

Twenty minutes later, as the light was fading from the sky, they pulled down the alley to the back gates of the clubhouse.

Yammer sat on the ground, leaning back against the wooden fence by the gate.

"Hey, Yammer. Open the gate," Ghost called, his bike idling.

Yammer didn't move, his head hanging as if he'd fallen asleep.

"Yammer!" Ghost barked.

When he still didn't respond, Ghost shut his bike off, and he and Jessie both climbed off as he moved toward the prospect.

Jessie watched as Ghost kicked him.

"Wake up, motherfucker."

Yammer slumped onto his side, and Ghost stepped back.

"What the fuck?"

A gloved hand clamped over Jessie's mouth, and a strong arm grabbed her around the waist, pulling her against a solid chest. She watched as another shadowy figure immerged from some bushes and charged Ghost. He was caught off guard as the man brought a pipe down on his head with a crack.

Jessie tried to scream as she watched Ghost crumple to the ground. A moment later, a dark sedan was barreling down the alley, its lights off. It stopped, and the man who had hold of her was suddenly shoving her face-down over the trunk, yanking her arms behind her back and cuffing her wrists. He yanked her back up, and she was able to see the other man rolling Ghost to his back and cuffing him as well. Then he dug in Ghost's pocket, pulled out his phone, and chucked it over the fence, into the clubhouse yard.

The man behind her held on tightly, his hand over her mouth while the driver popped the trunk open, jumped out, and helped the other man carry Ghost. They hefted him inside, the car dipping with his weight.

Then she was being shoved toward the trunk, lifted and tossed on top of Ghost. She landed with a thud against his chest. With their hands cuffed, she could do nothing to break her fall against him. She heard him grunt as she rolled partially off him, and then the lid slammed down, trapping them in utter darkness.

"Ghost," she whispered frantically, and he moaned. "Ghost, please, please, wake up."

She was afraid for him. She wasn't sure how hard he'd been hit, but it had been enough to knock him out, and that couldn't be good. And, as selfish as it was, the thought of going through this alone terrified her, and that's what she'd be if she couldn't get him to wake up.

The car rocked when the men climbed inside. She felt the car begin to move, slowly at first, and then making a turn and picking up speed.

"Ghost. Ghost. Baby, please wake up. I need you. You have to be okay."

He moaned again, and then he murmured her name.

"Jessie—"

"Yes, oh, thank God. Are you hurt?"

"My head feels like someone took a baseball bat to it." He squirmed, as if just realizing something wasn't right. "Where are we? What happened?"

"Some guys jumped us at the back gate. They hit you

over the head. We're in the trunk of a car."

"Fuck. You okay, sweetheart?"

"Yes, I'm okay."

"Did you see them?"

"No, they had ski masks on. Do you think it was the Death Heads?"

"Probably."

"Oh, God."

The trunk was completely dark, but she could already hear Ghost's breathing increase. His claustrophobia was taking hold. Already his breathing was rapid, sawing in and out of his increasingly sweaty chest.

"Jesus," she heard him whisper between his labored breathing. "It's like a coffin in here."

She felt his body tremble.

"Ghost, it's going to be okay. We're going to get out of this, right?"

He tried to laugh, but his teeth were clattering together as if he were shivering with cold. "Of course we are, sweetheart."

"You've got to slow your breathing."

"E-easy for you to s-say." He clamped his teeth together, and she heard him growl in frustration. "Goddamn it. I fucking hate this s-shit."

"You have to go somewhere else in your mind, Ghost. Close your eyes and think of something else."

He stuttered out another attempt at a laugh. "Your ocean?"

She grabbed at his example, the one she'd told him

about. "Yes. *Yes*. Imagine the water. You're floating. It's warm and lapping at your body."

"I'd rather imagine your tongue lapping at my body," he gritted out between clenched teeth.

She was tempted to ignore his comment, but in the end she decided to go with it. Perhaps his imaginations would work better that way. "Yes, Ghost, my tongue on your body. Close your eyes and feel it."

After a minute she felt his breathing slow. She didn't know what he was imagining in his head, but it was working. Her shoulders slumped in relief.

Her attention moved to the handcuffs that bound her. She worked her wrists, twisting and folding her thumb under. Jessie had always had small hands with delicate wrists; she used that to her advantage now. Twisting and pulling, she felt her wrist slide an inch and hope soared inside her. She closed her eyes and tried to concentrate. After a minute, she was able to slide the cuff down another half inch.

"Ghost?" his body still trembled, but he was managing to keep his breathing under control.

He grunted.

"I think I can get the cuffs off one of my wrists."

"Yeah?"

She struggled a moment longer and finally pulled her wrist free, groaning at the pain in her shoulders as she brought her arms around. But it only impeded her a moment, and then her hands were all over Ghost, his chest, his face. "Baby, we're going to get out of here," she assured him.

They felt the vehicle slow for a turn, and they shifted

against each other. The car rocked slowly over a bumpy road.

"There's a safety latch, Jess. Find it. Quick."

"Where?" she asked, frantically feeling around.

"It should be in the center, near the latch. It should be flat and T-shaped."

She felt around, and then her hand closed around something just as he described. "I found it."

"Good, baby. When you pull it, try to keep the trunk from flying wide open. Get a peek at where we are if you can."

"Okay." She pulled and felt the trunk pop. They hit a bump, and she felt the trunk try to bounce open, but she kept a tight hold and it banged down against her arm. She lay over Ghost's chest and looked out the opening. "An alley. We're in an alley."

They were going at a relatively slow speed, bouncing along the potholes.

Ghost threw a leg over the edge. "Ready?" he asked.

"Yes."

He struggled up and threw his body over the side, slamming hard to the pavement. Jessie scrambled out after him, dashing to him and helping him to his feet. They darted into a narrow gangway between two brick buildings.

Jessie glanced back around the corner. She could see the red taillights of the car as it continued moving down the alley, the men totally unaware that their prisoners had escaped. She turned back to Ghost to see him leaning against the wall, groaning in pain.

"You're hurt."

"Dislocated my shoulder when I fell," he said through gritted teeth.

"We need to get you to a hospital."

"No hospitals. The club. First, you have to help me with my shoulder."

"How?"

"I need you to hold it in position while I slam it against this wall. That should jam it back in."

"Have you done this before?"

"Yeah, unfortunately."

"Okay. What do I do?"

"Take my arm."

She slid her hands on his bicep.

"Push it up."

"Like this?"

"Yeah. Right there. Hold it."

"Okay."

"One, two, three."

He slammed it into the wall, and Jessie could hear it pop. It was a sound that had her wincing.

"Fuck!" He bent over stomping his foot as the pain shot through him. "Fuck. That hurts like a bitch."

"Are you okay?" Jessie asked, her hands cupping his face as he straightened.

"Yeah. I'll be fine. We need to get out of here and find a phone."

They stumbled down the gangway until it came out on the street. They paused at the corner of the brick wall, peering around.

"You see 'em?" Ghost asked, glancing around.

Jessie searched in both directions. "No."

"We need to find a phone."

"There's a convenience store on the corner across the street. I could go and make a call."

"You remember that number I made you memorize?"

"Yes."

"Okay. But be careful."

"I don't want to leave you here."

"I'll be fine. You have to hurry, Jess. They realize we're gone, they're gonna double back."

She nodded. "Stay hidden."

"You got it, cupcake." He grinned at her.

She lifted up on her toes, pressing her hands to his chest. He dipped his head and met her lips halfway.

"Go," he said, pulling back.

She dashed across the street.

***

A bell tinkled above the door as she entered the tiny store. There was metal gating across the front window cluttered with beer and cigarette ads. A counter stood to the left with a cash register. Jessie glanced around. There were no customers in the store.

"I need to use a phone. It's an emergency."

The man behind the counter eyed her with little sympathy.

"Please," she begged.

He huffed out a breath, but reached for a wireless phone and handed it to her. She frantically punched in the number

Ghost had taught her.

"Clubhouse," a deep voice muttered through the receiver.

"Ghost is hurt. We need help."

"Who the fuck is this?" came the reply.

"It's Jessie."

"Where is he?"

Jessie pulled the phone away from her mouth and asked the clerk. "Where am I?"

"Gip's. Fifty-Third Street. Fairfield."

She repeated the information into the phone.

"Okay. Hang tight, girly." With that nickname, she realized this must be Griz.

"Hurry, Griz, please."

The phone went dead. She shoved it at the man with a mumbled, "thank you," and dashed out the door. Terrified the entire way back that Ghost would be gone. She reached the gangway, and he stepped out of the shadows.

She flung her arms around him, "Thank God."

"You find a phone?" he asked, his head dipping next to hers as she held him. "You okay?"

She nodded against him, knowing her reaction must be scaring him. Everything was starting to catch up with her. She'd been running on pure adrenaline, but it was starting to fade fast. "They're coming, Ghost."

"Good, baby doll. You did good." He kissed the top of her head.

They waited in the gangway, the whole time she couldn't keep her hands off him. She needed to touch him.

About fifteen minutes later they heard the distant roar of several bikes approaching. They staggered out together into the street, and three bikes came to a stop, followed by a panel van. Hammer, Griz, and JJ were on the bikes, while Heavy drove the van.

Griz was off his bike in a flash, grabbing Ghost to him. "You scared the shit outta me, bro. What the fuck happened? We found Yammer by the gate. He's not sure what hit him."

"Death Heads. They're after Jessie. Get us the fuck out of here, before they come back."

Griz put his arm around Ghost and led him to the van. Hammer approached Jessie.

"You okay, darlin'?" he asked softly, studying her face.

"I'm fine."

Hammer put a hand on her back and guided her to the van.

***

It was late that night when Ghost finally rode them back to his place, escorted by two of his brothers who stuck around long enough to check the place over before leaving.

As Jessie's eyes followed their fading taillights, Ghost grunted, "You don't feel safe, I can call them back."

She shook her head. "It's fine."

"Is it, Jess? 'Cause tonight changed everything. They know you're here. They came for you. It's a whole new ballgame now."

She nodded. "I suppose it is."

He stared at her a moment as if trying to come to a decision, then jerked his head. "Come on. I want to show you something."

He moved around the side of the building, and she followed. Instead of moving toward the terrace, like she'd expected, he moved off toward the adjacent vacant land. It was part field, part wild bushes, and part overgrown underbrush. They walked through the knee-high grass some distance until they got to a tree line where he stopped beside a fallen log.

"See this?"

She nodded, wondering why in the world he'd bring her out here to show her a log.

He knelt down, dug around under some brush, and came up with what looked like a canvas backpack. Flipping it open, he pulled out a 9mm.

"It's got a full magazine. All you have to do is take the safety off. Aim and shoot."

She glanced around. "You think they'll come here?"

"Maybe."

She knew he was being honest with her, giving it to her straight, but that honesty was doing nothing to reassure her.

"They do, and something happens, in a way where I can't help you, you come here."

She understood what that hesitation in his explanation meant. That "something" meaning they'd killed him.

"Ghost—"

"They come, they'll have to go through me, Jess. But I want you prepared, just in case you're on your own."

She looked down at the gun in his hand and hugged herself. She couldn't bear the thought of something happening to him.

"Blood already taught you how to shoot it, right?"

She nodded.

"I wasn't too happy about that. Now, I'm glad. He's a smart man. Guess he saw this coming."

She glanced around as the wind whipped her hair across her face. She didn't want to talk about Blood, or her shooting lesson, or how smart the man was. She wanted to know about a gun in a bag in a field. "Why is it hidden out here?"

"Rally point."

"What?"

"We get separated and you make it out, you come here, get the gun and run. If you can't run, you shoot the shit out of whatever comes after you."

"Please stop talking." She closed her eyes.

"Not sayin' this shit to panic you. Sayin' it 'cause it might come to that. If it does, you've got a plan." He was silent for a moment. "Jess, look at me."

She shook her head.

"Jess."

She opened her eyes.

"You understand?"

She nodded. "Yes."

"Good." He put the gun back, stood, and closed the three steps that separated them.

She looked up at him. "I'm sorry about before, about not trusting you enough to tell you everything. I was ashamed, Ghost. Now I've brought all this trouble."

His hand came up and cupped the side of her face, his

thumb stroking over her cheekbone. "We done fighting?"

She nodded, and his head dipped down for a kiss. She went up on her toes, meeting him halfway. Then, suddenly, they were clinging to each other, standing in the scrub, crickets sounding all around them. Nothing existed outside this man. This man who'd always been there for her when she needed him most, and it scared her to think that may not always be the case.

She broke from the kiss and hugged him tight. "I'm scared, Ghost."

He rubbed her back, murmuring in her ear, "I know you are, baby. Couple more days, and this'll all be over. I promise."

CHAPTER TWENTY

Undertaker stood in Ghost's living room and shoved a white dress shirt at Shades. "Here, put this on."

"Why the fuck would I put this on, old man?"

"Cause he fucking told you to," Blood said, stepping forward.

Shades' eyes moved between Skylar's father and his right hand man. "What, is it picture day or something?"

Ghost fought a grin at Shades' joke, and he took in Undertaker's expression. The man looked like he was about to crack. He'd told the men what they were all there for, and warned them all that they'd better not do anything to fuck this up. Now he looked like he was the one they had to worry about.

Ghost knew he had to think of something quick, so he blurted out the only thing he could think of.

"I'm gonna marry Jessie."

The men all turned to stare at him. Undertaker finally

broke the dead silence that followed that announcement, as he played along, apparently grateful to be off the hook for an explanation in this play act they were all putting on.

"Yeah, he's marrying Jessie, and you're the best man, so shut up and put this on," Undertaker insisted.

"Damn, bro. You serious?" Shades turned, frowning at Ghost.

"Yeah, I am."

"Well, why didn't you say so you big secretive bastard!" Shades shrugged out of his cut and slipped the white shirt on, then put his cut back on.

Ghost dragged him to the courtyard, where he watched Shades' eyes take in the decorations.

"Damn, when'd you do all this?"

"Just shut up and stand here with me," Ghost grumbled, pulling Shades to the altar. They waited while everyone took their seats.

Ghost's eyes connected with Tink's at the back of the aisle, and he gave her a slight nod. She nodded back and disappeared out of sight.

***

Shades glanced at the minister standing at the altar as some recorded music began to play, and he leaned to Ghost's ear. "Think it through, bro. You sure you want to do this? Last chance to run for the hills."

"I'm sure."

Shades tried one last attempt. "Call me old fashioned, but what's wrong with living in sin?"

"Remind me later today that you said that." Ghost tried

to hold back his grin.

"Maybe there's a very small chance you aren't about to make the biggest mistake of your life," Shades continued teasing.

"You're right. I changed my mind." Ghost switched places with Shades, shoving him forward.

"Dude, I was just giving you hell," Shades tried to apologize. "I like Jessie. Hell, marry the girl if that's what you want."

The strains of *The Wedding March* began to play and everyone stood. Shades turned to look and saw Skylar standing at the end of the aisle. She was dressed in a long white wedding gown, a small bouquet of flowers in one hand and the other tucked in Undertaker's arm. She looked beautiful, and his jaw dropped.

"Close your mouth, bro," Ghost said under his breath to him.

"You know about this, asshole?" Shades whispered back, his stomach falling to the floor.

"Found out about fifteen minutes ago."

"Jesus Christ."

"Just breathe, buddy. You got this."

She came down the aisle on Undertaker's arm. And goddamn, if she wasn't the most beautiful thing he'd ever seen. She practically floated with the most radiant smile on her face.

"Surprise, baby," she whispered as they stopped in front of him.

He nodded, huffing out a laugh. "Yeah, I'll say." Then

he sobered. "You look gorgeous, Sky."

"Gorgeous enough to marry me, Shades?"

Undertaker glared at him. "Only one acceptable answer to that, Son."

"Yes, ma'am."

The ceremony was a blur. He remembered the minister asking him for a ring, and he'd looked at the man stupidly, with the panicked thought running through his head that *crap, he had no wedding band to put on her finger,* until Ghost had tapped his shoulder and extended a plain gold band to him.

Fuck, they'd thought of everything.

He took it, turning to smile at his best friend.

"Thanks, Brother."

Ghost grinned big. "Anytime."

***

After their first kiss as husband and wife, they pulled apart and Skylar stared up at him, grinning big. He'd do anything to make her happy, and apparently he'd just made her very happy. The woman was just full of surprises. Then she pulled his head down and surprised him even more when she whispered in his ear.

"Husband?"

"Yes, wife?" he whispered back, grinning.

"I'm pregnant."

He pulled back, staring at her with what he was sure was a stupid expression on his face. "Are you shittin' me?"

That was about as uncouth as he could get, but he was kind of at a loss and couldn't be held responsible for anything that came out of his mouth.

She nodded, grinning.

Jesus Christ, could this life get any better? Then he hugged her, lifting her clear off the ground, and whispered back, "I love you, wife."

When he set her down, he turned to the crowd and hollered, "We're havin' a baby."

A resounding cheer went up, and then Ghost was there, pounding him on the back. But the best part of all of it was the way Undertaker's face turned white as a sheet at his announcement.

Shades burst out laughing, happier than he'd ever been.

***

Ghost leaned his elbows on the railing of the porch that overlooked the terrace, watching the party below. The girls were dancing together while his brothers drank. Several prospects were posted around the edge of the property, standing guard.

His eyes lifted to a plane landing in the distance, the horizon a gorgeous midnight blue in the background as the last streaks of sunset faded.

He turned his head as Skylar stepped next to him.

"It's so beautiful," she whispered, taking in the view.

He smiled at her. "It's you who's beautiful tonight, Hotrod."

She grinned at the nickname he'd always teased her with. Then her gaze fell to Jessie, and Ghost's eyes followed.

"You two work everything out?"

He took a sip of his drink. "For the most part."

She frowned, apparently not satisfied with that answer. "Which part's not worked out yet?"

He shook his head.

"I'm not going to push you to tell me what it is, but whatever it is, you need to have a conversation with her about it."

He turned his head to glance over at her. "When I do, it'll all go to shit."

"If you don't tell her, it'll all go to shit."

Fuck.

His eyes returned to the horizon.

"Ghost, you once had a conversation with me about what it took to be an ol' lady. Remember? Back when Shades and I were struggling to work things out."

He smiled. "Yeah, I remember, Hotrod."

"Is that what this is about? That you don't think she has what it takes?"

He shook his head. "That's not it at all."

"Then what are you afraid of?"

She stayed quiet, patiently waiting for his answer.

"There's something from my past. Something she doesn't know about. Once I tell her…I'm afraid she'll never look at me the same."

"Maybe, maybe not. But you owe it to her to come clean. Only way this works, right?"

He turned to her, bumping her shoulder with his. "When did you get so smart?"

She bumped his shoulder back. "I had a good mentor."

"Is that what I was?"

"Friend?"

"Always." He pulled her into his arms. "Come here, girl."

She went, her head resting against his chest as his arms enfolded her.

"Have some faith, Ghost," she whispered. When he didn't respond, she said, "Promise me you'll tell her."

He replied, his voice soft at her temple. "I promise."

"Hey, you tryin' to steal my woman again?" Shades asked, coming up the stairs.

"Always," Ghost replied winking down at her.

Skylar laughed, pressed a kiss to his cheek, and then went smiling into her husband's arms.

***

As the party wound down, the cake cut, and the garter thrown, Skylar took one last minute to speak with Jessie before she and Shades made their exit.

She found her in the courtyard alone, looking up at the pretty lights.

Skylar hugged her, looking up at all the work that had gone into the decorations. "Thank you so much for doing all this for us. Everything was so beautiful."

Jessie hugged her back. "You're welcome. You are a beautiful bride."

Skylar grinned. "Thank you." Then she studied Jessie's eyes. "How are you doing?"

"I'm fine."

Skylar brushed a lock of hair back from Jessie's face. "Everything between you and Ghost okay? You work everything out?"

Jessie shrugged. "It will take some time for him to trust me again. I'm working on it."

Skylar nodded, searching her eyes. "Can I tell you something? A little advice about Ghost?"

Jessie smiled. "Sure. Apparently, I could use all the help I can get."

Skylar laughed. "Funny how we see others problems so clearly, and yet we can't see our own, isn't it?"

"I suppose."

Skylar put her hand on her arm. "Ghost is a good man."

"I know that."

She nodded. "I know you do. I just want you to remember that. With this life, things come up, things happen. Sometimes they want to talk about it, sometimes they don't. But I just want you to remember, if there ever comes a time when he needs to confess something to you, something he's done, just remember the man he is. He loves you. If he makes a mistake, if he pisses you off, just remember to give him the chance to explain. Hear him out before you make any snap decisions. Okay?"

Jessie frowned at her, not quite sure if there was something specific that Skylar knew about, or if she was just speaking in general about being a woman in love with a man in the life of an MC.

"I will," Jessie promised.

Skylar smiled. "Good. Now its time for me to go find my husband and take him home to bed."

Jessie grinned. "I'm sure it won't take too much

convincing on your part."

Skylar waggled her brows. "I'll probably just have to look at him that certain way, if you know what I mean."

Both girls giggled.

***

Ghost's brothers partied into the wee hours, but eventually he and Jessie said goodbye to the last of their guests.

They walked onto the terrace, and Ghost collapsed into a lawn chair. When Jessie began picking up discarded plastic cups, he caught her wrist and pulled her down to his lap.

"Ghost, the mess—"

"Leave it, brat. I'll have the prospects come clean it up tomorrow." He brushed the hair back from her face. "Did I tell you how beautiful you are tonight?"

She grinned. "Once or twice."

His hand squeezed her hip, his gaze on the cleavage he hadn't been able to take his eyes off all night. "Where'd you get the dress?"

She looked down, fingering the flounce. "Tink loaned it to me."

He nodded. "I need to buy you some of your own."

She shrugged. "I don't really have a place to wear them."

At that, his eyes moved around the terrace, taking in the courtyard in the background. "You do all this?"

"Tink helped."

He nodded. "You've got a knack for it."

She smiled at his compliment. "Maybe."

"You think I could make a go of this place? I mean as an event location. Put on parties like this one and shit?" He rubbed his hand up and down her thigh.

"I think you could do anything you put your mind to, Ghost." Her eyes took in the place. "I think it could be a huge success. It has such funky originality. There's no place like it. Maybe it would never make it as a restaurant, but I think you could do all kinds of events here. Weddings, proms, company parties… the list is endless."

He grinned, pleased with her enthusiasm. His hand slipped beneath the hem of her dress, his palm sliding up her thigh.

"You think you could help me with all of that? Do this with me?"

Her smile faded, a stunned expression on her face. "You…you want me to stay?"

He grinned at that. "Yeah, I want you to stay, Jess."

She kissed and hugged him.

He stood, tossed her over his shoulder, and slapped her ass. "Come on, woman. Your ol' man needs a back rub."

CHAPTER TWENTY ONE

Ghost stood at the windows overlooking the view, sipping on a cup of coffee, his thumb moving over his phone screen. He put the cell to his ear, telling Boo that he and Yammer were on party cleanup duty and to get their asses over here.

He smiled as he slid the phone in his pocket, thinking he'd make an extra tall stack of pancakes to make it up to them.

He took a sip of his coffee and watched the sun come up. He felt settled for the first time in a long fucking time. He knew how crazy that sounded, especially when shit was hitting the fan from, seemingly, all sides. But as happy as he'd always been with his life in the club, something had always been missing. Now, having Jessie back, it felt like he'd finally found that missing piece.

Yeah, they still had problems to work through. The

Death Heads problem had to be dealt with. That ball was currently in the DKs hands; they had to find that damn snitch. Once they did, both clubs could make their move. Ghost just hoped it didn't take too fucking long. He had no control over it, so he had to take a breath and let it sort itself out.

His problem with Jessie, on the other hand, was totally in his control. There was shit he hadn't told her, and it was eating at him, especially when he was demanding that she be upfront and completely honest with him. He saw the irony, the paradox, and he knew he had to come clean with her. He just needed to find the right time. Things had finally started to smooth out between them, and the last thing he wanted to do was rock the boat.

He took another sip of his coffee and felt Jessie's arms slide around his waist. Her lips pressed to the bare skin between his shoulder blades. He dropped one hand to hers and squeezed. "Get back in bed, babe. I was just about to bring you some coffee."

She stole the mug out of his hand and took a big sip, moaning. "Hmmm. That's so good."

He turned, taking her in his arms. "You sleep okay?"

She grinned up at him slyly. "You didn't let me sleep."

He dipped down and kissed the tip of her nose. "Then get back in bed."

"I need to get all these rental chairs back."

"Prospects can do it."

"I told Tink I'd help her with her nails today. She's got a hot date tonight. I don't think the prospects want to do *that* job for me."

He grinned. "Nope. Even I draw the line on putting that off on 'em. So, Tink's got a hot date, huh? With who?"

"I'm not telling."

"Bet I could get it out of you."

"You probably could, but do you really want to know?"

"If it's not Hammer, then probably not. I'd feel a responsibility to tell my brother, and then the shit would hit the fan. I'm in too good a mood to fuck it all up by trying to keep Hammer from killing some guy."

Jessie grinned at his logic. "Good. Then you'll take me?"

"To Tink's house?"

"No, I'm supposed to meet her at the clubhouse."

He huffed out a breath. "Shit, I was hoping I'd have you all to myself today."

"Take me to the clubhouse, I'll do her nails, we can return the chairs, and *then* you can have me." She kissed him on the nose. "Deal?"

"Finish your coffee, and we'll work out this deal in bed."

She grinned. "A little undercover negotiations? I'm up for that."

***

Outside the clubhouse, Blood stood by the open back gate, smoking a cigarette and shooting the shit with Yammer. Over on a nearby picnic table, Hammer sat talking with Tink, who was admiring her newly painted nails. It was a pretty, sunny day, unusually cool for this time of year in Alabama.

Blood's eyes moved to the end of the alley, which was actually just a dirt road that ran behind the clubhouse, cutting between two short side streets, a junkyard on the other side..

A dark panel van was pulling into the alley.

"You get much traffic comin' down here," Blood asked as he tossed his cigarette.

Yammer followed his eyes to the van. "Not much. Just the club."

A moment later they were both diving to the ground as the side door of the van slid open and several assault rifles opened fire on the clubhouse.

As Blood rolled and pulled his Glock out, he saw Hammer flip the picnic table over to its side, shoving Tink behind it. Then Hammer was up over the top of it, returning fire. Blood scrambled to the fence and peeked around the open gate. He was able to fire off a couple of rounds into the van.

Then his heart dropped as he saw the end of what looked like a goddamn grenade launcher poke out the open door. It fired straight into one of the clubhouse windows.

***

Inside the clubhouse, Ghost, Jessie, and Griz were at the bar laughing with Boo a moment before they heard the gunfire. Bullet holes began piercing the backside of the clubhouse that faced the alley.

Ghost grabbed Jessie's shirt and yanked her off her barstool, shoving her to the ground and covering her with his body. Then he, Jessie, and Griz all scrambled behind the bar.

They all sat with their backs to it.

Boo hunched over and ran to a cabinet. A moment later he was tossing shotguns to both Griz and Ghost.

"That's some high-powered rounds, bro. They're gonna

make Swiss cheese of this place," Ghost observed.

"Let's flip the pool table on its side. The slate will give us some protection," Griz suggested.

"That thing's gotta weigh over eight hundred pounds."

"Boo, get over here," Griz yelled.

The three men were able to flip it to its side. It crashed to the floor with a boom that shook the whole building, and Ghost was sure, cracked the foundation.

They all got down behind it.

Ghost pointed to the window on the left, pulled his 9mm, and handed it to Jessie. "Keep watch on the side yard, can you do that?"

She nodded, taking the gun.

"Anything moves, shoot the shit out of it."

"Got it."

"Stay with her," he ordered Boo.

"You got it."

Ghost grabbed Jessie by the back of the neck, pulled her close, and kissed her forehead. Then he scrambled toward the back door with Griz.

Ghost got in position, with his back to the wall under one of the windows. Griz crept under the other. The walls were being punctured by rapid fire in a zigzag pattern over their heads. He saw Jessie pop up and look out her window.

"Stay the fuck down, Jess!" he yelled. She dropped back down. He looked over at Griz as he busted the pump on the 12-gauge, slamming it down and up with a ratcheting sound. "You ready?"

Griz nodded, and they both rose up to shoot.

The blast was deafening when Ghost pulled the trigger, the recoil slamming into his shoulder. He got a look at the van where the fire was coming from as he and Griz both dropped back down.

"Death Heads?" Ghost asked.

"Gotta be," Griz replied. "Guess they've moved on from the *capture plan* to the *kill plan.*"

"Jesus Christ."

A second later the glass above them exploded, and a projectile went skidding across the floor. It spun in a crazy circle, and Ghost's heart stopped as he saw it was a grenade. His eyes connected with Griz, and they both dove into the side hallway.

The explosion was deafening, a white flash searing through the air. When the percussion faded, they both staggered to their feet. Half the back wall of the clubhouse was gone as was the ceiling to the second floor.

There was smoldering debris everywhere.

Ghost clambered across it, clawing his way to the other side of the pool table. Both Boo and Jessie were lying on their stomachs, Boo covering her, protecting her, half buried under the debris.

Ghost scrambled to dig them out, with Griz stumbling up to lend a hand.

"Jessie! Jessie, are you okay?" Ghost shouted frantically, his own voice sounding deaf in his ears. All he could hear was a roaring noise. He clawed his way through the debris and everything seemed in slow motion. He couldn't lose her. Not now.

Griz pulled Boo off her, and Ghost rolled Jessie over to her back. She began to cough, and he grabbed her up hugging her to his chest.

"Thank you, Lord."

She pushed back on him. He watched as her lips moved, and he knew she was saying something, but he couldn't hear a word through the deafening roar in his ears.

He studied her, his eyes moving over every inch, checking to make sure she was okay. He determined she must have had the wind knocked out of her. Her forehead was cut, blood oozing from it, but it didn't appear too deep.

"You okay, baby?" he asked, cupping her face and brushing her hair back.

Finally, his hearing started to return. Slow at first, like the sounds were coming down a long tunnel. But he could make out the words, distorted as they were.

"I'm okay. Are you hurt?"

He shook his head. "I'm good.

Griz was rousing a moaning Boo.

"You took a blow to the head by that two by four, Boo," Griz told him.

"Fuck, that hurts."

Jessie pulled at Ghost's vest. "Tink and Hammer! They're outside."

Griz looked at Ghost. "Blood and Yammer, too. Let's go."

Ghost looked back at her. "You okay?"

"I'm fine. They may need help."

The two of them moved toward the door, but the men

were already tearing in through the rubble, trying to see if they were hurt.

"We're all okay," Griz shouted to them.

"Tink. Is she okay?" Jessie asked, looking up at Blood.

He squatted down in front of her. "Yeah, babe. Hammer's with her. She's fine. Are you okay?"

"I think so." Her eyes took in her arms and legs, looking for wounds. Then they moved to Blood. "You're bleeding."

He glanced down. "Just a knick. I'm good. You're the one who needs a bandage." He pointed at her forehead.

She touched her head and then pulled her hand away, seeing the blood on her fingers. Before she could comprehend anything, Ghost bent and scooped her up in his arms carrying her to the bar that, surprisingly, was still standing. He sat her ass on the bar top and nodded toward the hall.

"There's a first-aid kit in the closet."

Blood moved off to get it.

Ghost ripped a piece from the bottom of his t-shirt off and pressed it to her forehead.

"Ghost, your shirt. You ruined it."

"Think that fucking matters? Look around, sweetheart. The place is blown to shit, and you're worried about my shirt?"

Blood chuckled. "Maybe she got knocked in the head."

She glared at him. "I'm fine. It's just a scrape." Then she looked at Ghost with a pout. "I didn't even get to fire off one round."

Ghost and Blood burst out laughing.

dept.

CHAPTER TWENTY TWO

After a long day of dealing with the fire and police departments, getting the prospects started boarding the place up, and sitting through a long meeting that involved a phone call to the DKs to set a meeting for retaliation, Ghost finally brought Jessie home, and she was so happy to be there.

They were out on the terrace, watching the planes land as the sun set. He stood behind her, his arms folded around her shoulders. His mouth at her ear, he said softly, "When that blast went off today, I thought I'd lost you. Never been so scared in my life."

She nodded, squeezing his forearm, feeling safe in his arms. "Me, too. We were all so lucky. I'm so grateful no one was hurt. I'd feel responsible. I'm to blame for all of this."

"No, babe. You're just an excuse. Hatred between clubs runs deep and goes back a long way. You did nothing to start any of this."

"Still, I feel like maybe I shouldn't have come here. I wanted to find you, but I've been nothing but trouble."

He turned her around. "Look at me. That's bullshit. Get it out of your head. I'm glad you came. Glad you found me. And I don't want you to worry. We're gonna take care of this. Understand?"

She stared up into his eyes, and his strength melted into her. She nodded. "I know. I just wish I'd told you everything right away. Maybe things would have been different. Maybe none of this would have happened."

"You don't know that, brat, so don't drive yourself crazy."

She nodded, but it was easier said than done. "I just want you to know there's nothing else. There are no more secrets. I promise I won't ever keep anything like that from you again. Do you believe me?"

He searched her eyes. "I believe you, Jess."

"Good. Thank you." She went into his arms, pressing her cheek against his chest, and felt his hand sink into her hair. He kissed the top of her head, holding on tight.

"There's something I need to tell you." His voice came out soft and serious. "Something I've wanted to tell you for a long time."

She nodded, perhaps knowing what was coming. He was going to finally tell her that big thing he said would drive her away when he revealed it. Well, at least after her talk with Skylar, she felt a little more prepared and hoped she handled it well.

"Okay," she whispered.

"Do you want to sit?"

She shook her head, her hair brushing across his jaw. She felt him take in a long, slow breath.

"Jessie, I've been lyin' to you about something, and I need to come clean." He blew out a breath. "Shit, it's so hard for me to tell you this."

"Just say it, Ghost," she encouraged in another whisper, her head still buried against his chest.

He blew out another breath. "I'm the one who talked Tommy into that recruiter's office."

"What?" She pushed back to look at him. That was the last thing she expected him to say.

"You remember the day Tommy went to enlist?"

She nodded. "Yes. Why?"

"I went with him."

This was news to her. She frowned. "You did?"

"Yeah. I was supposed to enlist with him."

"You were?"

He nodded. "Remember when he practically idolized me? I don't know, maybe you were too young to know that."

"He did. We both did." She felt his arms tighten in a quick squeeze.

"He'd been out of school for a year or two and just sort of floundering for what to do next. That's the summer I found the club."

"The MC?"

He nodded. "Yeah. I knew. Immediately. Everything just sort of…clicked into place for me."

"I didn't know."

"I kept it from you. Your mom, my dad, *no one* knew, except Tommy."

"Tommy knew?"

He nodded. "And I knew he'd follow me. Whatever path I led him down, he'd follow, if for nothing more than to have my back, even if it wasn't right for him. And the club... wasn't right for him. Tommy was always more the hero type. That's why the military was perfect. He got to save people. He got to stand up for right. That wasn't me."

"That's not true," she protested. "You've saved me. So many times."

He squeezed her again, snorting. "Saving you from a schoolyard bully? That's not exactly the same thing. I was never cut out to be anyone's white knight."

"You were to me."

He looked off at the horizon for a few minutes, his head turned toward a plane landing in the distance. When he spoke again, she heard the emotion in his voice, as if her words had affected him.

"Maybe. Anyway, I knew I couldn't let him follow me down that road. I had to make sure he took the path he was always meant to take."

"The military?"

"The military. Maybe you don't remember, but he used to talk about it all the time."

"I didn't know. It was such a shock when he signed up."

"I was supposed to go with him to the recruiter. I knew he wouldn't sign up if I didn't sign up with him." He paused, and she could sense he was struggling with his next words.

"And?" she prompted.

"So I went with him."

"You did?"

"When it was time to sign on the dotted line, I told him to go first. So, he did."

She swallowed, pain knifing through her. "You didn't do it, did you? Obviously, you didn't."

He shook his head.

"You just hung him out to dry."

He didn't deny it.

"Once he signed, I came clean. Told him that I never had any intention of signing up. I knew, even then, that my life was drawn to a different path, one that never would have been right for him. He needed to take the right path. I made sure he did." He paused, staring at the ground, perhaps reliving the moment. "He'd felt so betrayed."

When she didn't respond, his eyes lifted to hers. "You look like you just found out Santa Claus isn't real. Or maybe that I'm not the knight in shining armor you made me out to be. I'm not, Jess. Hell, I never have been. Maybe it's time you open your eyes to that. You're not a child anymore."

"No, I'm not. So, why don't you explain it to me?"

"I thought I was protecting him. Thought I was doing the right thing. I couldn't let him join the MC, and that's the road I was headed down." He shook his head. "I don't know. Maybe I was wrong…maybe if I'd kept him with me, I could have looked out for him."

She pushed away, spinning as fury consumed her. "He trusted you."

Ghost nodded, his jaw locked tight.

"All this talk about him wanting to have your back, what about when he needed *you* to have *his* back? You could have saved him. If you had been there with him, you could have saved him."

"Baby." He reached for her, but she stepped back, as if his touch was poisonous. And perhaps right then, to her, it was.

"I can't even bear to look at you," she hissed. As the words came out of her mouth, all his warnings flooded over her. He'd told her this would change things. That this would change *everything*. That this would *destroy them*. She shook her head, tears spilling over her lashes. He was right—this changed everything. Maybe it *had* destroyed them. It felt like it at that moment.

She took a step back, her brain scrambling for what to say, what to do. She glanced toward the road before returning her eyes to his. He didn't miss it.

"You're thinking of leaving, aren't you?"

She stayed silent, her eyes locked with his as she felt her heart breaking in two.

"Aren't you?" he repeated with a little more bite.

She nodded, giving him the truth he'd always asked for. "Yes."

He ran a hand through his hair. "You want to leave, I can't blame you, and I won't stop you, but before you do, before you go, I have something to show you."

She shook her head. What could he possibly have that she would want to see *now*? But then Skylar's words came back to her.

Give him a chance to explain fully. Hear him out.

"Please, Jessie," he asked quietly.

She found herself nodding once. "All right."

He led her inside, and surprisingly stopped in front of his computer. He hit a few keys until he had pulled up what appeared to be a saved file. He clicked on it, and an email popped up. Then he stepped back, nodding toward the screen.

"I saved this. You should read it."

She frowned at the screen. "What is it?"

He lifted his chin toward the computer. "You'll see."

He went to stand in front of the wall of windows, his hands in his pockets. Her eyes followed him, and then, as if drawn by a magnet, they returned to the screen. She sat in the chair and started at the top.

Billy—

You and I are through. You made sure of it that day in the recruiter's office. And I get it. You probably had a good laugh about it, huh? How I bought it, hook, line, and sinker. You in the military? Right. Only a fool would think you could ever be cut out for that kind of brotherhood—the kind that really counts.

So I'll never contact you again. And I'll never ask anything of you again. Except for one last thing. If something should happen to me over here, I want you to make sure she's okay.

I'm asking you, as a brother, to watch out for Jessie.

You do that and we're square.

—Tommy

She turned and looked back at him. "He never told me any of this. He never told me you'd had a falling out. He never let on. Not once."

Ghost nodded, not turning around.

"He told me…he told me if I ever got into trouble, if I ever needed someone while he was gone, I was to go to you. That you'd help me."

That had him turning, and she could see his glassy eyes. He nodded. "You know I'll always be there for you."

They studied each other for a long moment. All the feelings she had for him warred within her.

He lifted his chin toward the door. "And if you walk out, that's still true."

She stood frozen for a moment before her legs carried her to the door. When she reached for the knob, she heard his voice, gruff and thick.

"I love you, Jess."

She paused and looked back at him. "I love you, too. That's what makes this so hard. What you did? I lost my brother, Ghost. Because of you."

"You lost your brother because of a roadside IED."

She shook her head.

"Jess."

"I'll call a cab."

"Fuck. Babe. You don't have to do that. I'll take you anywhere you want to go."

She shook her head again and slipped out the door.

***

When the cab pulled in to collect her, Ghost sat

listening. He heard the the sound of the car door opening, then slamming, and then the tires crunching on the gravel as it pulled back down the drive. Suddenly the house felt so empty, and he felt more alone than he'd ever felt before. Maybe even more than when his mom died.

He strode out onto the terrace where he collapsed in a chair and stared at the runway lights, watching the planes land and take off in the darkness for what must have been hours. His mind went over every word they'd said, wondering if he'd lost Jessie for good. If he'd ever see her again, ever hold her in his arms, or taste her skin, or hear the breathy sound she made as he slid inside her.

He loved her, down to his soul, and to sit there imagining he'd never see her again drove an ache inside him so deep that he worried the pain might kill him.

Eventually, he heard the rumble of a set of pipes roll up the long drive. His hand automatically went to the gun he'd set down on the side table, his palm resting lightly over the cold metal. Most likely, it was a brother. But it could also be a Death Head, come to settle the score.

A dark shape moved around the side of the building.

"Ghost, you out here?"

Blood.

Not even in his top ten of who might come see him.

"Yeah," he called out, taking his hand off his piece. He was slouched back in his chair, his fingers laced together when he looked up at his visitor.

Blood's eyes move to the pistol, and then back to him with a grin.

"Expecting me?"

Ghost huffed out a laugh. "There might be a round in the chamber with your name on it."

Blood chuckled. "Right."

Ghost watched Blood's eyes move around the property, eying the dark corners, scoping out possible attack routes. "If that isn't for me, then you must be expecting trouble."

It wasn't really a question, so Ghost didn't answer it.

Blood plopped down in the chair next to him and dug something out of his cut's inner pocket. A moment later, he dipped his head, and a lighter flared as he lit up. Holding the joint out to Ghost, he offered, "Here, you look like you could use this."

Ghost took it, inhaling long and deep.

Blood eyed him, his eyes squinting through the smoke he exhaled. "I remember the last time we smoked a joint together. One of us had just pissed off a woman."

Ghost cocked a brow, his lungs expanding. "One of us? That was all you, bro."

Blood grinned, knowing the truth of Ghost's words.

Ghost remembered that night. It had been at the beach. They'd all been down at the Gulf Coast. Blood had pissed off Skylar, and the two had it out. Ghost couldn't help but smile at the memory. She'd been a little spitfire that night, all teeth and claws. Kind of surprised the hell out of him, since he'd thought of her as a scared little kitten back then. She'd proven them all wrong.

"So it's your turn, huh?"

"Guess so," Ghost admitted. "Apparently, I'm not

always the sharpest tool in the shed."

Blood snorted. "Tool being the operative word."

"Fuck you."

"Luckily, she seems to have smarts enough for both of you," Blood teased.

"Smart enough to walk out that door."

"What'd you do?"

Ghost shook his head. "Just something I did years ago comin' round to bite me in the ass."

"You want to talk about it."

"Fuck no," Ghost spat.

Blood grinned. "Thank God."

"Asshole."

"Hey, we both know I ain't Dr. Phil."

Ghost looked at him and chuckled. "No shit."

Blood huffed out a laugh.

"Was there a point to this visit?" Ghost asked.

"Yeah, came to tell you the Devil Kings found their snitch."

"Oh really?"

"Yup. Got all sorts of info out of him. Having a meeting about it."

"What time?"

"Now."

***

Ghost took his seat at the scarred wooden table in the dimly lit room that was crowded with his brothers—a room that wasn't damaged by the carnage from the attack. The common room of the clubhouse was currently in a state of remodel, plywood boarding up the gaping holes.

Butcher looked over at him. "Nice of you to join us. Think maybe next time you could answer your damn phone, so I don't gotta send a man clear out there to get you?"

Wasn't the first time his President had reprimanded him for something. Wouldn't be the last. And right now, with the mood he was in, he really didn't give a shit. He caught the smile on Shades' face as he tried to hide it. Then his eyes slid to Blood, who stood against the wall, his arms folded. The man winked at him and blew him a kiss.

Ghost made a kissy face back at him.

Judging by the laughter in the room, the rest of his brothers enjoyed it, which only seemed to infuriate his President even more. He slammed the gavel down.

"Knock it off! And come to fucking order!"

Everyone got quiet. Ghost's eyes moved around the room. Even Undertaker was there, which meant the New Orleans Chapter was going to play a part. How big a part remained to be seen.

"Most of you have already heard; DKs found their snitch. Guy named Mugs. Ran the Georgia Hell's Harvesters before the DKs patched them in. From what they got outta him, Florida's half crazy. His men are getting more and more leery of him. Seems their VP was trying to cut a deal with Mugs behind Florida's back. Trying to pull Mugs from the DKs, get him the fuck out of there. Deal was, if Quill did that, Mugs gets his men to throw in with Quill in a bid for the Jacksonville Chapter. Seems the VP has ambitions."

"Balls, too, if he was thinking to take the newly patched

over Hell's Harvesters out from under the Devil Kings."

"None of 'em were too happy with that deal. Seems if they gotta swing one way or the other, they'd all rather swing toward the Death Heads."

"Great."

"So, this guy was going to pull his whole crew and move 'em down to Jacksonville."

"Seems Quill promised him the VP position." Butcher shrugged. "A lot more power than he was ever gonna see with the DKs."

"How does all this bullshit work into our plan?"

He grinned. "Perfectly."

"So, you're sayin', we take out Florida, it falls right into Quill's plans?"

"Yup. He steps into the President's position without having to make a move."

"You think the Death Heads are gonna let us take out the fucking Jacksonville Chapter President and let it slide? No fucking way."

"I've got some news on that," a deep voice said.

Ghost and the rest of them turned to look. Undertaker leaned against the wall, his arms folded, his face in the shadows until he stepped forward into the glow of the light that hung over the table.

"Got some informants on the Louisiana/Texas border. Word out of Texas is the Death Heads were thinking about sending in their Nomads to Jacksonville. Lookin' to clean house. Seems their meeting with him in Sturgis opened some eyes to how fucking crazy the guy's becoming."

Butcher's eyes connected with Undertaker's, and he nodded. "Good news. Seems we'll be savin' 'em a trip."

Undertaker nodded.

"You gonna join us for this little party?" Butcher asked.

Undertaker grinned. "Wouldn't miss it, old man."

Butcher grunted out a laugh. "Look who's talking."

It took them another hour to work out the details.

CHAPTER TWENTY THREE

Tink pulled her beat-up old Rambler down the alley, stopping behind the clubhouse gates. Jessie yanked the door handle, looking over at her.

"Thanks for the ride. And for letting me stay with you."

Tink peered out through the windshield. "I'd go in, but I've got to get to work."

"I'll be fine."

"You sure?"

Jessie nodded.

Yammer approached the car, leaning into the doorframe and peering in at Tink. "Hey, doll. Ain't you stayin'?"

The prospect was a shameless flirt when it came to Tink—a factor that Jessie had already learned was a stupid move. Especially when Hammer seemed to have already staked a claim to her. One Tink was quick to deny, a little too vehemently. Someday, maybe she'd get the full story on those two.

Tink gave the man a sugary sweet smile. "Sorry, wish I could, but I've got to work, Yammer. But Jessie here can stay. Let her in, will ya?"

"Sure thing. Maybe I'll see you later tonight, after you get off work?" he asked hopefully.

"Maybe," she replied, waving her fingers as Jessie climbed out.

Yammer looked over at Jessie as Tink drove off. "She sure is somethin', huh?"

Jessie smiled. "She sure is."

Then he unlatched the gate and let her in.

She glanced around the yard. It seemed very quiet. There were only three bikes parked, and none of them were Ghost's. She moved to the back door and let herself in. It took a moment for her eyes to adjust to the dim lighting. When they did, she spotted Boo behind the bar and one man sitting on the other side, hunched over a drink. He was one of the older members named Boot.

He turned to look over his shoulder as she approached. "He's not here, darlin'."

She took the stool next to him. "Do you know where he is?"

Boot blew a stream of smoke at the ceiling and eyed her. "Maybe."

Boo walked over, his palms on the bar. "Can I get you a drink, Jessie?"

Before she had a chance to answer, Boot told him, "Set her up with a whiskey."

Boo connected eyes with her, then moved off to do as he was told.

"Maybe I don't like whiskey," she said.

"Maybe you'll drink it anyway." He downed his own drink.

"O-kay," she replied softly.

"Thought you ran off?" Boot asked her.

"I'm back."

"I see that. Question is, for how long?" He swiveled on his barstool to face her, leaning his elbow on the bar.

"As long as Ghost will have me, I guess."

"What makes you think Ghost wants you back?"

"What makes you think he doesn't?" she countered.

Boot chuckled. "Heard you were a feisty thing."

"Maybe that's what he needs."

"What he needs is a woman who's not gonna lie to him. A woman who's not gonna run at the first sign of trouble." He arched a brow at her.

"He lied to me, too."

"Yeah, heard he did. Also heard he *forgave* you. Way I heard it, you didn't give him the same courtesy."

Her chin came up. "Maybe I deserve that. Maybe I've made some mistakes—"

He laughed. "*Maybe?*"

"Okay, I have. We both have. I forgive him now. It just took me some time to come to terms with what he did. Can't a person realize they fucked up? Can't a person change?"

"Sometimes." He eyed her. "You grow up all of a sudden?"

"I guess you could say that."

"And what'd you learn?"

"I guess I realized that there are consequences. That my actions hurt people, hurt Ghost."

"Well, good for you."

"Where is he, Boot?" She searched his eyes.

"You in love with him, honey?"

She took in a breath, not wanting to tell him. That was between her and Ghost. Not anyone else's business, especially not one of his brothers. But the man seemed determined to put her to the test. Maybe this was all part of seeing if she was good enough for one of his brothers.

"If you must know, yes, I am."

He studied her, apparently waiting for more.

She huffed out a breath. "He makes me feel secure. I may never completely stop being bratty, but I won't ever lie to him again. I'm not afraid to let him in anymore, to see all my flaws, mistakes and all. I can't lose him now."

Boot reached for his glass.

She frowned.

Was he totally unaffected by her words?

"Please, Boot, tell me where he is so I can tell *him* that."

"You're too late."

She felt herself literally deflate inside. "What?"

No, she couldn't be too late.

"They pulled out an hour ago."

"Pulled out where?"

"Club business."

"Boot, tell me. Please. If anything happens to him

because of me—"

"He went to kill Florida…because Florida is trying to kill you."

"Oh dear God, no." She stared, unseeing over his shoulder.

Boot took another drag off his smoke, his eyes forward. "So, maybe his feelings for you are mutual. Nothing says 'love' like a head on a spike."

She knew he was joking. He had to be, right? He wouldn't literally… *Eww.* She grabbed his arm. "He's not alone, is he?"

Boot turned to look at her then. "Fuck no, darlin'. Got three chapters from two different states with him. And that's just *our* guys. Your friends in the DKs are joining in the fun, too."

She frowned. "Why are you telling me all that?"

He stubbed out his cigarette and turned to look at her. "Maybe I got a feelin' you're gonna be an Evil Dead ol' lady one day. Time to see if you can keep your mouth shut."

Her mouth dropped open.

"That is, if your man comes back alive." He grinned and slid her drink toward her. "Bottoms up, darlin'. Looks like you could use this."

CHAPTER TWENTY FOUR

The men squatted down and observed the house. It was a small ranch-style home buried back in the poor section just north of Commonwealth, on the northwest side of Jacksonville. The neighborhood was wooded, and Ghost was sure Florida liked it that way. Kept the nosy neighbors from seeing anything.

"The house is a ratty shithole," Hammer observed.

"Probably let it go to hell after his ol' lady died," Shades guessed.

"How the hell do you know that? This may be the best it's ever been," Griz joked.

His brothers chuckled.

"There's nothing behind it, just more woods and a sludge pond. The DKs got all streets in and out covered. Gulf Coast Chapter has the back covered," Shades advised them.

"Nearest neighbor is that house half a block down. JJ

just went in dressed like a gas company guy. Told 'em there's a leak in the neighborhood and that they needed to evacuate in case of an explosion," Ghost informed Shades.

"Oh, there's definitely gonna be an explosion," Hammer replied with a grin.

"Make sure he ain't got no dogs. I hate killin' animals," Griz grumbled.

"He got any dogs back there?" Shades said into his two-way.

"Nope," came the crackly reply.

He looked over at Griz. "Happy?"

"What? I like dogs, shoot me."

"Maybe later."

They moved in, closing on the front of the house. Ghost slid to the wall and peeked through the window.

"Looks like no one's home."

"Should I knock?" Blood offered sarcastically a moment before he opened fire on the door, the burst of firepower busting the doorknob and lock all to hell.

Shades gave him a barely tolerant expression. "A little dramatic, are we?"

He grinned. "Ding-dong, Avon calling."

The men moved inside.

"Do your thing, and be quick about it," Shades snapped at Heavy.

"It's gonna take a minute. Riggin' this to look like a gas explosion is tricky, boss."

"Well, we ain't got all day."

Ghost lifted his chin. "Search the place. May find

something of use."

A moment later Griz walked back down the hall, hefting an assault rifle.

"Back room's like an arsenal. Check out this M249 SAW. Be a shame to blow all this shit to kingdom come."

Blood walked in the room. "There's a safe in the bedroom wall, but it's locked tight."

Shades' radio crackled with a low voice. "We got a bike comin' in."

It was Reno's voice, one of the DKs posted out on the road.

Shades put the two-way to his mouth. "Just one?"

"Yeah."

"Is it Florida?"

"Yeah, but we got a problem."

"What's that?"

"He's got a chick on the back."

The men all looked at each other.

Fuck.

Ghost didn't have a problem killing Florida. He wouldn't lose one moment's sleep over it. But he didn't kill women.

"Collateral damage," Blood grunted.

"We're not killing an innocent woman," Shades growled at him.

Blood shrugged. "Your call. But how the fuck you gonna pull this off now?"

"You got sixty seconds. He's turning into the neighborhood," came the voice of a different lookout, one posted at the end of the street.

Shades looked over at Heavy. "You done?"

Heavy shoved some tools in a small black kit and jumped to his feet. "Yeah, let's get the fuck outta here."

They dashed out the back door, across the yard, and into the wooded tree line at the back of the property. Then they squatted down and watched.

Just like Reno had said, Florida rolled down the street with a blonde ridin' bitch.

"You got a plan, boss?"

"I'm thinkin'. Feel free to throw an idea out there if one comes to you."

"We separate 'em. Only solution."

"Yeah, that's what I'm thinking. Hammer, you and Heavy take the left—"

Ghost grabbed Shades arm. "No. Let me do this. I brought this down on the club, I need to fix it."

"You sure, Ghost."

"Yeah." He stood and jogged to the back of the house, hiding around the corner as Florida pulled in the drive. He waited until they climbed off the bike.

***

The men watched from the trees as their brother took up his position.

Blood looked over at Shades and whispered, "She's gonna be a witness."

Shades looked back at Blood. "Give him some credit, Blood."

Blood grinned.

***

Ghost peered around the corner. Florida took the lead, just like Ghost knew he would. No holding open doors and ladies first for *that guy*. He made the bitch trail behind him.

Ghost had a split second to move before they'd be inside. He jumped around the corner, catching the blonde with her foot on the step. He slammed the butt of his gun down on her head, and she dropped like a rock.

Florida, who was halfway in the door, turned, saw Ghost, and bolted inside.

Ghost jumped over the woman's slumped body and dashed after him. Apparently Florida had been caught without a weapon. Well, surprise, surprise.

The big man scrambled backward, stumbling down the hall, taunting Ghost.

"You ain't got the fucking guts, Son. You know who the fuck I am?"

Ghost's finger itched to pull the trigger, but he couldn't put a bullet in the man. The plan was to make it look like a gas explosion. Couldn't have the body turning up with bullet holes in it, now could he?

Florida kept backing down the hall. Ghost knew where he was headed—that fucking arsenal.

Ghost couldn't let him reach that room. This would quickly degenerate into a firefight, not just with him, but with all of his brothers. This entire fucking problem was because of him; he'd given Jessie protection, and that act had come with all this baggage. The last thing he wanted was one of his brothers getting shot because of his bullshit. He had to be the one to end this, and he had to do it now. Florida had about three more feet to go.

"You the one that took my Rose?"

That question would have thrown Ghost if Jessie hadn't already told him all about that shit.

"Yeah, ol' man, I took your Rose. What are you gonna do about it?"

Florida spit at him, "You the one that took her to the DKs? Think I didn't know about that? I know *all* about that. I know all of it."

"Maybe you need to worry about what *I* know."

"You don't know shit."

"I know your own VP was setting you up."

That had the man frowning.

"I know your club was five minutes from sending in their Nomads to deal with your fat ass."

The man was two inches taller than Ghost and had about a hundred pounds on him, with big beefy hands. When Ghost thought about those hands running over Jessie, manhandling and pawing at her, he saw red.

It was time to make a move. Another step and Florida would be at the door to that arsenal.

Ghost bum-rushed him, slamming him up against the wall where he fell to the floor, framed pictures crashing down around him.

When Florida saw the picture of his beloved Rose, the glass all smashed, he went over the edge.

"My Rose. You broke my Rose." He grabbed up the picture, hugging it to his chest. "I'll fix it, Rose. I'll put you back together."

"You'll meet her soon enough, old man." Then Ghost slammed the butt of his gun into the man's skull, and he slumped back against the wall, the framed picture falling into his lap. Ghost's eyes fell to the picture, and goddamn if she wasn't a dead ringer for Jessie. *Holy fuck. The old guy was right.*

His brothers burst in the door as Ghost stepped back, standing over Florida with his gun still in his hand.

Shades moved to stand next to him, looking down at the man. His eyes, too, fell on the photo, and then he looked at Ghost.

Ghost met his gaze. "Yeah, I know. Dead ringer, huh?"

"That's fucking weird as shit, man."

"I know. Gives me chills."

"Let's get the fuck out of here."

Ghost nodded, ready to get home. He suddenly needed to hold Jessie. He had to find her and make her see that they belonged together. Hell, they always had. And he was glad that she'd been smart enough to look for him in Sturgis. He'd always be grateful she'd had enough guts to do that.

Ghost looked back. "The girl?"

"The guys dragged her to the tree line. When the place goes up, she'll be far enough away. Saw you hit her, she never saw it coming. She'll think it was the explosion that knocked her out. Good thinking, by the way."

"I have my moments."

Shades grinned and slapped him on the back. "Let's light this place up and go home."

CHAPTER TWENTY FIVE

The bikes rode through the gates and into the yard, kicking up a cloud of dust. Jessie searched the men one by one as they roared in, looking for Ghost, praying he was okay. She knew the mission they'd been on was dangerous, and one or more of them could so easily have been killed.

The dust was so thick, and there were so many bikes, that she began to panic. He had to be here. He had to be. And then she saw him climbing off his bike, yanking his helmet off and throwing it to the ground, his eyes searching the compound as well. Was he perhaps looking for her? Hoping she might be here? Needing to see her, needing to hold her, like she needed to hold him?

She ran toward him, and the movement must have drawn his eyes for they locked with hers. A moment later he was catching her in his arms as she flung into him. He clutched her to him in a tight hold that told her everything she needed to know, and she felt safe again. Everything inside her settled.

His mouth dipped to her ear, and he whispered, "Brat."

She clung to him, unwilling to release her hold on him as she spoke against his neck. "I was so scared I'd lose you."

"Never," he whispered back. "I'm here. I'm right here, baby."

"I can't lose you, too."

At her reference to her brother, his hand came to the back of her head and stroked her hair.

"You won't, Jess." He was quiet a moment, and then continued in a rough voice, "I'm sorry about Tommy. Forgive me?"

She nodded against his shoulder.

"Baby," he whispered, and that one word was filled with emotion. The arms around her tightened, and she knew he'd needed that forgiveness.

"I need you," she whispered back, her face still buried in his neck.

"I don't know if I can make you happy. But if you let me, I'm gonna damn well try, Jess."

"You do already."

"Do I?"

She nodded, and finally lifted her head to meet his eyes, because he needed to understand the truth in her words. "You make me very happy, Ghost."

He took her face in his palms, looking deep in her eyes.

"We do this, there's no more running. I piss you off, you stay and fight it out with me," he ordered. Then added with a grin, "Seems you're good at that."

She let out a laugh, releasing the emotion that she'd barely been able to contain as she'd struggled to keep from falling apart. "Deal. We fight it out."

He studied her eyes, his thumbs caressing her cheeks, and he sobered.

"The trip we just took, brat. It doesn't mean it's over."

Her mouth parted. "It's not?"

He shook his head. "They'll probably regroup. Hit us again in the future." The palms on either side of her face tightened slightly, and he asked, "This really the kind of life you want?"

Her hands slid up, closing around his wrists as she looked back at him with clear, open eyes. "I want to be anywhere you are. If trouble comes, we'll face it together."

He studied her, and then nodded. "We will, and we'll get through it. We can get through anything as long as we've got each other. Right, babe?"

"Damn right," she agreed with narrowed eyes.

He grinned, and then burst out laughing. "You're gonna make a great ol' lady."

"Don't you forget it."

He hefted her up in his arms, her legs coming around his waist. "Time to break in that twin bed." He lifted his chin toward the clubhouse, referring to the tiny room he kept there.

She tilted her head to the side as if considering his suggestion. "Hmm, maybe, if you play your cards right, mister."

His palm came down with a hard smack on her ass. "Oh, I plan to play my cards very right."

Then she laughed, her arms wrapping around his neck as her *ol' man* carried her across the yard, his eyes never leaving hers.

EPILOGUE

Ghost—

I watched as Jessie paced the floor, rubbing her distended belly, while our dog, Shadow bounced next to her. I'd gotten her the Collie mix as a pup, and he'd lived up to his name, never leaving her side.

I leaned against the doorjamb, timing her contractions. "Two minutes apart, babe."

"I'm not going."

"It's time, Jess. Can't wait any longer."

"I changed my mind."

I grinned. "Little late for that, brat."

"I'm not kidding, Ghost."

I took her in my arms and attempted to talk her down. "You know I love you, right?"

She nodded.

"And I'm going to love this baby. And *you're* going to make a wonderful mother," I whispered in her ear. "But none of that can happen if we don't let the little sucker out of there." I patted her stomach.

She tried to muffle a chuckle, but bent when another pain hit her. "Don't make me laugh, it hurts."

I held her through another contraction, my hand on her belly, feeling it harden as the muscles tightened. When it finally subsided, I asked, "You okay, now?"

"Yes."

"Good. Now let's go get my son born, okay?"

"Okay."

"I love you, Jessie."

"I love you, too, Ghost."

***

Five years later…

Jessie—

I found Ghost out in the garage working on a bike.

"Your son is at it again."

He looked over at me. "How come when he's done something wrong, he's my son, and when he's being an angel, he's your son?"

"Ghost." My frustration bled through my voice. I was at my wits end with that boy.

"What's he done this time?" He went back to tightening a bolt on his bike.

"He's peeing in Mrs. Mitchell's yard again."

Ghost looked at me with a doubting expression. "No

way. He's forbidden to go over there anymore."

I pointed at the window that gave a view of the backyard. "Look!"

We'd moved to a cute house in a quiet, family-friendly subdivision not long after Ghost got the club he'd remodeled up and running. It was doing a great business, especially in special events.

Ghost rose to his feet, his eyes on me as he moved to the window and bent to peer out. I looked with him.

There was our son, standing on top of the highest part of the wooden backyard playset that Ghost and his brothers had built, peeing off the edge. The pee arced high up in the air, over the privacy fence, and straight into our neighbor's yard. Shadow, who'd promptly traded loyalties to my son the moment he was born, sat in the grass nearby, watching.

My eyes flicked back to my husband. He was snorting with laughter.

"Impressive."

"Ghost!"

"Come on, babe, that takes talent."

My hands landed on my hips as I glared at him.

"What? So the boy ain't shy about whipping out his dick. Takes after his old man." He was grinning. Ear to ear, I kid you not. Then he pulled me to him. "I seem to remember you not having a problem with that trait in me."

His hands landed on my hips, and he pulled me up against his crotch, letting me feel the erection that was building as his hands slid down and squeezed my ass. Insatiable. The man was insatiable.

I pushed against his chest, trying to keep a straight face. "Ghost, this is serious. You have to do something."

"I am doing something."

"I mean about your son."

"I'll talk to him, babe."

"You promise?"

"Promise. We'll have a little father-son chat about the 'whens and wheres' of proper peeing etiquette. Now, shut up and kiss me."

What can I say? I loved my man. So I shut up and kissed him.

***

GHOST—

I watched her strut away, and my eyes dropped to her ass. I quickly whipped out my cell and snapped a shot, zooming in on said ass. Then I looked down at the screen and grinned.

Two big greasy handprints stood out on her white shorts, perfectly framing that ass. I texted it to her. It didn't take long for my phone to ding with a reply.

My cute new shorts! You ruined them!

Looks good to me. Might make it my new screensaver.

Ghost! You're gonna pay for this.

I'll make it up to you tonight.

Not funny.

Sorry I ruined your sexy-as-hell shorts, babe.

No you're not.

True. Still the best ass I've ever seen.

I waited a couple beats before getting a reply to that one.

You're forgiven.

I grinned. What can I say? That woman cannot stay mad at me, and I loved her for it. Unshakably. Undeniably. Unashamedly. Head-over-heels, last-a-lifetime, till-the-end-of-our-days, *loved* that woman. But that was a lot to type for a guy who was all thumbs. Guess I'll just have to show her later. And that was a thought that had me smiling as I typed a reply.

Love you, babe.

My phone dinged one last time.

Back atcha, babe.

I smiled.

My girl. My love. My life.

Then, shoving my cell back in my hip pocket, I headed to the backyard to teach my son how to write his name with pee. Yeah, okay, it was gonna be a "don't tell your mom" moment. But those were the best kind between a father and son.

The End

PREVIEW
OF
BLOOD: An Evil Dead MC Story

Blood lay chained to the filthy iron cot, his wounds burning like fire. The room was like an oven in the humid New Orleans' heat. He knew it had to be late afternoon by the angle of the sunlight coming through the slats of the louvered shutters covering the windows. But the heat wasn't the only reason sweat was pouring off him; his fever was spiking as the infection took hold.

He heard the door lock rattle, and then the door was opening. He looked toward the sound, trying to focus, and saw a man shove a woman into the room ahead of him. He remembered the man, a sadistic son-of-a-bitch. But they'd never brought a woman in before.

He tried hard to make sense of what he was seeing, but she was just a pale green blur. *Were those hospital scrubs?* He knew the fever was starting to mess with his mind. It had to be, because when she hesitantly approached him, her blessedly cool hand pressing to his forehead, he looked up into the face of an angel.

Was she coming to take him to heaven?

A laugh bubbled up inside him. Heaven? More likely hell is where he'd be going.

Watch for
BLOOD: An Evil Dead MC Story
Coming 2016

If you enjoyed GHOST, *please* post a review.
Thank you!
Nicole James

Watch for
Nicole James' new four book tattoo series:
BROTHERS INK
Book 1— Jameson

Also by Nicole James...

The Evil Dead MC Series
OUTLAW
CRASH
SHADES
WOLF
GHOST

RUBY FALLS